PRINCESS OF EARTH

R.J. ROGAN

For twelve-year-old me.

Look what you did!

Pronunciation Guide

- Kira – Key-rah
- Maeteo – Mah-tay-oh
- Eyvlin – Eye-vel-lin
- Aepein – Ay-pee-in
- Eoghan – Oh-wen
- Saorise – Ser-sha

1
Before

They came on the eve of my fourth birthday.

My hand was clasped tightly in Emily's as she pulled me through the dimly lit hallways of the castle. The sounds of people screaming had woken me from my sleep minutes ago, only seconds before my bedroom door had been thrown open and Emily had taken me, barely awake, from my bed. I tripped over my feet as I tried to keep up with her brisk pace, eventually she had to pick me up and carry me towards my mother and father's bed chamber.

Through the darkened windows I could see the orange glow of fire over the castle walls. Soldiers running along the battlements, shooting arrows down into the blazing fires.

Candlelight licked the stone walls of the halls as we entered my parent's chambers. I had never been allowed into them before, and my eyes widened as I took in the sheer size of the room. The bed stood in the centre of the room, quilts and pillows thrown around in disarray, as if my parents had jumped from their bed as quickly as I had been taken from mine. My mother stood, fully dressed, in front of the roaring fireplace. It taller than she was and alive with flames. Strangely, she was talking to it. And there, talking back to her, was a man made entirely of fire, but I could not make out what either of them were saying.

Emily cleared her throat as she placed me on my feet again, and my mother turned quickly, the man of fire disappearing completely. Her eyes took me in, four-years-old, still rubbing sleep from my eyes and wearing my pink nightgown, and her face softened. The hard mask she was wearing as she spoke to the man in the fire disappearing and being replaced with the face I knew – soft, caring, a woman I could go to with all my four-year-old problems.

Without speaking, my mother knelt in front of me, pressing a kiss to my forehead.

"What's going on?" I asked, rubbing my eyes again as my mother pulled away, noticing the tears that started to brim around her eyes – my eyes, just with a few more lines around the edges.

"Aunt Emily is going to take you somewhere safe." Mother said softly, smoothing her hand over my hair and looking towards Emily, who just nodded. She was chewing her bottom lip, worried. "Remember, Kira.

You are so loved. Your father and I love you so much. You are our gift from the Heavens. Will you remember that darling?"

I did not have a chance to reply before a sound erupted through the room, the glass of the chamber windows shattering around us. My mother flung herself over me, sheltering me from the glass scattering, and the screaming from outside got louder.

"Go, Emily, you must go now. Keep her safe." My mother said, lifting me from the floor and placing a final kiss to my head as she passed me to Emily's waiting arms. "I promise, Kira, we will see each other again."

Tears fell from my eyes, and I called out to my mother as Emily ran as quickly as she could out of the room and down the hallway we had been in minutes ago. I watched as my mother stood inside the door, her eyes still on mine and tears streaming down her face.

My eyebrows furrowed as Emily turned down a passageway I had never seen before — my mother disappearing — and from that point, I did not recognise the hallways she took. They were smaller, darker, and quieter than the main hallways had been, but she knew them like the back of her hand as she ran through them, holding me to her tightly. The sounds of explosions, swords clashing and people shouting had faded to the point the loudest noise now was my sniffling, Emily rubbed her hand on my back as reassuringly as she could.

We did not speak as Emily weaved her way through the halls and down several staircases until we emerged into the castle kitchens. They were buzzing with life as people flitted back and forth, carrying bags of food and supplies, and jumping out of the way of passing soldiers. Emily chewed her bottom lip as she stood on the tips of her toes and looked around the mass of people.

"Leo!" She called, relief in her voice when she spotted the tall, sharp jawed male. His head spun, a look of panic on his face as Emily surged forward, pushing through people, and crossing the kitchen.

"Emily! What are you doing here?!" Leo's voice was thick with concern, his eyes flitting from Emily to where I sat on her hip, my own eyes wide as I took in his tall frame, his ice blue eyes, his slightly pointed ears. He was Fae. I had met a few of the Fae women who worked as my mother's aids, but I had never really seen any more around the castle — I was always told they were all incredibly busy out in the wilds of the Kingdom, keeping crops growing, medicine ready and easily accessible…

"I need to speak with your father," Emily was breathless, moving me on her hip so she could hold me more securely. "We have to get Kira somewhere safe."

Leo eyed Emily for a second, before he nodded tightly. He dropped the bag of flour that he was carrying onto the nearest table and wrapped his arm around Emily's shoulders. His arms were long enough that he managed to wrap me up in the movement also, his large hand falling protectively onto the back of my arm.

He steered us through the kitchen, past the line of soldiers who were tightening their shields on their arms, and through a thick, wooden door in the back. Leo led us down a twisting staircase made of mud, and through a corridor that was dark and smelled strongly of earth and smoke — an underground tunnel.

An almost Earth-shattering explosion above us made Emily drop down, one of her hands going to my head and Leo using his body to shield us. The screaming that followed made him curse loudly, and he grabbed Emily's arm, pulling the two of us up until we were standing. Leo's eyes were wild as he turned to look at us.

"We need to run." He whispered, barely audible over the noises coming from above us, "Give me her."

Emily passed me over into Leo's open arms, and he shushed me as I whimpered. "You're alright, Princess, I've got you." His harsh face softened. "You need to hold on to me. Nice and tight, okay?"

I nodded, throwing my arms around the man's neck, and nuzzling my face into his shoulder. There was a second of Leo lifting Emily onto his back, before my hair was blowing around my head like I had been swept into a windstorm.

Looking up in surprise, I saw the tunnel around us moving past so fast I would have sworn we were flying.

Emily loosened her grip on one of Leo's shoulders, bringing her hand to the back of my head again to either soothe me, or get me to put my head back down. I took it as the latter, burying my head back into the hard space below Leo's shoulder.

We ran until the sounds of fighting were distant enough that we could barely hear them. Leo slowed to a walk, his breathing barely laboured, and let Emily drop from his back. He slid me round until I was on his back, my arms wrapped tightly around his neck and legs around his waist and let his free hand slip into one of Emily's.

The pair talked quietly among themselves, about people I had never heard of, and about how when this was all over, Leo was going to take Emily to see the dragon's nest at the top of Lides mountain. Emily laughed quietly at him, shaking her head, and calling him an idiot.

The dark of the tunnel was broken by a flicker of orange candlelight, and Emily sucked in a breath. Leo shushed her, reassuring her that it was just his father, and that they must have tripped one of his alarms without noticing. It took a few minutes for the tall, slender figure to appear in the opening to the tunnel.

Leo's father was taller than him, with white hair to the back of his shoulders and intricate tattoos down the front of his neck and onto his arms. His face was lined with age, and his eyes the same bright, icy blue as Leo's. He watched us as we drew closer, his face grave with worry while he, not so subtly, checked over Leo for any signs of injury. When he was satisfied that his son was not hurt, his eyes fell onto me, his whole face softening as they did so.

"Princess." He greeted me in a gruff voice that almost sounded like one my mother would have used while telling me bedtime stories. "Leo, Emily… what is the meaning of this?"

"The castle is under attack, Father." Leo said stiffly, standing up a bit straighter so I could barely see over his shoulder. "Emily needs to take the Princess somewhere safe."

"You know I would never ask if it wasn't an emergency, Alexandre." Emily smiled sadly at the man in front of us, reaching to take me from Leo's back and hugging me close to her. A frigid wind blew from the entrance of the tunnel, and I shivered against it, trying to curl tighter into Emily's warmth.

Alexandre was quiet for a moment, before he nodded and motioned for us to follow him. Emily breathed her thanks, almost running after the Fae male as he took long strides across an open meadow, toward a small, wooden cottage hidden just behind the tree line. The long grass tickled my ankles where they hung by Emily's waist.

Leo held open the cottage door so Emily could step inside, the warmth of the fireplace hitting me as soon as we stepped into the small living area. Emily let me down, my slipper-clad feet landing on a plush, rose-coloured rug, and I looked around as she headed towards the kitchen with Leo and Alexandre.

The room I was left in was full of bottles, potions and books covering every surface I could see. Dark wooden beams stretched across the ceiling, and instead of doors, thick woven curtains hung between the rooms; the windows were covered with a thick layer of frost, despite the warmth coming from the small, iron fireplace tucked in the corner between two armchairs.

I was halfway across the room, making my way to one of the chairs, when Emily came back into the room, a smile on her face that did not reach her eyes. She held her arms out to me, and I let her pick me up again so she could sit on one of the chairs with me in her lap. Leo and his father spoke in hushed voices as the smell of jasmine started to drift through from the curtained off kitchen. Emily pulled me against her chest, her hand stroking my hair.

"Alexandre is making you something to drink, okay?" I looked up at Emily, my brows knotting together, "It'll taste nice, and it'll keep you safe for a long time."

Her voice shook, but the reassuring smile on her face made me nod. Emily placed a kiss to my forehead, and the curtain to the kitchen pulled back to reveal Alexandre carrying a steaming mug. Leo was chewing on his bottom lip.

"Now, Princess." Alexandre's gruff voice was soft as he moved a chair from the small dining table and sat in front of where Emily and I were curled in the armchair together. "This is a special drink. It will make you feel sleepy, so you must go to sleep straight away, okay? And when you wake up both you and Miss Emily will be safe from what is happening at the castle. How does that sound?"

I eyed the mug he was holding out to me, crinkling my nose at the strong smell coming from it. Alexandre chuckled softly; "I know, it doesn't smell the best, but it tastes better, I promise."

Nodding, I took the mug from him, barely managing to wrap my small hands around it. Emily placed her hand on the bottom of it, helping me take a sip. The smell was indeed the worst part because it tasted like berries and my favourite sweeties from the castle. I smiled, licking my lips, and drinking more deeply.

"Emily, when she is asleep, I will make sure you have everything you need to put the correct wards around the safe house." Alexandre's voice sounded farther away the more I drank of the delicious tea.

"Can I go with them?" Leo asked.

"No, Leo. You will be needed here."

I slurped the last of the tea from the mug, wiping my mouth on my arm and handing the mug back to Alexandre. He grinned at me, looking even more-so like Leo when he did.

"Well done, Princess. Now, go to sleep, and we will see you soon."

2
Kira

Sunday mornings were always market mornings in Green Haven.

The market always appeared before six in the morning and was gone by the time it hit one in the afternoon. It sat nestled between the village church and the stables behind the only pub. It was not big, but it had bakers and cloth merchants, and every so often a fortune teller would arrive with them. Emily never let me visit her after she had told me I was being lied to by a motherly figure.

My hand gripped my small money pouch that was tied to my belt as I weaved my way through the crowd of people. Emily and I usually came to the market together, but this week she had sent me by myself, claiming she had something to do at home. I had not questioned her — I was thankful for the freedom. My eighteenth birthday was three sleeps away, and this was the first time she had sent me out on my own. Maybe my turning into an adult was enough for her to finally loosen her strings.

I loved Emily, really, she had raised me since I was little, but sometimes she felt very... smothering. Our cottage had multiple locks on the doors — both physical, made from brass and copper, and ones conjured by spells Emily had purchased from a traveling mage. She knew my every move, had walked me to and from school every morning, and triple checked her locks every night. No one could talk to me without Emily knowing about it.

The smell of freshly baked bread stopped me in my tracks as I passed the baker's stall. The heat from the fire hitting me in the face, I stepped forward, inhaling deeply and having to stop myself from groaning aloud. The baker laughed, holding a beautifully golden loaf out towards me — as if I would need more than the smell to convince me — and thanked me when I handed him two copper coins.

Sudden shouts made me turn my head, my eyebrows furrowing as I looked towards the clock tower. A stream of horses flew through the middle of the market, their riders shouting to people to move out of the way, to watch where they were going, and disappeared into the forest on the other side of the square. I blinked, stunned at what had just happened, and finished putting my bread into the cotton bag I had slung over my shoulder.

"What do you suppose *that* was about?" A voice from beside me asked, and my face broke into a smile, rolling my eyes as I looked around at him.

Stood leaning against the wooden beam of the baker's stall, his arms crossed over his chest and a questioning frown on his face as he watched after the horses, was Dane. His usually dirty skin had been cleaned, and his freckles stood out against his pale cheeks, the perfect match for the fiery red hair that sat atop his head in a mix of braids. He turned to look at me, his eyes lit up with mischief.

"Maybe they found one of the hunters traps you set." I shrugged, pulling my bag back up onto my shoulder. Dane laughed, pushing off the beam he had been leaning against and slinging an arm around me.

"Don't be silly, Ki, no one ever finds my traps." He winked, sending a blush across my cheeks.

Dane had been my first, and only, friend when I started at Green Haven village school. For some reason, the rest of the kids in attendance had looked at me like a circus side-show. But not Dane. Dane had sat himself right down next to me during the first break of the day and offered me a bite of his apple, promising me he had not poisoned it. Since then, he was *my* Dane. We had grown up together — his father owned the stables and the pub, making enough money from drunk soldiers wanting to leave their horses in the stables overnight that Dane had never wanted for anything — with only a few months between my birthday and his, and we had spent our time raising Hell until we hit our teenage years, when girls started to realise how heartbreakingly attractive Dane's smile was, how his eyes on you could make you feel like the only person in the room, and suddenly... he wasn't just my Dane.

He was Jamie's Dane. And Liza's Dane. And Poppy's Dane.

We started walking, his arm still tight around my shoulder as he led me through the middle of the market, past the farmers who had everything Emily had told me to get. I tried to protest, looking back over my shoulder, but he just tsk'ed, telling me there was plenty of time for me to get what I needed, and that he had something to show me.

I sighed, but went with him anyway, shrugging his arm off my shoulder and walking alongside him. He grabbed my hand as we neared the stables, pulling me along to the farthest one with a grin on his face. I grimaced as I stepped in a puddle of mud and hay, the insides of my boots now soggy.

Inside the stable stood a mare with a coat as white as snow with flecks of grey scattered across her back. Her mane and tail matched the grey perfectly, both tied into tight braids. I gasped, leaning my arms on the top of the stable door, and lifting myself to stand on the metal beams of the door to get a better look at her.

"Where did you find her?!" I asked, my voice barely above a whisper in fear of spooking the beautiful creature. Dane lent on the door next to me, smiling at the horse.

"She was going to slaughter, but you know my dad — he won't let a perfectly healthy horse go." Dane's voice was gentle as he extended a hand, clicking his tongue to get the horses attention. She lifted her head, huffing through her nose and bumping her head against Dane's knuckles. I watched as he smiled, his eyes crinkling at the corner. I reached my hand out and placed it against her neck gently, the warmth radiating from her seeping into the palm of my hand.

"Why was she going to slaughter?"

"Because her owner died, and his son didn't want to keep her." Dane shrugged, running his fingers along her soft coat. "Her name is Dusty."

He turned his head to look at me, still smiling.

Dane had always loved animals and had always been against his uncle's weekend hunting activities. He had started setting hunter traps in the woods when he was thirteen, catching hunters unawares and scaring their prey away in the same pop of smoke. No one, apart from me, knew it was him setting the traps in the woods.

I pushed myself away from the stable door, sighing.

"As wonderful as it was to meet you, Dusty, I *really* have to go and get my things from the market." I raised an eyebrow at Dane, who just laughed, shaking his head. He patted the horse's neck before he pushed himself off the door, landing on the ground with a cloud of dust. "You don't have to walk me back, Dane."

"I know," he shrugged, pushing his hands into his pockets, "I want to, though. Poppy will be in the village by now."

He wiggled his eyebrows at me, and I laughed, shaking my head.

We walked in silence back into the village centre. Despite us only being in the stables for no more than ten minutes, the market felt busier. It was buzzing with people's voices, shouting from vendors, children running in between stalls, and it brought me back to reality with a harsh slap.

I sighed, my shoulders slumping slightly when I spotted the group of girls gathered by the fountain in the middle of the square. Their hair all tied into intricate braids, finished with bows the same colour as their dresses. Poppy stood in the middle of them all, wearing a lavender dress with woven flowers and giggling into her hand. Dane nudged me with his shoulder, grinning at me when I looked up at him again.

"I'll see you later, Ki." He grinned, kissing me on the forehead and leaving before I could even reply, his voice carrying over the crowded square as he called out; "Pops!"

Poppy's head shot up, a cheek-splitting smile on her face at the sight of Dane crossing the square to her. I swallowed harshly, looking away when he reached her, his hand going to the small of her back and his head dipping to kiss her cheek.

Shaking my head at myself, I pushed my way through the ever-growing throngs of people in the market. I could not remember the last time it had been this busy, and my eyebrows furrowed as I realised every single person in the village must have been here. Racking my brain for why so many people had needed to come out today, I could only think of one reason. A reason that hit me square in the chest.

The lost princess's birthday was in three days.

It would be fourteen years since the Fire Kingdom had attacked the Earth castle in the middle of the night, leaving the king and queen, and ninety percent of their staff and armada dead. No one had ever been able to find the princess. There were rumours, of course, that she had been taken by the Fire Kingdom and raised to be a kitchen maid or left to be a street rat in their city, but everyone knew she had been killed alongside her parents, her body burned in the fires they left behind.

Every year as her birthday neared, people would gather in the square and dance and sing into the little hours of the morning. Stories of the king and queen were told, wishes for the Princess to return would be shared, and a feast that we could only dream of the rest of the year would be enjoyed by all on the day.

Years ago, when Dane and I had been lying in the hay of the stables, laughing and joking and sharing a slice of my birthday cake, he had suggested that I was the lost princess. I had laughed so hard I was almost sick, throwing a handful of hay and dust at him.

"Princesses don't wear dirty socks!" I had shrieked at him, sending us both into giggles. We never spoke of it again after that.

I stopped in front of the farmer stall, a row of caged chickens clucking at me as I stood there. I tried my hardest to avoid looking them in the eye as I handed over gold for twelve of their eggs, the guilt I would feel for it would settle in my stomach all day. I tried not to think on it, focusing instead on the strong smell of smoke; the kind of smoke that only came from burning wood.

The sound of hooves hammering against the cobbled streets filled the village square again, making everyone look towards the clock tower.

A single horse, with a coat darker than a moonless night, came streaming into the square. It's rider sat tall, silver armour glinting in the afternoon sun and two swords strapped to his waist. His face was set in a scowl as he slowed his horse, pulling the reins until it halted by the fountain. Dane's eyes went wide, his arms tightening around Poppy's waist as she hurried to try and get out of the way fast enough.

The mystery rider searched the crowd, his eyes running over the faces of everyone in front of me. I ducked behind a small family, the father holding on tightly to the children's shoulders, silently hoping he had not seen me hiding.

"I'm looking for Kira Dagon."

The rider's voice carried across the silenced square. I stilled, a cold shiver running down my back. Quiet voices repeated my name over and over as people in the crowd looked for me. I did not have much time if I wanted to get out of here. I turned on my heel, holding tightly onto the straps of my bag and dodged my way through the tightly packed bodies.

A hand slammed onto my shoulder, stopping me in my tracks and taking my breath away in the same action.

I looked to the side, meeting the harsh blue eyes of a local vendor. His grey beard was tied into a knot at his mid-chest, and his nails were caked with dirt. I knew him well enough to know that he was a coward.

"*Please.*" I whispered; my voice barely audible to even myself. The vendor's eyes glinted, a small smirk on his face as his grip tightened on my shoulder and he spun me in place.

"I have her!" He bellowed, and my heart stopped in my chest.

The crowd around us parted down the middle, people scurrying to get to the side as the rider dismounted from his horse. His armour clinked as he walked, one hand on the hilt of one of his swords, his eyes trained on me where I stood.

A cold sweat broke out across my hairline.

"I have gold." I said quietly to the vendor. "I will give you it all if you let me go, right now."

He chuckled darkly, his hand staying planted firmly on my shoulder. Frantic, I searched for Dane in the crowd. He had let go of Poppy and was staring at me with wide, wild eyes; one arm stretched out as if he could grab me from where he stood. I swallowed roughly; my throat suddenly dry.

The rider stopped in front of where I stood and removed his helmet, his harsh face giving away nothing as to why he was here for me. My heart hammered in my chest as I stared at him. His hair was slicked back with sweat, and dark enough to match his horse. He was taller than me by at least a foot.

"Kira?" He asked, his voice quieter than before, but still loud enough for the people in our immediate vicinity to hear. I nodded; my own voice completely lost to the fear that was creeping up the back of my neck.

Then, suddenly, he dropped to one knee in front of me, his head bowing.

I blinked.

The crowd around us watched in stunned silence as he kept his bowing position for several seconds, before rising and glaring at the vendor still holding my shoulder. His jaw ticked slightly.

"Please, remove your hand."

The vendor hesitated, but his grip on my shoulder eased, and the residing ache told me that it was going to bruise. I frowned at the dirty hand print he left on the clean material of my shirt.

"Who are you?" I asked, my voice sounding a lot more confident than I felt as I looked back to the man stood in front of me. His armour carried the royal army symbols, and his importance radiated from him just by the way he stood. He smiled lightly, his entire face changing with the small gesture.

"I am Maeteo Stoll, General of the Royal Army."

"What do you want with her?"

Dane's voice shocked me, and my eyes flew past Maeteo to find him standing significantly closer than he had been before. Poppy was staring after him with a look of shock on her face, as if she could not believe what she was seeing. I could not, either.

Maeteo turned where he stood, his face hardening and shoulders squaring as he took in Dane. If it came to blows between the two — Dane did not stand a chance.

Not bothering to answer before he turned his attention back to me, Maeteo held out his hand.

"Come, Kira. There is much to discuss and not much time."

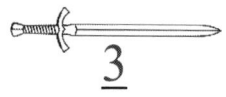

3

Maeteo

When I was ten, I saw my parents murdered in the raid on the Earth Kingdom castle.

My father, the General, had been woken by one of his soldiers slamming his fists against our front door at nearing two in the morning. We lived on the outskirts of the castle wall, tucked behind the thick line of trees, in a clearing that was big enough for the army to set up targets for archery practice. The soldiers lived in the barracks at the other side of the clearing, but due to my father's high status and the fact he had a family, the Earth Queen had ordered a cottage to be built for us. It was not much, only one bedroom for the three of us, but my mother cooked in the kitchen and when my father came home from work, we would sit in front of the fireplace and listen to his stories. It was home, in the truest sense of the word.

I had been tucked into my bed in the corner of the room, awoken by the sudden shouting as my father ran back into the room. He woke my mother, telling her to get up quickly, to get dressed and to get out somewhere safe with me. He had kissed her on the forehead and promised her he would see her soon.

Mother scooped me into her arms once she had dressed and attached her sword – for protection only, my father swore -- to her belt. Even though I was ten, I was small and skinny enough that she could sling me round onto her back without any issue. I wrapped my arms around her neck and my legs around her waist as she ran from the house. I reached out my hand as we left, catching my bow and hauling it over my shoulder, the taught wire digging into my chest.

The air was full of smoke and screaming, and I watched as my father ran through the line of trees, shouting commands at the soldiers alongside him. The last I saw of him, he was unsheathing his own sword, disappearing into the orange glow on the other side of the trees.

Mother ran across the clearing, towards the barracks and against the tide of soldiers running towards the castle. I saw a few I knew, men who had taught me how to shoot an arrow when my father was not looking, and men who had taught me how to fight with my fists properly, always saying I would need to know how to throw a decent punch in case I never got any bigger… all men I would never see again.

We ran until the screams from the castle were far enough away to just be background noise, and my mother stopped to let me down from her back, taking my face in her hands and checking me over. Her eyes were filled with tears as she looked at me, and I could see the fear written all over her face. When she believed me to be okay, she stood straight, looking around us to try and find somewhere safe to hide.

That was when we heard it.

The unmistakable sound of hooves riding towards us. Mother cursed, something I had never heard before, and hoisted me into her arms again. Instead of running she lifted me into the air, onto the lowest branch of the nearest tree.

"Climb, Maeteo!" She whispered urgently, pushing me up with all her strength. I scrambled to get a good grip on the tree, climbing as fast and as high up as I could.

When I looked behind me, mother was still stood on the ground at the base of the tree, her hands trembling as she unsheathed the sword my father had given her for protection. I panicked when I saw her standing still, the sounds of hooves getting closer, and my foot slipped from the branch it was on. Mother looked up; her eyes wide. I gestured for her to please, *please,* follow me up the tree. She shook her head, holding her hand to her heart and blowing me a kiss, before looking back to what was coming towards her.

An arrow came through the gap in the trees, hitting my mother square in the chest before I even had a chance to blink. Slamming my hand over my mouth, I held in a scream as I watched her drop to her knees, blood starting to come from her gaping mouth.

A troop of riders passed by then, all of them wearing Fire Kingdom armour, but only one of them laughing as he reached down and pulled the arrow from my mother's chest, kicking her down to the ground fully. Tears streamed down my face as I had to sit and wait until I could no longer hear the soldiers' horses until I could climb down to her side.

I landed on my knees beside my mother's body, the pain of stones and branches dull in comparison to the anger I felt in my chest. I crawled over to her body, my hands covered in dirt and blood, and rested my head on her chest. Sobs racked through my body as I clung to my mother's bloodied shirt, and I stayed there until the morning sun broke through the trees, and the screams from the castle had stopped. Taking my mother's sword from where it lay in the dirt, I placed a kiss to her forehead and closed her eyes gently with my fingers, and then I stood.

***

The sun was sitting high in the sky as I pushed the youngest entries of my army to their limit. Sweat dripped down my brow, and my throat hurt from shouting directions — but training days were my favourite days.

Lift your shield! Duck away from him! Faster!

I called out another round of instructions, watching each sparring pair closely as I wandered around between them, correcting postures and kicking shields until they were lifted.

The training space we used was not big, if it were the whole battalion in here, we would be squashed together like sardines, but for days like today it was enough. Once at the end of summer and once at the start of the year we took in every male from the kingdom who had turned eighteen in the six months before, we put them through eight weeks of intense training, and then we held the war games in the castle grounds. The men would be given a sword and would fight it out until there were only a handful remaining, and then they served with us until they either died or turned twenty-five, when they got the choice of staying or returning to their family to continue their fathers' works.

Next to none chose to return home.

I leaned against the wall nearest the gate, picking up the skin of water I had left here for myself, and sipping at it slowly, the heat of the day baring down on me. I did not need to be in full armour for training, really, but it showed my status; to scare the intakes into behaving.

Lifting my head towards the sun, I closed my eyes.

I had never been one for fitful nights of sleep. Usually, I would fall into bed and be asleep within seconds, and most of the time would wake up in the same position I fell asleep in. But last night… last night I had tossed and turned and wondered all night. I had been lost in my head, in thoughts of the Princess that would be turning eighteen this week, until the light outside my window had turned the dreary grey of early morning, and I had forced myself out of bed and down to the kitchen for an early breakfast.

I let my hands fall by my sides as I sighed, my eyes traveling along the stone walls around the training space.

A scream pulled my attention back to the training in front of me. Swords had stopped, and bodies had moved so they were standing in a loose circle to the far left of the grassy field. I rolled my eyes — no doubt one of them had been nicked by a blade and felt like their life was ending.

Walking across the grass, my steps became more hurried as a dark pool of blood started to seep out from under the soldier's feet.

"What happened?" I asked as I approached, several pale faces turned towards me, their eyes wide and their jaws slack. I pushed my way through them and stopped in my tracks.

Lying on his back on the grass, a boy stared at me with a sword sticking out from just below his collarbone. He was panting, his hands balling into fists around the grass. I had seen men die from less.

"What happened?!" I demanded again, glaring at his sparring partner; an arrogant eighteen-year-old from a more well-off family. He had his arms crossed over his chest as he stared down at the boy. "Well?"

"He insulted my mother." He shrugged; his voice infuriatingly light despite having just stabbed someone through the chest. I lifted my head slightly, narrowing my eyes as I took in his words.

"What's your name?"

"Cooper Fox."

I nodded my head, turning my attention back to the boy lying on the floor. He had closed his eyes and was sucking breath in through his teeth. I knelt next to him and placed my hand on his forehead, his eyes snapping open at the contact. Sweat from his brow soaked through my gloves.

"One of you get Merethyl from the hospital wing. Tell her to bring plenty of Valerian root."

Bodies scuffled as three different boys took off towards the castle.

"Cooper says you insulted his mother. Is that right?" The boy nodded, "Well, she probably deserved it."

A muffled chorus of laughter filtered through the gathered crowd as Cooper opened and closed his mouth in shock at my words. The boy on the ground laughed lightly, his breath hitching in his throat and his face scrunching up at the pull on his wound. I winced for him, knowing from experience that a sword wound was not exactly pleasant.

The sounds of shouting had me lifting my head and scanning the expanse of grass in between the training fields and the castle to see if Merethyl was on her way. The boys who had run off earlier were returning but there was no sign of my favourite medic following them. I frowned at them, raising an eyebrow as they all panted their excuses as to where she was, why she had not followed them, and that if I wanted to see her that badly, I was to go to her.

I rolled my eyes. The boy lying in front of me was losing too much blood much too quickly for me to move him, but if Merethyl was busy, then I would have to.

I swore under my breath, pulling off my armoured vest before my under shirt, balling it up in my hand.

"Okay…" I started, pulling the boy's attention back to me. "This — this is going to suck, all right? I am sorry."

Before he had a chance to reply, I had grabbed the hilt of the sword and pulled it free from his shoulder. He screamed, blood curdling and devastating, before his body fell limp into the grass. I used the balled-up shirt in my hand and pressed it onto the wound with as much pressure as I could manage. Blood soaked through it instantly. Shouts came from the group surrounding us as I slipped my free arm under the boy's waist and lifted him up, propping him against my shoulder so I could pick him up properly.

I eyed the pale faces that stood around us still, their eyes still wide and all of them sweating, and wondered how they were going to fare on a war field.

"You are all dismissed. Go and report to Hollis in the barracks."

They all scattered as I took off at a jog towards the castle, trying not to jostle the boy in my arms too much. His blood had soaked through my shirt completely and was starting to run down my chest. *Great.*

I shouldered my way through the back kitchen entrance, the smells of lunch hitting my stomach and making it grumble angrily. Chef and staff members jumped out of my way as I passed through and took the stone stairs two at a time up to the servant's tunnels.

When I was young, these tunnels were where Tarian, Hollis and I used to play hide and seek, so making my way through them now was like muscle memory. I knew every turn, every dip in the stone flooring, even every gap in the wall where the wind would come through a bit too loud, like the back of my hand. I took the stairs up to the main hallways as quickly as I could, inwardly pleased with myself for finding the hospital wing first try.

Using my shoulder again, I grunted as I pushed open the heavy wooden door to the lower level of the hospital wing. The strong smell of disinfectant burned my nose as one of the nurses looked up from her patient and gasped loudly; she stood so quickly her stool fell out from under her.

"General! What happened?!" She asked, starting to make her way towards me and the boy I was carrying.

"Accident in training." I grunted through my teeth, the muscles in my arms were starting to ache. "Where is Merethyl?"

The nurse in front of me pointed towards the curtained off stairs, and I took off at a jog again, despite the fact it looked like she was about to say something else. I pushed the curtain back just enough for me to slip through and started up the stairs, my pace starting to slow.

"Mer?!" I shouted as I reached the top of the steps, the empty ward making me stop in my tracks.

"Coming!" Merethyl's voice called from the far corner of the room. She emerged from behind another curtain, her hands pulling at her hair as her eyes fell on me, covering the pointed tips of her ears in case someone with an aversion to Fae had come in. Her face dropped when she saw the blood dripping onto the floor at my feet. "Lides! What happened to him?!"

"Long story, he got ran through with a training sword." I followed her to one of the empty beds, nearest the back cabinet where she kept all her potions and healing fixes. Merethyl had trained under the Fae healer Alexandre for years before I was even born, despite the fact she barely looked a day over twenty.

She gestured for me to place him down on the bed and handed me a clean roll of cloth, ripping the bloodied shirt from where I had placed it and throwing it into the metal bin beside the bed. I pressed clean cloth to the wound, but I knew it would not slow the blood flow until Merethyl had a chance to work some magic.

I watched her closely as she moved towards her cabinet, grabbing bottles and bowls, and muttering to herself as she lay them all out on a small metal trolley that she used to wheel between patients' bedsides.

"Why did you pull the sword out?!" She grumbled at me, nudging me with her hip to move me out of the way.

"Well, I wouldn't have needed to if you had come out to the field." I lifted a brow as she scowled at me, "What were you doing up here?"

"It is coming up for the Princess' birthday, is it not?" She ripped off a piece of cloth and dipped it in a metal bowl, the red liquid soaking into the material before she lay it across the wounded boy. "If she is to return, she will need a full health check, I was checking my supplies."

I blinked, surprised by her response. The Princess would be turning eighteen in three days, and I had every intention of bringing her back to the castle and her people before then, but Merethyl's readiness threw me.

No word had been sent yet from Emily about where they had been living. All anyone in the castle knew was that they were in one of Earth's many villages, under one of Alexandre's protection potions that was due to wear off on Kira's eighteenth birthday. If I did not manage to get her home, into the castle walls, before then... She would be traceable by the Fire Kingdom, and knowing she was in the Kingdom somewhere on the edge of having no protection made me feel uneasy.

I swallowed as I turned my attention back to the boy lying on the bed. His breathing had shallowed, and the bleeding slowed, but Merethyl's hands were pressing gently around the wound as she frowned at him.

"This is going to take time to heal, and when it does... He will not have full use of this arm. He might've if you had left the sword in."

I winced at her words, the ache in my chest for the boy overwhelming. He would be sent back to his village, shamed, and made to work wherever his father found his trade if he was not part of our ranks.

"We could get him into stable work here, couldn't we?" I asked, catching Merethyl's attention, she laughed lightly.

"Feeling guilty, Maeteo?"

I rolled my eyes, grumbling about needing to go and clean up and turning on my heel.

Trying to keep my pace casual, I took the stairs one at a time as I made my way back down to the lower level of the hospital. The floors were similar, lined with beds and cabinets, but this floor had several nurses flitting between castle staff and lightly injured soldiers, getting pain killers and headache treatments. My boots scuffed at the floor as I made my way across to the main door, very aware that I was still covered in blood that was not mine and nodded quickly to the nurse who had greeted me when I had arrived.

The hallway outside the hospital was cold enough that I was shivering by the time I made it to the doors leading to the gardens.

The gardens had always been my mother's favourite place in the castle grounds. We would spend hours here every day when she was not helping the queen dress, with her teaching me about her favourite flowers, or playing games of hide and seek, or simply listening to me tell her stories while she brushed my hair. My heart ached every time I stepped foot onto the lush, green grass.

Flowers lined the sides of the stone paths leading to the white marble fountain. Perfectly trimmed hedges covered with white and pink roses boxed the gardens in, making them feel like something from the fairy tales mother used to tell me when I had nightmares. I smiled lightly to myself as I passed through the beautiful space, admiring the lavender plants as they swayed in the light breeze. I knew I looked entirely out of place in the gardens now, especially covered in someone else's blood, but the calm they brought me was unlike anything else.

I stilled by the fountain — the sun beating down on my shoulders warming me again — and sat myself on the edge. The blue water shimmered as I crossed one leg over the other, leaning back against the cool wall. I tilted my head back, letting the sun warm my face again, memories of times spent with my mother in this exact spot running through my head.

"If you weren't covered in blood, I'd say you looked a vision."

Tarian's voice made me sigh heavily, opening one eye to glare at him.

My second in command, and the most talented swordsman in my ranks, Tarian had been my best friend since he enlisted at eighteen. I had been working my way up the ranks already, having been raised by the commanding General since my parents died, and had been put in charge of helping the new recruits find their bunks. I had fought him, of course, because I was eighteen and was convinced that I was better than I was, but he simply shook his head.

"Friendship is just as important as your position, Maeteo."

Tarian sat himself down beside me, mimicking my position and crossing his own legs over each other. He bumped me with his shoulder.

"Hollis is furious with you, by the way."

"I thought she would be." I laughed, closing my eyes again. Hollis was Tarian's twin sister, who had absolutely refused to stay at home when Tarian got to come and train. She had shaved her head, flagged down an intake wagon and pushed her way into the training ring, and was the first woman to ever fight in the Earth Kingdom army. "Any news yet?"

Tarian cleared his throat, making me look at him. His face was sharp, his blue eyes staring at me fiercely. I sat up straighter, my attention peaked.

"The Princess was spotted in Green Haven village half an hour ago."

My heart stopped in my chest. The thought of the Princess being in the village by herself making me feel instantly unsettled. Tarian watched me closely.

"Was Emily — "

"She wasn't there. The Princess was by herself, and then met with, I'm assuming, a friend. They went to go look at a horse in a stable together."

I nodded, swallowing the unease in my throat, and pushing myself up from where I sat on the fountain edge. Tarian followed suit, falling into step beside me easily as we made our way out of the gardens and towards the barracks.

"We will head to the village." I started, pushing through the barracks door, "Send one of the new men to the stables to get the horses ready. Have everyone ready to go in thirty minutes."

Tarian nodded and broke off from my side, heading into the mess hall and starting to shout commands.

I walked to my private room, the red, plush carpet soft under my feet when I kicked my boots off and all but ran to my bathing chambers to try and rid myself of the blood coating my chest. I did not even wait for the water to heat before I jumped into the copper tub that sat in the middle of the room, cursing to myself as I scrubbed myself clean.

Today was the day the Princess of the Earth Kingdom would be coming home.

4
Kira

My knuckles turned white as I clung to the front of the saddle.

General Stroll had lifted me onto his horse before I had the chance to object. Climbing up behind me and making sure I was comfortable before he took off at speed through the village square, leaving behind the baffled faces and whispered gossip. I had hunted for Dane's face as we had fled the square, catching a glimpse of him just before we sped through the trees. He was watching after us with a frown on his face despite Poppy pulling at his sleeve, her own face a mix of shock and amusement.

The village streets made way to the lush green of the forest trees as we flew through them, the houses all blurring into one mix of white and brown stone and their window boxes of flowers a blur of multi-colour. General Stroll did not slow the horse once the smooth terrain of the streets gave way to the uneven dirt of the forest floor, the ride becoming a lot less smooth, and a lot more stomach-turning as my hands tightened on the front of the saddle. The horse's dark mane whipping in every which way as the wind seemed to move with us, propelling us forward.

My eyes streamed as I fought to keep them open against the bitter cold wind. It had not felt cold when I had been walking through the village, if anything there had not been enough of it, but now, as we almost flew through the trees, it was bone chilling.

The lingering smell of smoke got stronger the farther into the forest we rode, and a feeling of ease settled through my stomach. We were heading in the direction of the house that Emily and I lived in.

I gasped as we broke through the trees into the familiar meadow, the horses speed finally slowing. The normally welcoming sight of the cherry trees completely thwarted by the sight of our cottage burning in bright orange flames. My scream got caught in my throat as one of General Strolls hands let go off his reins, squeezing the top of my arm in what I am sure was meant to be a comforting gesture, but it sent a shock through my body so strong I jolted away from him.

Swinging my leg over the saddle, I threw myself from where I had been sat onto the grassy ground. Pain shot through my legs as I landed awkwardly on my knees, rolling far away enough from the horse that I did not get trampled. General Stroll's curses reached my ears as I stopped, pushing myself up from the grass and hissing at the pain in my legs.

I made my way towards the house frantically, my eyes not focusing on any one thing long enough to take in what was happening in front of me. Emily stood chest to chest with a soldier much taller than she was, a finger pushed into their chest and a snarl on her face unlike any I had ever seen on her before. Emily had never been one for anger, always saying there was nothing that could not be solved through sitting down and talking. There was no trace of that Emily in the woman stood before me now. Her cheeks red, eyes puffy and wild, and her teeth bared.

"Emily?" I whimpered, my legs starting to shake as I drew closer to her. Emily's head whipped to the side, her features softening when she spotted me. She dived forward, her arms catching me by my elbows and pulling me into her chest. Instant comfort filled my body, but it was not enough to stop the growing devastation at watching my house burn to ashes.

"Kira, love." Emily's voice was soft as she stroked my hair with one hand. "Why are you limping?"

"She threw herself from my horse." General Stroll's voice came from behind us. Emily's grip on me tightened momentarily before she looked over at him.

Emily let me go, her face falling into that hard mask again as she stepped towards General Stroll, who squared his shoulders in preparation for whatever she had ready to throw at him.

"Care to explain why your band of bastards showed up at my house three days before schedule?" Emily bit out, her face flushed.

Schedule?

I frowned, my eyebrows furrowing as I watched General Stroll swallow harshly, his eyes fleeting between Emily, myself, and the burning house behind us. The man's confidence from earlier seemed to have completely disappeared under Emily's harsh gaze. Hot embers drifted through the wind as the soldiers from earlier in the village stood in a solid line, blocking me and Emily from getting too close to the house.

"We couldn't risk word of her being unprotected getting out." General Stroll's voice was soft but there was a harshness to his tone that made me wonder if that was why he was in charge.

"Do you think I'm stupid enough to let that happen?!" Emily spat, smacking at his chest. He lifted an eyebrow.

"Emily, she was in the village. *Alone.* If it can reach the castle that quickly, it would only be a matter of hours before… others, found out." General Stroll flicked his eyes to me briefly before he focused on Emily again. "This was my call."

"A stupid call, Maeteo!" She smacked his chest again, but he did not move an inch.

My voice was stuck in my throat as I watched the two argue. Their words sounded almost foreign as my eyes travelled over the burning foundations of the house I grew up in. The cherry red front door was now charred black, the window frames stood without their glass, and the roof had started to collapse in on itself with an earth-shattering crack.

Memories of years gone in that house flooded me as I stared. Emily and I watching the snow fall in the meadow, cups of steaming hot chocolate clutched in our hands, the fireplace crackling beside us. Dane, sprawled out on the floor of my small bedroom, his hands over his face while I tried — and failed — to explain the work our teacher had sent home with us. My favourite chair, sat in the corner of the main room surrounded by my piles of unfinished books.

I gasped aloud, whirling on the spot.

"My books!" My voice was near hysterical as I grabbed Emily's arm. Her eyes went wide. "I hadn't finished them!"

"The castle has an extensive library, Kira —" General Stroll's voice stopped as Emily sent him a look I could only describe as death. I stared at him, blinking as his words settled into my head.

The castle. Emily had told me stories of the Earth Kingdom castle since I could remember, about the night it was attacked, about how beautiful and extravagant the balls there had been before that night. She never, ever, told me how she knew so much about what the inside of the castle walls looked like, or how she knew the kitchens always smelled like bread on Sundays, but I hung onto every word of her stories like they were facts.

"I don't understand." I started; my voice surprisingly calmer than it had been before. "Why would we be going to the castle? What have we done?"

Emily shook her head at me, wrapping a reassuring arm around my shoulders.

"We haven't done anything, love." She glared at General Stroll, "There is… a lot, that you need to know. That I was *planning* to tell you before this happened."

I frowned at her, stepping away from Emily's warmth and crossing my arms over my chest. Her face fell as her arm dropped back to her side.

"What's going on?" I asked, looking between Emily, her face a mix of hurt and anxiety, and General Stroll.

He stood tall, his shoulders back, but his eyes were warm. The pair of them were staring at me like I was precious metal they feared scratching.

"This isn't really the place for this conversation." Emily said softly, reaching her hand out to touch my arm and then stopping herself, her hand lingering awkwardly in the air for a second before she let it fall again. "But seeing as we can't go inside," Another glare at General Stroll, "it seems like we have no better option."

"The castle is a much better option."

Emily rolled her eyes at General Strolls words but did not respond. I almost laughed at the exasperated expression on his face.

For a minute, the only sounds were the angry crackling of wood as the house burned behind us, the wind blowing smoke and ash over everyone who stood too close. Emily chewed on her bottom lip as she wrung her hands together, her eyes locked on something in the grass. I had never seen her so nervous.

"You remember the stories I told you, don't you? About the Princess stolen from the castle the night the

Fire Kingdom attacked?" I nodded, "Well, I may have left out a few details."

It was General Stroll's turn to roll his eyes as he crossed his arms over his chest and looked over his shoulder to his horse, who was happily grazing on the daisy's that scattered the grass of the meadow amongst the other horses. The fire did not seem to bother them.

"You see, the night of the attack… you were in the castle, Kira. Your mother and father were the most respected, fair leaders the Earth Kingdom ever had. They loved the kingdom, and everyone loved them. When you were born the kingdom celebrated for a week straight; parades, and parties, and so many gifts sent to the castle the kitchens could not house them all. You, my love, are the first female born into Earth's royal family in five centuries."

Emily's voice shook as she spoke. Her eyes searched my face, but I simply gestured for her to continue, my eyebrows furrowing.

"The — the Fire Kingdom, King Conleth, was adamant that you would marry his son, Prince Cyrus. He sent five marriage proposals to your parents before you had turned three. When your parents turned him down that fifth time... he lost his patience. He started sending his fire birds to burn down the farms to the West, to pressure them into agreeing. Your father, the fool that he was, sent our army to capture one. He ripped the feathers from its wings and sent its body back to Conleth.

"Conleth did not take it well, obviously. He went silent for months, and your mother and father thought he had gotten the message; the marriage was not going to happen, and he had to stop asking... But it was not that simple. Conleth gathered his own armies and sent them across the ocean on silent ships, no word of them being in our Kingdom reached us until the day before the attack, and by that point it was too late. They had set up camps all along the outskirts of the castle walls, across the fields, through the villages, even at the base of the Lides mountains... there was no way to get around it.

"When the attack came, your mother and I had been talking, *planning,* about how I was to take you to the eldest Fae in your mother's court, Alexandre, and he would help me keep you safe until your eighteenth birthday. I fetched you from your rooms and took you to her to say goodbye, and then we ran. We went with a... friend of mine, Alexandre's son, to see him. He gave you a tea to drink that held the protection spell we needed, but also clouded your memory of that night and anything to do with your heritage. It was safer for us for you to believe you were just Kira, not the Princess of Earth.

"I brought you here. Alexandre's son owned this cottage, and he sold it to me for three gold pieces. He... we were mad for each other, but after that night we never saw each other again. Every day of my life for the last fourteen years has been dedicated to keeping you safe, love. Conleth died about five years ago, and Cyrus took over his father's throne even though he won't be coronated as King until he marries -- and the betrayal of your parents declining his marriage proposal... he is out to finish what his father started. Either marry you, merge our Kingdoms and turn Earth into nothing more than a production line for Fire, or make sure our whole kingdom burns. Maeteo was not meant to show up today, he was not meant to be here until your birthday."

Emily took a deep breath. Her hands were clasped together and shaking in front of her as she stared at me, trying to gage my reaction.

"We got word of you being in the village today — *alone* — and decided to move early. When Cyrus and his forces find out that the spell has worn off and there is nothing to protect you from their spies anymore, they will move in. They will stop at nothing to get you, Princess."

The story they told me made sense in my head, like it was tugging on an old, distant memory that had been taken and locked away somewhere, just waiting to be brought forward and thrown out onto display. I blinked a few times, looking between Emily and General Stroll — Maeteo, as Emily had called him, not once but twice now.

A feeling grew in my throat, that I was sure was going to be a sob, but when I opened my mouth to let it out, a shrill, almost shrieking laugh burst from me. Emily startled, stepping back slightly with wide eyes. Maeteo stared, before a slow smile started to spread across his face.

I laughed until I was breathless, tears streaming from my eyes and my hands on my knees as I tried to catch my breath. I could hear Maeteo talking to someone beside us, the second male voice muttering something about me being in shock, and that there were horse sedatives in one of their packs should I need them. Maeteo chuckled, telling whoever he was talking to that they would not be necessary, and that he was sure it was illegal, if not extremely frowned upon, to drug a princess.

The word '*Princess*' had me straightening up, still giggling, and wiping my eyes. Every person in the meadow was staring at me. Some looked amused, but most wore a more concerned expression, like they were worried I had gone round the twist with the story Emily had spun me.

"Are you alright?" Maeteo asked, reaching out a hand and setting it gently on my arm.

"Yes, yes I'm fine," I giggled, wiping under my eyes again to catch any stray tears. "What are you saying, Emily? That I *am* the lost princess?"

The ridiculous theories Dane and I had shared as children suddenly did not feel all that ridiculous.

Emily did not reply, just nodded her head with the same worried expression that most of the guards were wearing. Another almost hysterical laugh.

"That's not possible," I shook my head, shaking Maeteo's hand off my arm, "I can't be a Princess. I don't know the first thing about ruling a kingdom."

"You will be taught everything you need to know by the castle elders. They tutored your mother and father, and your grandparents… they are the most knowledgeable people in the Kingdom." Maeteo's voice was serious enough that I stopped laughing to look up at him. His bright blue eyes were tinged with orange reflecting from the fire, and he looked as though he was ready to scoop me up, throw me back onto his horse and run off with me.

"I know this sounds bizarre, Kira…"

"Bizarre?!" I cut Emily's sentence off midway through, throwing my arms in the air. "I only wanted to get *eggs*, Emily! Eggs so you could make me a birthday cake, and I got kidnapped and told I'm not who I believed myself to be."

Emily's cheeks flushed at my words, her mouth straightening into a tight line. She clasped and unclasped her hands, like she did not know how to explain the events of the day any more than I did.

I turned my head to look at Maeteo, crossing my arms over my chest.

"So, what now?"

Maeteo lifted his chin slightly, his expression becoming more serious. The soldiers all shifted slightly, their relaxed stances stiffening into ones of squared shoulders and sharp eyes.

"Now, Princess," Maeteo started, his voice dropping into, what I assumed, was his commanding voice, "Now we return to the castle and let the Kingdom know you have returned."

I blinked at him, my heart beating at a thousand paces a second in my chest, but my head fell into a nod. Maeteo held out a hand for me to take as he whistled for his horse, the beautiful creature trotting over at the sound and stopping beside where we stood. I took Maeteo's hand slowly, trying my hardest not to think too much about what was happening, or where we were heading. Emily nodded at me, a tiny smile playing around the corners off her lips, but it was not enough to rid her eyes of her concern.

Maeteo slid a hand around my waist as he helped me up onto his horse, the strong body beneath me feeling no less intimidating than it had an hour ago. The soldiers that stood around the house moved to their own horses, falling into a formation that placed Maeteo and I in the middle of them all.

Emily joined the guard to our left, her hands gripping at the front of the saddle with ease as she hoisted herself up in front of the rider. I met her eyes for only a second before I looked away, my gaze focusing on the burning house behind us. My heart ached as Maeteo whistled again and the guards all moved their horses forward, the strong wind moving with us and keeping the smoke at bay as we moved away. Flurries of ash and embers floated alongside us for a while, until we were deep into the forest surrounding the meadow.

We were headed in the opposite direction to the village, and I frowned. Turning my head to look at Maeteo over my shoulder. He raised an eyebrow at me, questioning.

"Why aren't we going towards the village?"

"It is quicker for us if we go around the outskirts and through the forest as opposed to through the village." He explained, his eyes returning to the rocky path in front of us. Through a gap in the trees ahead, I could see the outline of the castle looming in the distance, its walls and turrets standing strong and proud at the top of a hill and the early afternoon sun casting its shadow across the valley. "It will still take us an hour or so to get there at this pace, though."

I nodded, swallowing as I looked to the front again, the horses' muscles moved beneath my legs as we kept up the swift, but somehow still leisurely, pace.

The sounds of birds and creatures of the forest all stopped as we passed through, the only sounds now being that of the horses' hooves cracking twigs and kicking stones. I looked over every guard in our strange procession. Near the front, sat tall on the back of a snow-white horse, was the only woman beside me and Emily. Surprise rushed through me at the sight of her and I wondered how I hadn't noticed her at the cottage, but the armour she wore matched that of the rest of the soldiers, and I figured no-one would be able to tell who she was if she hadn't taken off her helmet and hung it on the side of her saddle.

As if she could feel me watching her, she looked over her shoulder suddenly. Her eyes met mine and she grinned, looking almost feral as she did so, nodding her head at me. A blush crept up my neck at being caught staring, and I quickly looked away.

I felt, rather than heard, Maeteo laugh behind me.

My stomach churned unsteadily as I wondered what was awaiting me at the castle.

My castle.

5

Looming above us, taller than I could see from where I sat on Maeteo's horse, was the castle.

Stone walls taller than I had ever seen stretched in both directions, cutting through the forest like an unwelcome visitor. The stones near the top of the wall looked more recent than the ones nearer the ground; they were grey with moss and signs of weather wear, but the ones nearer the top were cleaner, less worn, and brighter in the small slips of sunlight coming through the trees. The thought of why they had to add those extra feet of wall made my stomach drop uncomfortably. We had come to the back entrance, apparently, as it was closer to the stables. The gatehouse that stood in front of us was made of worn, white stone and two faded flags swayed in the wind. I eyed them closely, seeing the same emblem on them that was at the top of the clock tower in the village; a mountain, a deer and a solid, full moon.

Dust floated up through the air around us as the gates creaked open. I squinted into the cloud, desperately trying not to end up with a stone in my eye. The guards had stopped the horses in the same formation we had travelled through the forest in, the only difference now being the dark green, velvet cloak that sat on my shoulders. Maeteo had pulled it from a saddle bag I hadn't noticed just before we got out of the forest, despite the warm summer sun. I had frowned at him, raising my eyebrows at the garment and scrunching my nose slightly; the feeling of velvet had always made my skin crawl. He had only laughed, taking one hand off his reins to place the heavy fabric across my back and pop the buttons together at the front.

Emily coughed from the horse next to us, waving a hand in front of her face to rid some of the dust from around her nose. She had been given a cloak matching my own, but she had pulled the hood up over her hair. I wondered for a second how she didn't appear to be sweating nearly as much as I did.

The dust around us cleared enough for me to see through the large iron gates that towered in front of us. They opened to reveal a bridge made of stone that travelled through the gatehouse, lit on the walls by sconces lit with orange flames. The large river that Dane and I had spent so much time at during the hot summer months as children now flowed along underneath the structure, the sound of lapping water echoing through the stone chamber as we passed through.

Armoured guards met us at the other side, their swords sheathed at their sides, but they gripped the hilts tightly. Their eyes searched over the guards as we passed by, finally settling on where I sat in front of Maeteo. If I had blinked, I would've missed the way the guard to the left gasped, his face lighting up as he walked through the horses to our side. He bowed his head, crossing a single arm across his chest as he did so. I just stared, completely baffled by the strange display.

"Princess," His voice was gruff, like that of a man in his mid-forties, "Welcome home."

I simply smiled at the man, unsure the correct response he was looking for. Maeteo cleared his throat.

"This is Mac, your majesty." He explained. "Mac was a commander under my father. He's one of the few who survived the raid."

My eyes widened as I looked at the man in front of us. He had a sad smile on his face, but his eyes were fierce underneath his helmet.

The horses started moving again, but Mac didn't go back to his position by the gate. He stuck by our side as we made our way up a stone path lined with trees, pink and white flowers growing on bushes, and long grass swaying in the wind. It felt like Green Haven — the cottage — was a thousand miles away, even though if I looked through the trees on the other side of the walls, I could still see the smoke billowing towards the sky.

The sounds of people shouting reached us as we turned a corner, and into the horse yard. The flurry of activity stopped as we all crowded into the small square and every person in the space turned their attention towards us; towards me.

I felt the blush rise up my cheeks before I could stop it. Guards started to dismount their horses, handing the reins off to stable hands and giving the horses sugar cubes from their saddle bags. Maeteo jumped down from the horse we shared and held out a hand to help me down. I thanked him, slipping off the side of the beast and losing a breath when my feet hit solid ground. My legs felt like jelly, and I rubbed my hands on the fabric of my trousers to try and bring some feeling back to them.

A hand on the small of my back made me straighten up, my eyes meeting Emily's. She stood beside me with a small smile on her face, but her eyes were still as weary as they had been back in the meadow.

"How are you feeling?" She asked, just quietly enough that only I could hear.

"I'm fine," I smiled lightly, "I didn't think horse riding would be quite as tiresome."

Emily laughed, reaching her arm around my shoulder, and pulling me into a tight hug.

"I will explain everything this evening, alright?" She smiled as she pulled away, "But for now I have to go and make sure they have your chambers ready."

I did not get the chance to reply before she took off through the yard, her cloak reaching out behind her as she moved between people and horses. I watched her go, unsure of what to do with myself. Turning, I walked over to where Maeteo's horse was getting taken care of — his saddle had been removed, and he was happily munching on some straw. I smiled at him as I reached him, running my hand up his long nose and grinning when he huffed happily.

Workers continued going about their business, the yard now incredibly busy with the new influx of horses, and the guards were all starting to make their way out the same way Emily had gone. I was half tempted to duck down behind the small wall in the stable I stood in and hide out here for a while, just to get my head around what had happened in the space of a few hours.

Running my fingers through the horse's main, I pursed my lips. Wondering how exactly my life had been flipped so dramatically since this morning.

"Don't be fooled by how handsome he is," Maeteo's voice made me jump as he appeared at the stable door. "He's an old grump." He grinned at the horse, running his hand down his neck.

"I don't believe that. He's been a perfect gentleman."

Maeteo laughed, hoisting a bucket of water up onto a small metal ledge on the wall across from me.

"You hear that, Fenrir? She thinks you're a gentleman."

Fenrir huffed a breath through his nose, nudging my arm with it as he did so. I laughed lightly, returning my hands to his mane and stroking my fingers through it. Maeteo went about his business in the stable; emptying the water he had brought with him into a trough that stretched along the back wall, hanging his reins and bridle on a metal hook, and finally taking a pink sugar cube from his pocket and holding it out in the palm of his hand for Fenrir. Maeteo grinned at the horse, touching his forehead to the space between the horses' ears before he looked at me again.

His face was softer now, like the stress of the day had melted away from him just by spending some time alone with Fenrir.

"You'll get your pick of the horses when you're settled in, Princess." He smiled, holding his arm out for me to take. I hesitated but hooked my hand into the bend of his elbow and let him lead me from the stable.

"I don't know how to ride." I blurted; my eyes wide as I looked up at him.

"We have wonderful riding instructors here, don't worry."

We walked through the yard, passing guards still with their horses and some that were leaving the same as us. The ones that were leaving all stopped where they were, standing up straighter and raising a hand to their brows in salute. Maeteo nodded his head at them as we passed.

The route Maeteo led me on towards the castle was lined with the same flower-covered bushes as the road we had arrived on. White marble statues cut between the bushes at irregular intervals, and a matching fountain sat off to the side in the middle of a section of grass. Birds flitted between trees, twittering away between themselves happily, all the while bees buzzed around the pink flowers of the bushes. I eyed every statue, different depictions of fat babies with wings and bows and arrows, and finally settled my view on the castle in front of us.

The same stone as the walls and gatehouse, the castle stood proud and solid. Ivy climbed the side wall, wrapping itself around the iron window frames and almost reaching the roof. Flower boxes lined every window and wrapped around the columns outside the doors was a perfect display of roses, lilies and hydrangeas. I could see the crescent shaped arrival area to my left, with perfectly trimmed grass and perfect cobblestones.

I expected Maeteo to take us that way, but instead he turned to the right, to the much less impressive — but still stunning — wooden door carved with roses that smelled amazingly like freshly baked bread.

"This is the kitchen entrance," Maeteo opened the door with his free hand and gestured for me to go first. "Most of the castle staff are busy so it's quieter to come through this way just now and have you meet everyone once you're comfortable."

I nodded as I stepped into the warm kitchen, inhaling deeply. The wooden tables and counter tops were filled with copper pots, freshly chopped vegetables, and more bread than I had ever seen in my life. I could've stopped to drool over it all, but Maeteo's hand on my back nudged me forward.

We moved from the kitchen through a small hallway, managing to avoid bumping into anyone, and emerged in the main lobby. The large iron doors were closed with a bolt across them, but there was a group of people gathered in the middle of the marble floored room, all talking in hushed voices. Maeteo cleared his throat, and the group disbanded from their gossip circle into a straight line, the six of them staring directly at me.

I wanted to plant my feet, refuse to move forward until they stopped staring or until someone convinced me this wasn't a fever dream; but once again, Maeteo moved me forward towards the small group.

"Your Majesty," An elderly woman, with grey hair that reached her ankles and simple white robes, greeted me first, bowing at the waist. "I am Eyvlin, your head of house. What a great pleasure it is to have you returned to us."

"Thank you." I managed to whisper, my hands clutching to the inside of the cape I was wearing. The rest of the people in front of me introduced themselves one after the other, but the only one I caught straight away was Hollis — the small woman on the end was the woman that had been part of our horseback procession earlier, and she gave me the same wild smile as she bounced on the balls of her feet slightly. Maeteo rolled his eyes at her.

A girl with skin a few shades darker than the tunic she was wearing stepped forward and dropped into a curtsy. Her hair was tied tight into a knot on the top of her head, but she wore a smile brighter than any I had seen.

"Gracie is your personal staff, Your Majesty." Eyvlin explained, gesturing towards the girl who stood up straight again. "Anything you need, you tell her."

"Thank you," I repeated, my voice starting to warm up and not sound as terrified, "but please, call me Kira."

Eyvlin blinked at me like I'd slapped her, and Maeteo chuckled from behind me and covered it stealthily with a cough. Eyvlin glared at him.

"I'm afraid I can't do that, Your Majesty." Eyvlin's voice was tight as she ran her hands down the front of her robes, ironing out invisible creases. She stepped forward, gesturing for me to walk beside her. I looked back at Maeteo with wide eyes, but he just nodded at me, a small smile on his face.

Eyvlin whisked me away, up one of the curling staircases lined with red, plush carpets and walls full of intricate oil paintings of flower filled fields, animals grazing at a lake, and people gathered around a campfire. Maeteo stayed at the bottom of the stairs with two of the guards and Hollis, while the man introduced as the chef excused himself back to the kitchens. Gracie kept pace with us and followed Eyvlin and me up the stairs.

The hallways of the castle were full of the same red carpets as the stairs, but the walls were full of sconces, flickering brightly with orange flames, and portraits of men looking stuffy and uncomfortable in high collars and heavy crowns. We passed several heavy wooden doors as we walked through the castle hallways, and Eyvlin did try to list off what was behind each one, but they went right over my head. I would need to explore more by myself when I got the chance.

Something at the back of my mind placed these hallways as familiar, like I should feel more at home in them than I did.

Eventually, we turned down another hallway, and the space opened. The floors changed from the red carpets to cream, and the portraits on the walls gave way to light, floral wallpaper. At the end of the hallway stood double doors carved with flowers that were painted gold to match the handles. Crystal lamps sat at either side of the door, casting the hall in bright light, and there were white vases full of flowers lining the sides of the hallway. It was almost ethereal.

Eyvlin moved forward, her hands clasped in front of her. When she reached the double doors, she gestured for me to push them open. My eyebrows furrowed, but I placed my hands on the golden handles and pushed forward.

The smell of lavender hit me first while my eyes took a second to adjust to the sunlight streaming in through the windows in front of me. The flooring was the same cream carpet as the halls, and there were two plush sofas sat around a coffee table in front of a fireplace larger than I had ever seen. A desk sat to the left of the room, and gauzy, light pink curtains swayed in the breeze coming through the open windows — but my attention was snagged by the bookcases. Three large, wooden bookcases with gold flowers dancing up the sides stood proudly at the back of the room, and I itched to run my fingers over the spines, read the titles, and lose myself in as many of them as I could.

Plants covered almost every surface, all in small, golden pots that shined in the afternoon sun.

Two archways stood at either side of the fireplace, both covered by the same gauze curtains as the windows; through one I could see marble floors and a standing bathtub, which meant through the other had to be the bedroom. The room seemed bigger than our cottage had ever been.

Emily appeared from through the bedroom doorway and her face split into a smile when she spotted us standing there. She clapped her hands happily, lunging forward to grab my wrists and pull me into the room.

"Isn't it beautiful?" She asked, her tone light as her eyes roamed the room. "I knew you wouldn't want it to be too dark, and I made sure there were plants."

"It's…" words left me as I stepped onto the plush rug, the same shade of pink as the curtains. The whole room reminded me of spring, light and relaxed. "It's unbelievable."

Emily's grin got somehow bigger, and she wrapped her arms around me in a tight hug.

"Gracie, why don't you go and draw Her Majesty a bath?" Eyvlin's voice came from the doorway where the two still stood, watching the scene between Emily and I unfold. Gracie nodded, excusing herself and quickly disappearing behind the gauzy curtain to the bathroom.

The sounds of running water started, and Emily finally released me from our hug.

"Thank you, Eyvlin, that'll be all." Emily smiled at the elderly woman, who bowed her head and turned on her heel, closing the doors with nothing but a swish of her hand.

I stared; my mouth open. Emily laughed, putting a hand on my shoulder, and guiding me towards the sofas. I let myself fall onto the nearest one, my tired legs glad for the soft cushions. Emily sat on the one across from me, her hands folded on her knees. I unclipped the velvet cloak from around my neck, thankful for the drop in weight as it fell onto the sofa behind me and looked towards the windows.

"Are you alright, love?" Emily asked, her voice quiet.

I tore my eyes away from the view out the window. Way in the distance I could see the village, the square and clock tower looking minuscule from where I sat. The Lides mountains sat even farther beyond that, the tops dusted with snow, despite the heat of the summer. I could even see the farms scattered across the fields, separated by dirt tracks and forests.

My eyes trailed back to the village square, the colourful stalls of the market were gone now, meaning it was after one. I wondered briefly if Dane was still at the fountain with Poppy and her friends, or if they had left after we had, anxious to spread the news of my being taken by royal guards.

Emily raised her eyebrow at me.

"I'm fine." I nodded, smiling lightly. "A little… baffled, I guess."

Nodding her head, Emily stood from her seat on the sofa.

"Understandable, love." She started towards the door, "If you need me, send Gracie to find me. If not, I'll see you for dinner, all right? Chef will bring it up to your room about six."

I simply nodded, watching as Emily left the room, opening one of the doors and closing it behind herself quietly. The quiet of the room left me feeling anxious, the only noise being the running water and Gracie's humming coming from the bathroom. I stood from the sofa, my legs feeling like they were made of jelly, and made my way across the lush room towards the bookcase.

Scanning the titles, I spotted several from my childhood, all stories Emily had told me in front of the cottage fireplace during thunderstorms to keep me calm. The familiar titles made me smile, and I was going to turn away from the shelf when I noticed the small pile of books stacked on the floor in front of the farthest away case. When I looked at them closer, I realised it was the same pile I had on my table next to the chair at home. Relief flooded me that someone had managed to save them.

"Your bath is ready, Your Highness."

Gracie's voice made me jump, a hand on my thundering heart as I spun on the spot. Gracie laughed lightly, drying her hands on her apron.

"Sorry, I didn't mean to startle you."

"No, no it's fine. I was in a world of my own." I smiled, leaving the bookcases, and following Gracie into the bathroom.

It was grander than it had appeared through the curtain. The sinks and bath had matching golden hardware, and the floor was a slick, grey and white marble stone. The bath stood in the middle of the room, golden claw feet keeping it up high. I wondered briefly if I would be able to step into it, but Gracie quickly grabbed a small stool from under one of the sinks.

Steam and the smell of citrus and florals rose from the water, and I was instantly thankful for Gracie and her wonderful choice in bath oils.

"Is there anything else, Your Highness?" Gracie asked, standing by the door with a smile on her face.

I nodded my head, looking round at her.

"You can call me Kira, for one." I smiled, and Gracie laughed lightly, "Two, if we're going to be spending a lot of time together, would you like to join Emily and I for dinner?"

Gracie hesitated, but eventually nodded her head, a smile on her face.

"I would like that very much, Your Majesty. Thank you."

Gracie excused herself then, the curtains falling closed behind her as she left. I waited until I heard the main doors close before I turned to the bath. Steam filled the room as I got myself out of the clothes I had on, the thin summer leggings covered in horsehair and sweat. I crinkled my nose at them as I placed them in a pile beside the sinks and let my hair out of the ponytail it had been in.

Using the stool to reach the edge of the bath, I stepped over into the hot water. The instant relief from the heat flowed through my legs as I sat down, and I sighed aloud. Sinking down into the water, I noted how much deeper the bath was than I had originally thought, the water reaching my chin with ease before I started to run out of room to sink farther down. I closed my eyes for a second, relishing in the warm water before I dunked my head under completely, blocking out the outside world for a few seconds before sitting up properly, running my hands over my face and opening my eyes again.

Part of me had thought that, if I had gone under that water and closed my eyes, when I re-emerged, I would be back in the tin bathtub of the cottage, separated from the living area by only a thin wooden divider. But the bathroom remained as grand, and the bath stayed white and gold.

<u>6</u>

The castle library was the most unbelievable room I had ever seen.

Three stories of fully packed bookcases made of deep oak, alcoves with leather armchairs and reading lamps; tables for groups of four and six sat between cases, some left empty and some with people pouring over the contents of some old books. The running theme of red carpets continued into here, but the ceiling was painted into a brilliant mural, rather than the stone of the rest of the castle.

I had been sat back in my chair, my eyes roaming over the paintings of kings, queens, armies, and battlefields when Eyvlin found me. She cleared her throat, making my head snap forward and a blush run up my neck at the look on her face.

"Good morning, Your Majesty." Her voice was curt as she smiled a tight smile at me.

"Good morning." I stood from my chair, "Is everything okay?"

"We have been looking for you all morning. It is not wise to leave your chambers without alerting someone."

I shrank slightly at her scolding, feeling more like a child than someone who was turning eighteen in two days. Her eyes bore into me as I stepped away from the table, pushing my chair under it to keep anyone from tripping over it.

"I'm sorry, Eyvlin — "My apology was cut off by the arrival of someone else.

"Oh, Eyvlin, lighten up." Emily's voice was cheery as she appeared at the gap between bookcases, "Did I not tell you she'd be in here?"

"It is not *wise* — "

"For her to leave her rooms and not tell us, yes, she knows that now." Emily rolled her eyes at the elderly woman, who looked as if she was going to combust if Emily did not stop sassing her.

Smiling, Emily linked her arm through mine, leading me from the space we were in. We passed several groups of people as we left, all of them standing from their tables and bowing their heads at me. I kept my eyes forward, still unsure of how they wanted me to react.

I could hear Eyvlin huffing as she kept pace behind us, and eventually Gracie appeared by her side, her usual smile on her face. Emily led us down the main stairs, into the open lobby of the castle. People were rushing about on their daily tasks. Staff wearing the same tunics as Gracie ran back and forth with folded towels and empty trays. Soldiers in full armour were heading out of the front doors, laughing, and pushing each other, and I could hear shouting coming from the kitchens; words so foul my eyes went wide as we descended the stairs.

Emily laughed, patting my arm, and directing us in the opposite direction, down a hallway that matched the rest of them, and into a room with only a large table in the middle of it. The table was lined with chairs, and they were all full of people. Elderly men who looked like they would rather be off having a nap, some younger ones who were almost vibrating with excitement, and at the very end, on the right of the open head seat, was Maeteo.

Everyone around the table stood as we entered, the sounds of chairs scraping across wooden floors lasting for only a second.

I froze on the spot, staring as they all bowed their heads. Thankfully, Emily gestured for them all to sit, and when they did, she nudged me towards the empty seat at the head of the table. I took the seat quickly, folding my hands on my lap.

Eyvlin took a seat at the middle of the table, her hair draping over the back of her chair as she sat. She cleared her throat, sitting forward slightly so I could see her face clearly.

"Welcome to your first council meeting, Your Majesty." She said in a clear voice, "As you haven't gone through your coronation yet, the council will discuss all matters with you, but unfortunately you will not be able to vote on movements."

Emily and Maeteo both rolled their eyes at the statement, and a couple of the younger members of the council looked uncomfortable. The only people who seemed okay with the statement were the elderly gentlemen… apart from one. He sat at the far end of the table, his hair snow white tucked behind his pointed ears and tattoos on his neck and shoulders. His beard was tied with a piece of string, and he wore a dark green robe. He appeared to be the only Fae sitting at the table, and instead of looking at Eyvlin like everyone else seemed to be, he was staring directly at me.

"Shouldn't we discuss the coronation first, then?" Emily's voice pulled me from my thoughts, my eyes tearing away from the elderly Fae male.

Eyvlin nodded, shuffling a small pile of papers she had on the desk in front of her.

I looked around the room, only then noticing that Gracie still stood by the door. She grinned at me, but I frowned, wondering why she had not taken a seat with the rest of us.

"Sorry, before we start," I started, placing a hand on the table. Everyone at the table froze, "Can we bring another seat in here, please? For Gracie?"

Eyvlin bristled slightly, her shoulders squaring, but it was one of the men who spoke next, his voice nasally and annoying.

"Staff don't sit with council, Your Majesty." He snickered; his face amused as he looked at me.

"Why not?" I asked, my eyebrows furrowing.

"These meetings do not concern them."

"Ah," I nodded, sitting up straight, and bringing my hand back to my lap, "but you see, Sir, — if Gracie is to know my every move and attend my every need, shouldn't she be involved? She will need to know where and when she is needed."

The room fell into silence as the old man stumbled over his next reply, the only noise beside his fumbling for a reply being Maeteo's chuckle.

"That is not — She cannot — "

"She can have my seat, Brond." Maeteo stood from his seat, gesturing for Gracie to come and sit in it instead.

Gracie moved across the room slowly, her hands gripping at the apron she wore as she sat gingerly in the seat, as if it would open from underneath her and let her fall through the floor.

Everyone in the room stared as Gracie sat and Maeteo went to lean against a side table, his arms crossed over his chest and a smirk on his face. He locked eyes with me for a second and his grin grew even larger as he nodded his head.

I looked back to Eyvlin, tilting my head slightly as a way of telling her to continue. Her face was red, and her breaths were coming fast as she looked at the man Maeteo had called Brond. He was glaring between myself and Gracie but nodded also.

Eyvlin stood, her hands shaking slightly. Whether it was from anger or old age, I could not tell.

"The coronation for Her Majesty will take place four weeks from her eighteenth birthday. That gives us enough time to send invitations to those of nobility through the Kingdom and the royals of Air and Water, as well as time to train the newest intake of soldiers in case a threat from Fire emerges in the upcoming weeks."

The council all muttered agreement, and Eyvlin looked at Maeteo.

"Will the young ones be trained to acceptable standards by then?"

"Do you doubt me, Eyvie?" Maeteo smirked, "Of course they will be."

"Well, given one of your intakes is lying in the hospital wing with a nasty stab wound, gained from another intake, doubt is to be expected."

Maeteo's face fell, and I saw the anger flash through his eyes for a second before he schooled his features back into neutrality.

"That has been dealt with, darling." Maeteo's use of nicknames seemed to ruffle Eyvlin to the point I half expected steam to come from her ears and her hair to curl. She turned away from him, huffing.

"The coronation will of course be marked with a ball, the theme of which shall be left for Her Majesty to decide."

The morning continued in that fashion, Eyvlin rattling off points of importance and the council around the table either agreeing or disagreeing. More than once an argument between one of the elders and a younger council member erupted and had to be calmed down. The old Fae at the end of the table did not say a word, just nodded or shook his head when he was expected to.

I heaved a heavy sigh through my nose, my eyes traveling around the room for what felt like the millionth time that hour. Topics of conversation had gone from my coronation to staff uniforms, to the menu for the week — which apparently was the highlight of Maeteo's day, given how much he had to say about it — to the added stress it would put on the castle's resources if Air and Water were invited to the festivities over the coming weeks.

"Next," Eyvlin's voice was hoarse as she stood, using the table to lean against with her hand. "Her Majesty's training."

I looked at Emily, my eyebrows furrowing in confusion, but that was the moment Emily seemed wonderfully content to examine a knot in the wood of the table.

"Training?" I asked, turning my attention back to Eyvlin. She cast her eyes downwards, clearing her throat.

"Your training will consist of horseback riding, sword fighting and physical combat, and war strategy."

Silence swallowed the room as twelve pairs of eyes looked my way. I felt my stomach drop.

"If we are expected to go into battle, which is looking more and more likely by the day, you are going to need to be at least somewhat trained." Eyvlin's voice grew more and more hoarse as she spoke, and a glass of water appeared in front of her as if from nowhere. "Thank you, Alexandre."

The name tugged at my memory from yesterday, the story Emily told of the man who helped us escape and his father, who was the one behind the protection spell. Alexandre waved his hand nonchalantly, as if it had been nothing for him to produce the glass from thin air. I watched him closely, noting the way he moved.

"There will also be the matter of your eloquence lessons, your history lessons, your dress and crown fittings, and your audiences with the people of Earth."

My eyes went wide at the list Eyvlin was rattling off. Emily bumped her knee to mine under the table comfortingly, but I was still staring at Eyvlin. She sat back in her chair with a groan, the man next to her — I'd heard Eyvlin call him George — held her elbow as she sat, and for the first time since I'd met her, I saw her properly smile.

Alexandre cleared his throat, standing from his chair at the end of the table.

"Before we end things," His voice was like gravel under horse hoof, rough and scratchy, "I would like to say what an honour it is to have you back with us, Your Majesty."

Everyone at the table mumbled their agreements, nodding their heads.

"It has been a dark time without your parents, but we are certain you will lead with the same grace and dignity that your mother did before you."

He sat back in his seat, and I felt my cheeks heat at his words. There had been no mention of my father.

"Thank you, Alexandre." I said quietly, right before Eyvlin called the meeting to a close.

Emily placed a hand on my arm, gesturing for me to wait before I stood. She had us sit until everyone except the two of us and Gracie had left the room.

I let out a heavy breath, slumping in my chair and covering my face with my hands. The sounds of chairs scraping on the floor again let me know that Emily and Gracie had stood. I let my hands drop before I followed their lead, pushing my own chair back and standing, despite the protests from my still sore legs.

We had barely stepped out of the room when Alexandre appeared beside us, his long beard tucked into the rope belt he wore around his white robes.

"Your Majesty, may I have a word?" He asked quietly. I looked at Emily, but she nodded her head and took Gracie by the arm, leading her away with talks about the seamstress and the dresses she would need to create for me.

I nodded at Alexandre, and he gestured with a hand towards the hall leading in the opposite direction. My head was screaming at me not to follow this man, that I didn't know him at all, but if Emily trusted him — and had been in love with his son, from what I gathered — then I knew I would be safe.

We walked in silence until we reached a set of curved, stone stairs. Alexandre gestured for me to go first, and I held tightly onto the oak handrail curling up the stone wall. We were going farther and farther up into the towers of the castle, and my hands started to sweat with anxiety.

The sounds of people chattering, birds singing, and what sounded like metal hitting metal rose from somewhere on the castle grounds, the noises filtering through the small windows that were sporadic throughout the tower so far.

When we reached the top, I was out of breath and sweating under my light dress I'd chosen from the already stocked wardrobe this morning. Alexandre pushed his way through an old door, holding it open for me to step in after him. My stomach flipped as I stepped into the strange room.

The room was dark, but small jars filled with what looked like fairy light were placed around enough so I could see. There was a pair of large, worn armchairs sat in the corner of the room next to an old, iron fireplace and stove top. A bed sat under a pile of blankets against the back wall.

Alexandre motioned for me to take a seat in the armchair whilst he filled a tea pot and sat it gingerly on top of the stove. I crossed my hands in my lap, feeling like somehow, this whole room was familiar too.

"I hope you don't mind me bringing you up here, Your Majesty, but I don't much like the tea Chef makes." Alexandre crinkled his nose at the mere mention of it, and I laughed lightly, shaking my head. "I trust Emily has filled you in on who I am."

I nodded, taking the steaming mug he handed me and sipping at it gingerly. The taste of chamomile and peppermint burst into my mouth.

"You are the one who put the protection spell on me." I stated, and Alexandre nodded his head with a small smile on his face.

"I must say I am glad it held up so well." He sighed as he sat down in the matching armchair across from me. He seemed so old in that moment; I wondered if he should have been using some kind of walking aid. "How did my son's cottage treat you?"

"It was wonderful." I smiled, sipping at my tea again.

"I wish Maeteo and his brutes had more sense than to burn it down." Alexandre grumbled, more to himself than to me.

"Your son… He and Emily were close?"

Alexandre's smile turned sad as he stirred his tea with a spoon that he wasn't touching. His hands stayed wrapped around the mug and he was moving the spoon with only his eyes. It was entrancing to watch.

"Ah, they were very much in love with each other, yes."

"Is he still in the castle? Emily hasn't mentioned him."

Alexandre's eyes moved to me, his spoon stopping its rounds of his mug and clattering against the side.

"Leo never made it back to the castle the night he helped get you two free."

My heart dropped in my chest as I looked at Alexandre's face, seeing suddenly the depth of the lines by his eyes.

"He was told to return to me once he had escorted Miss Emily and yourself to the cottage, but he never showed. He was a foolish boy, so I have no doubt he would have gone straight to help those at the castle rather than keep himself safe. I... I have no idea if he was killed, or if he was captured and taken back to the lands of Fire, but I have not seen or heard from him in fourteen years."

My throat went dry at Alexandre's words, and I placed my mug down carefully on the small table between the two chairs, reaching over and placing my hand on Alexandre's knee in what I hoped was a comforting gesture. The old Fae smiled at me sadly, placing his own mug beside mine and taking my hand in his own; squeezing my fingers tightly.

We sat in silence for a minute, the distant sounds of outside barely audible over the crackling of the fire in the fireplace and the sound of an old clock ticking from beside Alexandre's bed.

I could still feel my heart hammering my chest as I watched Alexandre closely, he was staring blankly into the fire, his bottom lip pulled between his teeth as if he were mulling something over.

"How old are you, Alexandre?" I asked, my voice sounding louder than I would have liked it to. Alexandre laughed once, but it was a laugh with no sign of humour in it.

"Older than I would like to be, my dear." He smiled, patting my hand again. "Much older than I would like to be. I started working at the castle when I was a boy, with my father as your great-great-grandfather's apothecary." I started at the realisation that Alexandre must have been coming up for his two-hundred-and-something birthday. He laughed again, sounding slightly more chipper, at my reaction. "Fae lives are much longer than human ones, Your Majesty."

"I've never met many Fae, I won't lie. Emily always told me that they lived farther South."

Alexandre frowned, his eyebrows furrowing together as he mulled over what I just said.

"The Fae people of Earth left a long time ago, Your Majesty – most of us now reside in Fire. Your grandfather was not our biggest fan."

He let go of my hand, and I sat back in my chair, watching him as he pushed himself up from where he sat and walked across the room to the crowded bookcase behind the door. He ran his hands over several books before he decided on one, blowing enough soot and dust off it that it reached where I was sitting.

The book he was holding was thick, much thicker than any I had in my rooms, and its red cover was faded to the point it almost looked brown. Alexandre held it out to me, and I took it gingerly, eying the cover closely. There was no title, no author; just a picture of a golden crown above the same emblem from the flags outside.

"That is the book of your ancestors. Everyone from the first King of Earth to your father is found in these pages, how they lead, their downfalls, their marriages and children… it's all in there."

Alexandre sat back down with a huff of air, closing his eyes momentarily as I stared at the book in my lap.

"You are the first female born to the Earth line in five-hundred years, Your Majesty. Only you have the power in you to stop the horrors Fire intends to bring to our shores."

"I don't know —" My sentence was cut off by the sound of light snoring, and I lifted my head from the book in my lap to see Alexandre's head tilted to the side, his eyes closed and his breathing deep and shallow.

Standing from my chair, I took my mug from the table and placed it in the small metal sink beside the stove top. Quietly, I tiptoed across the room, picking up the book as I went, and let myself out of his room, closing the heavy wooden door behind me with a *'thunk'*.

The book in my hands didn't seem to weigh as much as the words Alexandre had left me with.

7

Gracie sat on the end of my bed with a smile, a pile of discarded dresses scattered next to her on the quilt. I had invited her in to help me decide on something to wear for the castle wide dinner this evening, the anxiety of having every single member of staff coming to meet me after the meal making me feel faint.

Emily had left that little detail out until fifteen minutes ago when she excused herself to go and get ready.

Now I stood, hands on my hips in a white, fluffy robe with my hair in wild curls around my shoulders. Not very princessy, Emily had commented, but I had simply rolled my eyes at her, more interested in asking her about the book Alexandre had given me. She claimed she had no idea about it.

I reached into the wardrobe, grabbing a pale blue, silk gown from the back of the racks and holding it up in front of myself, turning to Gracie for her opinion. She pursed her lips, tilting her head to the side in thought.

"It's... nice." She said slowly, her nose crinkling, "But I don't think it's right."

I shook my head, throwing the dress to pile and huffing out a sigh. I felt like I had gone through every single dress in this godforsaken wardrobe so far, and none of them felt right enough for an evening such as this.

Emily had said that I would be getting fittings with the castle dress maker, Anya, before my coronation, but I could have used her now. I drummed my fingers against the fabric of my robe before diving back into the wardrobe and grabbing my last option.

The dress I pulled was a mauve purple, with thin double straps and the bodice covered in floral lace. The lace fell onto the skirt before starting to disperse, scattering across the skirt, which was several layers of tulle and organza. I held it up in front of myself again, looking to Gracie, who's face seemed to light up at the sight of the dress. She nodded excitedly, her ebony hair bouncing around her face as she done so.

Relief washed over me at her approval of the dress, and I hung it on the door of the wardrobe. Gracie stood from where she sat, taking the skirt of the dress in her hands and holding it out to examine it properly.

"It's perfect!" She grinned, letting the dress fall flat back against the cupboard door.

"I'm glad you think so," I nodded, "I haven't had the chance to meet the seamstress yet, so I'm working with what was here already."

"Oh, don't worry about that. Mother rarely gets sizing wrong even if she hasn't met the person she's making for yet."

I stopped in my tracks on my way through to the main room of my chambers, my eyebrows furrowing at Gracie's choice of words.

"Did you say 'mother?'"

"Yes, Anya is my mother." Gracie smiled. "She was born in the castle, as was I."

My eyes widened, and Gracie motioned for me to keep moving through to the bathroom. I let her guide me into the small wooden stool, facing myself in the large, golden mirror on the wall. The dressing table was scattered with different creams and cosmetics, hair pins and brushes and glittering pearls. Gracie grabbed the nearest brush, pulling it through my hair gently.

"My grandmother was one of the elder Queen's ladies in waiting. She was always by her side, but she fell pregnant to a fisherman, my grandfather, when she was in her twenties. The Queen, your grandmother, was furious, but she let her stay in the castle. She didn't think it proper to have a pregnant, unmarried lady at her side, so she let her work in the kitchens instead, which gramma didn't mind, really, she ended up happier.

"Mother was born on Gramma's twenty-fifth birthday, and the Queen had sent for my grandfather to be present during it, but he never arrived. He was never seen again, actually."

Gracie placed the brush back on the dressing table, starting to twist and curl my hair into intricate swirls.

"Anyway, Mother was raised alongside the rest of the staff children. She took all her classes with them, and when she was a teenager, she asked to shadow the castle seamstress. She shadowed her for years before the elder Queen passed, and your mother and Father were to be married and put into power. The seamstress, Miss Dawn, took one look at my mother and told her to make your mothers wedding dress, and if she could, she could take over as seamstress.

"Mother was beside herself. She didn't sleep for weeks, constantly at her sewing machine trying to get your mother's dress perfect. A guard, Jackson, got put in charge of her, making sure she ate and slept. Jackson was absolutely head over heels for her from the minute he saw her, but mother didn't even notice his compliments.

"When the dress was finished, mother slept for days, only barely waking up in time to help your mother get dressed on the day of the wedding. Jackson asked to escort my mother to the wedding and the ball afterwards, and mother said yes… and the rest is history. I was born two years later."

Gracie had a smile on her face as she spoke about her parents, her hands still working quickly over my hair, pulling it this way and that until it was piled on top of my head in the most stunning style. Purple flowers, the same colour as my dress, were weaved through the braids alongside the pearls from the table. My mouth hung open as I looked at it all in the mirror. Gracie disappeared for a second, returning with a silver tiara in her hands which she placed gently on top of my head.

My stomach dropped, and I took in a breath of air. The tiara sparked no matter what way I turned my head, sending shimmers across the walls and mirror in front of me. Gracie grinned, clapping her hands before she spun me around in the stool to face her.

"How old were you when — you know…" I asked, closing my eyes so Gracie could dust a light cosmetic powder over my eyelids.

"When the Fire kingdom attacked?" Gracie asked, her voice even and unwavering. "I was ten, the same age as Maeteo — I mean, General Stroll."

"You know him?" I opened my eyes, blinking in the light of the bathroom. Gracie nodded.

"Oh, yes. We were in lessons together as children and our fathers fought together," Gracie's smile turned sad, "They both died the night of the attack. Mother took Maeteo in, she and Annabelle, Maeteo's mother, had been close so when she was killed trying to flee with

Maeteo, Mother thought it only right she take care of him."

My heart broke in my chest at the thought of Maeteo as a child and losing both of his parents in one night, because of me. I swallowed harshly, letting Gracie continue to sweep powders over my skin until she deemed me acceptable. When she spun me on the stool to face myself in the mirror, I started. She had managed to even out my usually red complexion completely, the only colour being a light peach across my cheekbones and tip of my nose. My eyelids were painted in shades of brown and grey, and my lips were a natural pink.

I blinked in the mirror, leaning in to examine myself more closely. Gracie stood behind me, ringing her hands nervously until my face split into a grin. She let out a heavy breath, laughing lightly.

"I was terrified you wouldn't like it — I've never done anyone else's before." Gracie's words came out quickly, and I shook my head.

"I love it," I smiled, standing from my stool, "Thank you, Gracie."

Gracie's grin was beaming as she led me back through my chambers to my bedroom.

The four-poster bed looked incredibly inviting as I stepped into the room, even with the scattering of discarded dresses along the bottom. Its white sheets and pink cushions had been made perfectly by a member of the castle staff before I got the chance to even look at it this morning, and right now I wanted to go and climb under the thick duvet and sleep.

I was still struggling to wrap my head around everything.

Gracie helped me out of my robe and into my dress. The soft fabric gliding over my skin like a glove as she fastened the buttons up my back and handed me a pair of shoes to put on myself. I sat on the end of the bed, pushing some dresses to the side as I did so, leaning down to slip the silver shoes onto my feet.

The main door to my chambers knocked loudly, making me jump where I sat. Gracie excused herself to answer it, leaving the room quickly on near silent feet, her hair falling over her shoulders as she did so.

Voices filled the rooms, Gracie's sweet laugh and that of a male. I stood from the bed, smoothing the fabrics of my dress and followed the sounds into the living area.

Maeteo stood by the door, dressed in dark trousers and a tight-fitting jacket. His sword was still sheathed against his back, but there was no sign of any other weapons on him. His hair was damp, as if he had just finished bathing not long ago, and he had a smile on his face as he looked at Gracie, who was still laughing. He looked up at the sound of my entrance, revealing the bruise across his cheek and the cut in his eyebrow. My eyes widened.

"What happened to you?!" I asked, concern coming through in my voice as I walked around the cream sofas toward where he stood just inside the door.

"Ah," He reached up to touch his eyebrow lightly, "Nothing to concern yourself with, Princess."

"He got in a fight with his girlfriend." Gracie laughed still, wiping tears away from under her eyes, "She threw a vase at him."

Maeteo rolled his eyes, shaking his head at Gracie. I raised an eyebrow.

"Essie is not my girlfriend, Gracie."

"Certainly not anymore." Gracie giggled, "Excuse me, Your Majesty, I have to go and dress for this evening."

Gracie bowed her head, still chuckling as she side stepped Maeteo and made her way out of the main door into the hallway beyond, closing it behind her. Maeteo looked at me again, and I suddenly felt very aware of myself. I straightened my shoulders and lifted my chin slightly, meeting his eyes when he finally looked up from my dress.

"You look lovely, Princess." He smiled, one side of his mouth kicking up more than the other. I felt the blush starting at the base of my neck.

"Thank you, General." I stepped closer to him, "To what do I owe the pleasure?"

"I'm here to escort you to the main hall this evening, if that's alright with you?" Maeteo's eyes rolled down my dress again, lingering on the exposed skin above the neckline.

"Oh," I swallowed, nodding. "I assumed Emily would escort me."

Maeteo did not reply, simply held out his elbow for me to take. I slipped my hand around his arm, gripping it tightly as he turned us back towards the doors and opened them for us.

We walked through the halls together in silence, the only sounds being those of his sword against his back and the bottom of my dress across the floor. In the short time I had been in the castle, the halls had never been this empty; staff usually going between rooms, but as Maeteo and I walked, we didn't see a single other person.

Maeteo's arm flexed around my hand as we started to descend the stairs towards the main foyer, his grip on me completely unwavering even as I struggled with the skirt of my dress. He only smiled, taking the steps as slow as needed,

A girl with white blonde hair appeared at the bottom of the stairs from the corridor to the left, her hands full of white plates. She shot a glare at Maeteo before bowing her head at me and took off into the main hall. I frowned, watching after her as I took the last step into the foyer.

"Who was that?" I asked, looking from the now closed doors to Maeteo.

"That was Essie, Princess." He replied, his tone light and expression unchanged despite the wounds on his face, inflicted by the blonde girl.

"Ah," I nodded, swallowing, "Your girlfriend."

Maeteo looked at me, raising an eyebrow.

"No, Princess, she isn't my girlfriend."

"She was, though?"

"She thought she was." Maeteo shrugged, his nonchalance on the matter making my skin crawl uncomfortably. I planted my feet where I stood, letting go of his arm. Maeteo turned, tilting his head. "Are you alright?"

"Fine." I gritted out through my teeth, "You should apologise to her."

Maeteo's eyebrows shot up to meet his hairline, his crooked smile from earlier returning as he turned to face me fully, his hand reaching out towards me to usher me forward again.

"Why should I do that?" He half chuckled, "She was the one who threw a vase at my face."

"It doesn't seem to be without reason." I grumbled, squaring my shoulders, and slipping my hand into the crease of his elbow again. He just laughed loudly, guiding me to stand in front of the large, double doors. The intricate carvings of two stags took my breath away.

They faced each other on the opposite doors, each stood on top of a hill with crowns atop of their antlers. The edges of the doors were adorned with carved flowers, much like the rest of the doors in the castle, but these flowers had large, unblinking eyes between the petals.

I stared at the flowers, the eyes giving me a feeling of unease in the pit of my stomach.

Suddenly, music flared from the room in front of us, and the doors opened, and my heart all but stopped.

8
Maeteo

The grand hall had long been my favourite room in the castle.

The high ceilings were full of lit, golden chandeliers between heavy wooden beams. Scarlett banners holding the Earth Kingdom emblem hung on the walls every few feet, only broken up by large, glass doors that had been thrown open to allow the cool evening air to mingle through the crowded room — an armed guard stood outside each one, their backs turned to the festivities inside. It was mostly younger guards, still being put through their paces. I eyed Cooper Fox where he stood at the far end, a sour look on his face as he looked out over the gardens. The stone floor was worn down but perfectly stable beneath my heavy boots.

At the very back of the room, on a raised platform, stood a table covered in a cloth the same colour as the banners. A golden throne sat in the middle, taller than the chairs to either side. Behind the table hung a portrait of the late King and Queen, and in the Queen's, arms was a baby girl with chubby cheeks and sparkling eyes. A baby Kira.

Long tables filled the room, and every seat at them was occupied with people from the castle, nobility from the Kingdom, and army members that I had given the night off. They all cheered wildly as we entered, the music from the string quartet situated by the doors completely drowned out by the sheer volume of them as Kira stepped into the hall.

I chanced a look down at her face as I escorted her into the room. Her eyes were wide, and her knuckles had gone white with the grip she kept on my arm. I placed my other hand on top of hers, squeezing it lightly as we walked down the middle of the crowded room. I could still feel her furious glare at me from the hallway when she told me to apologise, and a laugh bubbled in my throat that I covered with a sly cough.

Escorting Kira to her seat, I kept my grip on her hand until she was safely situated in front of the throne. She looked at me, panicked as I stepped away from her and clung to my hand.

"I'll be right there, Princess." I said softly, gesturing to the table directly across from where we were standing now. Hollis and Tarian and the rest of my inner circle were all stood, clapping excitedly and grinning at Kira.

Kira nodded, and I watched her throat work as she swallowed, letting go of my hand slowly.

I stepped down from the raised platform, bowing at the waist to Kira before taking my seat beside Tarian. The cheering in the room died down as Kira sat in her throne, Emily on her left and Eyvlin on her right.

Eyvlin raised her arms in the air, and the room fell into silence.

"Welcome!" She grinned, the woman's voice carrying surprisingly well through the large room. "What an evening indeed. Thank you, General Stroll, for ensuring our Princess's safe return to us."

I nodded, raising the glass in front of me to the sounds of applause, Tarian clapping me on the shoulder.

"Fourteen years ago on this very evening, our beloved Kingdom suffered an attack of catastrophic evil. We lost many, our late King and Queen sacrificing themselves to the Fire Kingdom to keep their daughter,

Her Royal Highness Kira Dagon, Princess of Earth, safe. Many thought we lost her, too, but she is here, returning to our court on the eve of her eighteenth birthday, ready to lead our Kingdom to the victory we crave."

Eyvlin's words caused an uproar, people stomping their feet and battering their glasses on the tables. I eyed Kira, who was looking at Eyvlin like she had just thrown her into a coliseum full of lions.

"As the threat from our enemies to the south grows closer, we must remain vigilant in keeping our Kingdom safe. Any person, of nobility or otherwise, suspected of passing information from within Kingdom limits to those against us, will be dealt with quickly and efficiently."

The crowded room grew silent at the words, eyes flitting between friends and family members alike around the room. Eyvlin's stern face disappeared as quickly as it appeared, a grin causing her eyes to crinkle more around the edges as she clapped her hands. The doors at the back of the room, painted the same colour as the walls to make them harder to spot, flew open, and staff members carrying plates piled high started to filter in.

The string quartet started playing again, softer now so conversations between people could still be enjoyed.

Instinctively, my eyes scanned the open doors for any sign of threat. The sun had dropped low enough in the sky that the room was cast in an orange glow, making the silverware sparkle in the still stifling heat. I hated summer; hated the heat and the memories this time of year brought with it.

A plate of roasted meat and potatoes got placed in front of me, and I turned to smile at the girl who had brought it to me. I was greeted with Essie's furious face, her eyes focused on the plate in front of me rather than on me.

"Thank you, Ess," I said, my voice low. She did not respond, simply straightened up and took off back towards the doors at the back of the room to collect more plates. Hollis's laugh from beside me made me roll my eyes.

Hollis was Tarian's twin sister, but the pair were more unalike than any two people I had ever met. Where

Tarian was quiet and collected, Hollis was loud and scattered. Tarian favoured the quiet of the library to the barracks on a weekend night, whereas Hollis could be found at the Poker table, cussing and slamming her cards down, laughing as she took everyone else's money. No one knew when, or how, she got so good at Poker, but almost all the longer-serving members of our army refused to play against her.

I lifted my eyebrows at her, stabbing at my plate with my fork and bringing it to my mouth, chewing slowly.

"Yes, Hollis?"

Hollis snickered, her braided hair falling over her shoulder as she took a drink from the glass in front of her.

"Nothing, nothing." She laughed, placing her glass back on the table and picking up her cutlery. "Just be sure she hasn't slipped a laxative into your gravy."

Tarian snorted beside me, one of his hands coming up to cover his mouth as he laughed.

The rest of dinner continued in much the same fashion. Jokes were shared between the soldiers at my table, and the occasional person of nobility would leave their table to come and clap me on the back, thanking me for my services to the kingdom.

Even after nearly four years as General, I never knew how to reply to that statement. It was mostly a nod or a shrug, but sometimes I felt my cheeks flush, and my words came out mumbled.

Turning my attention to the top table, I watched as Brond made his way around to the side of Kira's throne. She turned her head to look at him, her eyebrows knitting together in confusion as the elderly man pushed his way between her and Emily, whose eyebrows shot up to meet her hairline at the sheer audacity of him. Kira schooled her features into neutrality, keeping her face calm as Brond spoke about whatever was so important that he had to interrupt her dinner.

Brond stayed nipping Kira's ears for long enough that I could see Emily and Eyvlin growing more and more frustrated beside her. Kira, to my surprise, kept her face calm the entire time. Talking softly back to Brond when he stopped long enough to take a breath. Eventually, though, Emily stood from her seat, her hand under Brond's armpit and hauled him up alongside her. Brond yelled, causing everyone in the room to turn their attention towards the scene in front of them, but Emily did not stop. She dragged him away from the top table, muttering curses to herself as she frog-marched him out of the dining hall entirely.

A beat of silence passed, before the room erupted into loud laughter, people clapping their hands at the sight.

Kira had her head angled away with her hand over her mouth, but everyone knew she was laughing by the way her shoulders shook in her seat.

I stood from my seat, laughter still bubbling from my throat as I pushed my chair underneath the table, making sure no one passing by would trip over it.

My boots were heavy against the stone floor. I made my way up to where Kira was sitting and slid myself into Emily's now vacant seat that was still pushed back from the table. Kira turned to look at me, raising an eyebrow. I grinned back at her.

"How are you finding it?" I asked, gesturing towards the room full of people.

Conversations had started back up now, and no one was looking in our direction. Kira's eyes ran over the room, her lip pulled between her teeth. Her red hair had been pulled into an intricate style on top of her head, and the colour of the dress she had chosen made her skin look flushed. I let myself take her in for a moment, admiring.

"It's... strange." She said softly, her eyes landing back on me. "I feel like I'm dreaming. Or like someone is going to shout, 'Just kidding, you can go home now'."

I nodded, crossing my arms over my chest and sitting back in my chair, my legs stretched out under the table.

Dinner flowed in much the same fashion. Emily never returned to her seat, so I had one of the staff bring my plate to where I was now sat beside Kira and listened to the conversations going on between the people sitting close enough to us. Kira was quiet for the rest of the meal, apart from thanking the staff for replacing her finished dinner plate with a dessert bowl full of chocolate cake and ice cream.

Once the empty bowls had been removed, everyone in the room stood from their chairs and stepped away from their tables. Kira started as the table in front of her was pulled away by two of the castle staff and watched on as several more filed in through the doors to remove the large dining tables that filled the space.

The sun outside had dropped low enough that the sky was turning an inky black, the moon lighting the back patio now. The scent of the florals from the garden floated through the room on the low, slow breeze, and as everyone filtered from the room, Emily re-entered. A smile on her face and her hands clasped in front of her.

"Darling," Emily started, holding out her hand to Kira, "It's time for you to meet your people."

9
Kira

The evening dragged on.

After I had met everyone from the castle staff and chefs to the farmers who kept their livestock within the castle walls, to the market stall keepers who provided the fresh fruit and vegetables every morning, my head felt like it was going to split open.

I stood from my throne, my legs feeling numb from sitting for so long, and groaned at the movement. Emily had stood beside me the whole evening, and even she had started to look weary. Eyvlin had excused herself not twenty minutes into the stream of meetings, and I had not seen her since.

Stepping down from the dais where my throne had been placed, I wobbled slightly. My legs had taken on the feeling of jelly, and I stopped to rub my hands on my thighs, trying to coax some life back into them. A deep chuckle from nearby had me looking up, and I frowned as Maeteo made his way towards me. His boots were loud against the stone floor, and I straightened up as he got closer, clasping my hands together in front of me.

"Princess," He greeted, dropping into a dramatic bow. I rolled my eyes.

"General." I smiled tightly, waiting until he stood up straight before I kept walking. He kept pace beside me easily, his hands swinging by his sides comfortably.

"How did that go?" He grinned, opening the door to the great hall for me and letting me walk out past him. "Were your people everything you expected them to be?"

I moved to the side of the hall to let a few members of staff past, and blushed when they all stopped to curtsy to me before they continued on their way. Maeteo waited beside me, a smirk on his face.

"They were all lovely." I finally answered, my voice the only sound beside our footsteps on the floor as we made our way through the entrance hall towards the stairs. "I'm not sure what they were expecting from me, though."

"What do you mean?" Maeteo asked, taking the steps slowly. I had a feeling he was moving deliberately slow to keep pace with me in my dress again.

"I mean I'm not sure how to act with these things. It's not exactly something I do every day." I shrugged, lifting the skirt of my dress to take the last step into the upstairs hall. Maeteo nodded, slipping his hands into his pockets.

"It will come, don't worry. You'll be a natural at this soon enough."

I rolled my eyes at him, feeling my chest flush at his statement. If he were right, I would welcome that day sooner rather than later. The feeling of being an impostor, like someone was playing a very elaborate prank on me and would come swinging in with eggs and feathers to ruin my day was still settled heavily in my stomach. The open castle hallways and the views from the windows did not feel any more real than the strange creatures Emily used to tell me about in her bedtime stories.

When we reached my doors, I stopped, looking at Maeteo with a raised eyebrow. He grinned, leaning against the door frame with his arms crossed over his chest.

"Do you intend to stay there all evening?" I asked, my hand on the golden door handle, hesitating to push it open.

"Not unless you'll have me." He winked, a laugh rumbling through his chest when my eyes widened. "No, Princess, I do not. I'm simply letting you know that we have a riding lesson tomorrow morning, as soon as the sun is in the sky."

I nodded my head, anxiety flaring to life in my chest. Beside the ride to the castle with Maeteo, I had only ever ridden a horse with Dane, and even at that I had clung to his back like a scared child while he flew through the meadows. The thought of being by myself, on a beast the size of Fenrir, had my heart racing uncomfortably.

"You don't need to look so scared, Princess. I won't let you fall." Maeteo stood straight, bowing his head slightly. "I'll take my leave now. See you in the morning, Your Majesty."

I watched his back as he walked away, taking in the way he moved with such confidence and assurance even when no one else was around to see him. Once he had turned the corner away from my hallway, I let out a breath and pushed the door to my chambers open.

Thankfully, the windows had been left open, so the evening air moving through the living room was comfortable and enough to cool the sweat that had started to bead against the skin of my forehead. I wiped it away with the back of my hand, glad that there was no one to see me do so. The rooms were quiet as I padded across the carpet into my bed chambers.

All the dresses I had tried on earlier had been removed from where I had left them on the bottom of the bed, and the crumpled sheets had been straightened, it looked as if no one had been in this room at all. I sighed, sitting myself onto the bottom of my bed and slipping my shoes off my feet, rubbing at the uncomfortable skin where the silver slippers had been pinching.

A crash from the bathroom made me still, my head leaping into my throat as my head shot up.

Silence followed for a few seconds before the sounds of shuffling and quiet laughter filtered through the empty chambers. I furrowed my eyebrows, standing from my bed and gathering the skirt of my dress into my hand, moving as quietly as I could out into the main room. I stood for a second, listening to make sure I was not imagining things with exhaustion, but when another loud crash came from the bathroom again, I moved towards the gauzy curtain that acted as a door.

I grabbed the nearest vase on the mantelpiece, the weight of it heavy in my hand. It would certainly knock someone out if I hit them hard enough.

Taking a few deep breaths before I moved again, I ripped the curtain back and jumped into the room.

Gracie, who was being held up against a wall by a man I had yet to meet, let out a shriek. Slapping her hands at the man's back, making him drop her to the ground. His shirt was unbuttoned, and her skirt had been pushed up to the middle of her thighs.

My eyes went wide at the sight before me, and Gracie tried her hardest to flatten out her unruly hair, her words tumbling out over each other as her male friend quickly buttoned his shirt. A shattered bottle of lotion lay on the stone floor.

"Your Majesty! I'm so sorry — I didn't know you were back already — I didn't hear the door — "

Laughter bubbled in my throat, and I threw my head back, letting it out loudly at how flustered she was.

Gracie stopped her fussing, her hands falling to her sides. Her friend let out a small laugh, followed by one that filled the room instantly.

"Callum!" She hissed, hitting his chest, but that only made him laugh more. I wiped at my eyes, giggles still rippling from my chest as I looked at the red-faced pair in front of me.

"Callum, is it?" I asked, a grin still on my face. He nodded his head, licking his lips and trying his hardest to school his face into a serious mask when he looked at Gracie, who was still glaring at him.

"Yes, Your Majesty." He nodded, bowing his head.

"It's nice to make your acquaintance." I laughed, stepping forward and holding my hand out for him to shake. Gracie's face remained in a mask of shock as he took my hand and shook it forcefully. "Am I interrupting something… important?"

Gracie shook her head quickly, her curls bouncing around her face wildly.

"No! No, Your Majesty, we were just…"

"I know what you were doing, Gracie." I laughed, letting go of Callum's hand, "Callum, would you please go and ask chef to make up a tray of tea and some cake?"

Callum nodded his head, quickly scurrying from the room, leaving a very embarrassed looking Gracie and myself. I raised my eyebrow at her, pressing my lips together to stop another laugh from bursting out. Gracie stood, her eyes wide and her chest rising and falling heavily as she watched me. It was about a minute before she spoke again.

"Please don't tell my mother." She whispered, and the laughter that I had been trying to hold back burst out of me, sending both Gracie and me into fits of giggles.

"I won't, don't worry." I laughed, wiping my fingers under my eyes and catching the tears from laughing so hard. "Help me out of this dress, will you?"

Once Gracie had undone the back of my dress and I had changed into a pair of soft cotton trousers and matching top, we sat in the comfort of the living room, chatting and sharing the cake Callum had returned with. The red blush had left his pale cheeks, and he wore a grin when he reappeared, presenting the cake to us with a flourish.

The pair sat beside each other now, Gracie's legs draped over Callum's lap as she licked chocolate off her hands. Callum watched her intently, wrapping and unwrapping some of her curls around his fingers with a smile on his face. They were almost sickeningly sweet. From what I had gathered in the ten minutes it took for Callum to return, Gracie was hesitant about telling her mother about their relationship, knowing her mother thought relationships in their place of work would never last. Gracie had rolled her eyes, muttering about that being how she had met her father, but decided to keep it as secret as possible.

Callum had introduced himself properly when he had sat on the sofa beside Gracie, wrapping an arm around her shoulders. He worked in the stables, mostly with the horses that were used to bring supplies from the quarries a bit farther afield. I listened intently as he explained the ins and outs of how and when the horses were sent to retrieve their cart loads of stone and iron back to the castle blacksmith, how often they brought in coal to keep the castle fires lit, and my brain spun with it all.

Once they got into the topic of their relationship, I was much more interested, sitting forward in my chair with my hand under my chin.

"We mostly try to stay in the stables," Callum explained while Gracie had a mouthful of cake, her curls bouncing as she nodded, "But Gracie had said you would be busy meeting the rest of the castle staff this evening…"

"So, you defiled my bathroom." I nodded, giggling when Gracie choked on her cake. Callum laughed loudly, his hand rubbing circles on Gracie's back as she coughed.

"I'm really, really sorry." Gracie wheezed, wiping tears from her cheeks.

I laughed, dismissing her with a wave of my hand.

"You're more than welcome to hide in here, Gracie," I smiled, placing my now empty teacup onto the coffee table in front of me, "I would, however, appreciate some warning next time."

Sighing, I stretched my legs out in front of me and let my head fall back against the padded sofa, my eyes slipping closed. Exhaustion settled heavily in my bones, and I was sure if I were left to it, I could have slept exactly where I was. The thought of the next morning, spending time with Maeteo and the horses, made me feel sick to my stomach.

I heard rather than saw Gracie and Callum stand from where they had been sat and start to clean up the tea tray and empty cake plates. I snapped my head up.

"You don't need to clean this up right away, Gracie." I smiled, but she shrugged her shoulders.

"You look exhausted, Your Majesty. We'll take this away and let you get settled for the night." Callum nodded at Gracie's statement, and I felt utterly useless as I watched them take the plates and empty tea pot from the room, closing the large doors with a soft click.

10

"I'm not getting on *that!*"

My voice carried around the yard, echoing off the empty stables in the quiet of the morning. Dew clung to the grass and the horses munched sleepily on troughs full of food. The sounds of the castle kitchens were faint, but Chef's explicit tongue was still loud and colourful enough to make me blush from afar.

The sun had barely risen above the trees when Maeteo had knocked on my doors, the noise carrying through the quiet rooms and scaring me out of bed with my heart hammering against my rib cage. He had been stood with a grin on his face, arms crossed over his chest as he took me in, my hair still knotted and rubbing the palms of my hands against my eyes. I had grumbled about the ridiculous time of day and waved him into the living room, shuffling back into my room as he laughed and flopped down onto one of my sofas.

It had taken me all of fifteen minutes to get myself ready, much to Maeteo's annoyance. I had raided my wardrobe to find something suitable for a day of learning to ride horses, and settled on a pair of brown leggings, a white button up shirt that was longer at the back than it was at the front, and brown calf height boots. I had been mid braiding my hair when Maeteo grumbled that we needed to go. I had stuck my tongue out at his back as we made our way out of my chambers, Gracie only just arriving to turn down my bed. She giggled as she caught me with my tongue out, and I flushed a deep pink.

He stood in front of me now with an eyebrow raised. In his hands was a thick, twisted rope attached to the bridle of the smallest horse I had ever seen.

"Why not?" He asked, reaching his free hand over and offering a small, pink sugar cube to the tiny creature. "Jakob is great with beginners — we use him to teach the children how to ride."

I rolled my eyes, throwing my hands in the air and letting them slap down on my thighs.

"He barely reaches my waist!"

"Less distance for you to fall."

"I thought you wouldn't let me fall." I snapped, crossing my arms across my chest, repeating his statement from the night before. Maeteo let out a deep chuckle as he led Jakob back into his stable.

I turned on the spot, chewing on my lip as my eyes ran over the several horses still in their stables. Most were occupied eating their breakfast, but as I scanned the last block, one caught my eye.

Tall, with a sandy white mane, and a coat that looked almost golden, the beautiful beast was watching me closely. I crossed the yard as quickly as I could without spooking the animal, but it kept its eyes trained on me as I walked, like it was as nervous of me as I was it. Reaching my hand up slowly, I ran it gently down the side of its neck. The horse huffed through its nose, but it did not move away from me, and I smiled gently as I ran my fingers through its silky mane.

"What's your name, huh?" I asked quietly, moving to the other side of the door, pulling myself up on the half open wood to get a better look at the beast in front of me. Muscles and slender legs greeted me, and I was taken aback for a second.

"That's Freya." Maeteo's voice behind me made me look over my shoulder. His eyes were flitting between me and the horse beside me, a small knot between his eyebrows. "Her rider died a few months ago from a fever that he just couldn't beat... She hasn't let anyone near her since."

"Freya." I muttered, gently running my hand along the bridge of the horse's nose. Her eyes closed in a slow blink. Keeping one hand on the side of her long neck, I reached over the stable door and slid the lock across. Freya watched me closely as I slipped through the smallest space I could manage, her eyes warm and now without a hint of fear in them.

Standing next to her, I realised that Freya's back came in line with the top of my head, just enough that with a good saddle, I would be able to pull myself up without needing a step. I ran my hands along her back, enjoying the feel of her soft coat. The sound of Maeteo coming closer to the gate was met with a sharp huff from Freya, her big body starting to move as she tried to rear away from him. I jumped back slightly, just enough to avoid her hooves crushing my feet and put my arms around her strong neck.

"Hey, now!" I hushed, looking at her closely. "There's no need for that. He's not as awful as he looks."

Maeteo grumbled something explicit from behind me that had me chuckling as Freya calmed down, shaking her mane out and making me release my arms.

I turned to Maeteo, gesturing for him to move so I could slip back out of the stable, leaving Freya to calm herself down more. Dusting my hands on my leggings, I stood straight. Maeteo lifted an eyebrow at me, shock still evident on his face.

"She hasn't let anyone in to even groom her in months." He explained, his eyes traveling back over to the beautiful horse in her stable, "That was incredible."

I followed his line of sight, a small smile finding its way to my face as I watched Freya.

"I want to take her," I nodded my head, and Maeteo's eyebrows went up slightly, but after a second of watching Freya closely, he nodded as well, a smile blooming on his face.

Maeteo grabbed the arm of a stable hand as they walked past, making the small boy jump nearly a foot in the air. He could not have been older than twelve, and his eyes went wide at Maeteo's hand. Maeteo asked him to fetch the gear so he could show me how to get Freya ready for riding, and the boy's eyes nearly bulged out of his head as they flicked over to look at me. I smiled a little, my cheeks burning as the boy dropped into a deep bow before taking off at a sprint.

He was back before I even had the chance to think about what I was about to do, handing me a bright pink lead rope and bundling a bridle and saddle into my arms as well. Maeteo smirked, shoving his hands into his pockets and tipping his head towards Freya's door.

"Go on, then."

"I don't know how!" I panicked, turning on my heel and shuffling towards the door, trying to balance everything I was holding in my arms.

"She won't let any of us near her to do it." Maeteo shrugged, following behind me at a distance. He held the door open for me as I slipped inside, closing it behind me and sliding the lock back into place. "I'll tell you how from here."

I nodded, swallowing deeply, and placing the saddle over the top of the door, the weight of it making my arms burn already. Turning my attention to Freya, I startled to find her already watching me. If she could talk, I was sure she would have been telling me to get away from her.

To my surprise and Maeteo's, Freya stood perfectly still while Maeteo talked me through how to place the bridle over her head, what way her saddle needed to go, and why the girth was not something to be giggling over.

Quicker than expected, I was sat on top of Freya, fitting snuggly in the saddle the young stable hand had somehow managed to size just by looking at me. Maeteo was holding the stable door open, a small smile on his face. I straightened, tightening my grip on the reins and letting out a heavy breath. Squeezing my thighs gently just like Maeteo had told me to, I nudged Freya forward. The sound of her hooves against the ground was comforting, just because I knew I had done something right.

Crossing the yard, I met the eyes of several of the workers there, all of them smiling and nodding, some dropping into deep bows. My ears turned pink as I managed to get Freya to stop at the gate to wait for Maeteo.

It took him significantly less time than it took me to get Fenrir tacked up and ready to go.

Two elderly men opened the large gate into the field, and Maeteo called his thanks before he moved Fenrir forward, I patted Freya's neck and followed close behind.

Fenrir's head turned to look behind him more times than I could count, and every time he did, Freya would lift her head a little higher and huff through her nose, like she was reassuring him that she was okay.

Maeteo led us through the open fields beside the castle, the stone wall disappearing behind us as we trekked over muddy paths and winding roads and through a thick, seemingly unending, part of the forest, until we reached an open meadow a few hours later. Yellow wildflowers swayed in the light breeze, and the sun had finally reached a point in the sky where it could be considered daytime to me. I pulled Freya to a stop at the same time Maeteo took off at speed.

I watched as he leaned forward in his saddle, his hair behind thrown back off his forehead at the speed Fenrir was galloping. He was nothing but a streak of darkness through the bright field, and my eyes went wide as they turned and flew past where Freya and I stood at the tree line. Freya, to my surprise, did not spook when Fenrir went past. Instead, she followed him with her eyes, chewing on the bit in her mouth, completely unfazed.

Grinning, Maeteo slowed Fenrir to a trot, and then to a complete stop in front of us. His cheeks were flushed pink and his hair wild and windswept. It was the most genuine smile I had seen on him yet, and my breath caught in my throat for a second. Freya huffing and moving underneath me pulled me back to reality.

"You ready?" Maeteo asked me, reaching down to scrub his hand across Fenrir's thick neck. I nodded, the anxiety in my stomach settling.

The sun moved across the sky, and by the time it reached its midway point, sweat was dripping down my back. Freya was panting, but she was flying through the meadow at a speed I would not have ever imagined.

Maeteo called encouraging words as he flew along beside us, Fenrir's powerful legs managing to keep up with Freya's pace, no matter how hard she tried to lose him.

The Lides mountains were closer than I had ever seen them, and once Freya had slowed to a walk, I looked up at them properly. The green grass of the meadows and surrounding fields gave way to dark dirt, and instead of full, bright trees, there was bare trunks and branches. No flowers grew on the small bushes, and even the birds flying overhead seemed to avoid getting too close. I pulled Freya's reins, slowing her to a stop and pushing my sweaty hair from my face.

Maeteo came to stop beside me, his eyebrows furrowed as Fenrir stopped side by side with Freya, who — to my amusement — moved her head swiftly to the side, flicking her mane in the male horses' face.

"Are you alright?" Maeteo asked, looking at me closely.

"I've never been this close to them before," I nodded my head towards the mountains, still miles away but looming above us like a shadow. "Emily used to tell me dragons lived in the caves, and nothing ever grew on them because of it."

"Well, she's not wrong."

My head snapped to the side, staring at Maeteo as he looked up at the mountains, his usual smirk missing from his face. He let his eyes roam over the bare grounds, his hands gripping Fenrir's reins tightly.

"No one has seen any of the dragons in years, though. They all disappeared when the Fire Kingdom attacked. The night Emily took you into hiding." Maeteo's eyes flicked to mine, a sad smile on his face. "Aepein was the last one anyone seen. She was flying over the valley with her eggs, crying, and looking for something."

The entrance to the nearest cave was at least two hundred feet up from where Maeteo and I were, but I strained my eyes to try and see anything inside it. Nothing but darkness stared back at me.

"What was she looking for?" My voice was quiet, barely above a whisper.

"Some people think she was looking for Gavrun, her mate. Others think she was looking for you."

I frowned. Emily had always told me that the dragons of the mountains were just a bedtime story, made up by parents to make their kids behave. But standing there now, staring up at the barren mountainside and listening to the wind pass by, I knew Maeteo was telling the truth.

11

Every year on my birthday, I would pretend that the bells ringing through the village from the church were for me. Dane and I would run through the village square early in the morning to the sounds, laughing and dancing and eating the birthday cake Emily had made and left in the kitchen the night before.

But waking up on the morning of my eighteenth birthday with the ringing bells echoing through my rooms felt different. Emily threw my main doors open, calling out my name and clapping her hands as she pushed through the curtain into my bedroom area. I rubbed my palms against my eyes, sitting up in my bed and letting my pillows fall back onto the mattress.

Emily opened my curtains, the morning sun streaming into the room making my eyes burn. I groaned and fell back against the bed, burying my head under the full, fluffy quilt. Laughter filled the rooms, Emily's voice loud as she called to Gracie to send for breakfast. The weight of her flopping onto my bed was followed by her ripping the quilt off me in one quick movement. If I had been more awake, I would have shoved her onto the floor.

"Happy birthday!" Emily squealed, wrapping her arms around my neck and pulling me into a tight hug.

"Thank you," I laughed, patting her back softly until she let me go. Her hands on my shoulders, Emily grinned at me.

Emily had always looked younger than her years. Fifteen years separated us, and as a child I had never questioned the slight difference in her accent, or that I had hair as red as fire while hers was such a dark brown that it looked black. Her eyes were sharp and green, while mine had always been brown. She was just my Aunt Emily. When I had been a bit older, I had asked about her accent, and she had simply told me she had not been born in the Earth Kingdom, but had come here when she was thirteen, two years before I had been born.

She had told me about the times when I had been learning to walk, and she had followed me around with a pillow to make sure I was not hurt if I fell. Or, when I had started talking, she taught me to say her name before she taught me *"Mama"*, or *"Dada."* It never occurred to me that she had left out every detail about my parents. Sitting with her now made me feel like a child again. She would always come bursting into my room on my birthday, her arms full of wrapped presents and a full cooked breakfast lay out on the dining table.

The cake she had made the day before was always the centre of attention.

Slipping from my bed, I put my feet into my slippers and stretched my arms above my head. Emily gripped my wrist with a grin on her face, dragging me from my bedroom into the living room. My eyes went wide at the sight in front of me.

On one of the sofas sat several golden wrapped boxes of different sizes. The fireplace was decorated with white and gold banners, and balloons of every colour were scattered around the floor. The windows were wide open to let the morning breeze into the room, and the bells from the church were still ringing happily. The sounds of people celebrating were faint enough that I almost missed them.

In the corner between the fireplace and the bathroom door stood a mannequin, and my breath caught in my throat as I eyed the dress on it. The neckline was made of gold, tightly packed jewels, and the white fabric flowed down to the floor, pooling around the bottom like a cloud. I took a step towards it, taking in the details of the small flowers in between the jewels, trailing my fingers over them as they continued over the bodice and around the waist. The sleeves sat mid-bicep and opened out to flow behind the dress. It was one of the most stunning things I had ever seen.

The doors opening pulled my attention from the beautiful dress in front of me, and I blinked as Gracie re-entered the room with — what looked like — the entire kitchen staff following behind her. They carried trays upon trays of food. Sausages, toast, mushrooms, eggs, and the like were expertly arranged on the coffee table before a chorus of *'Happy birthday, Your Majesty'* filled the room and they left. Gracie grinned at me.

"Good morning, Your Majesty."

I returned her happy smile, a flush working its way up my cheeks as my stomach growled loudly, the smells of the food in front of me making me realise just how hungry I was. Gracie and Emily laughed, sitting themselves down on a sofa each, and starting to pile their plates high with food. I followed suit, sitting down beside Emily and taking the plate she held out to me.

We ate, and laughed, and shared stories until the sun had made its way to the middle of the sky, the warm air blowing in through the open patio doors.

A heavy knock on my door made me turn my head, and Gracie wiped her hands on her skirt as she stood to answer it. Maeteo stood with his shoulder against the door frame, his casual stance at complete opposites with how he was dressed. I hadn't seen him since our horse riding lessons days ago, and his riding trousers had been replaced with close fitting black ones, covered with silver gauntlets. He was dressed as if he was going into war, his helmet tucked under one arm as he smiled at Gracie.

My heart flipped in my chest.

"Is she ready?" He asked, looking over Gracie's shoulder to see me still sat on the sofa in my pyjamas. I blushed a deep shade of pink.

"Ready for what?" I asked, standing. Gracie slapped a hand over her mouth, a gasp leaving her. My eyes widened as she turned on the spot, almost sprinting across the room to me and taking my arm in her hand, pulling me into my bedroom. Maeteo's loud laugh filtered through from the main room, followed closely by the sound of Emily excusing herself.

Gracie flurried around my room like a storm, grabbing different brushes and clothes, leaving me standing there completely unknowing.

"Gracie?" I prompted, letting her sit me down in a stool and start to run a brush through my unruly hair.

"You are meant to be up on the Queen's balcony at noon," Gracie rushed, her voice muffled through a mouthful of hair pins, "So the people of the Kingdom can come and pay their birthday respects."

I blinked at her in the mirror, my stomach dropping into my toes at the thought of standing in front of thousands of people. My hands started to sweat, and I rubbed them against the fabric of my robe, trying to calm my nerves.

Gracie worked on my hair until it was tamed into a sleek bun atop my head and disappeared from the room quickly. I heard the sharp word she snapped at Maeteo, followed by a muffled laugh, before she came back with my new dress draped over her arms, an exasperated look on her face.

"Maeteo is helping himself to our leftovers." She grumbled, motioning for me to stand from my stool, and I laughed.

"I can get dressed myself, Gracie. Go on, get yourself ready." I smiled; taking my dress from her hands. She hesitated but nodded her head and dashed from the room again. The main doors slammed closed seconds later, and I was suddenly extremely aware that the only other person in my quarters was Maeteo. I tried my hardest not to think of it too much as I slipped out of my robe and stepped into my gown.

The silk like material slid up my body like a glove, the skirt filling out as I put my arms through the sleeves, settling them where they sat on my mid-bicep. I turned on the spot, trying my hardest to get to the closings on the back, but without Gracie there to help me it was impossible, my fingers not quite reaching the small golden buttons.

Huffing out a sigh, I stepped out of my room into the living space, seeing Maeteo sitting on the sofa with his arms crossed over his chest and his head against the back. My heart fluttered in my chest for a second before I cleared my throat, his head snapping up from where it was resting and his eyes meeting mine. A small smile came to his lips, and he stood up, his hands by his side.

"You look beautiful," His voice was soft, and a blush crawled up my cheeks at his words.

"I, uh — I can't get the buttons at the back." I stumbled over my words as I turned, and Maeteo's light laugh filled the room before I heard him moving closer.

His gloved hands were cold against my back, and I started at the sudden contact. He paused, waiting for me to relax again before he reached for the buttons again, fastening them up with surprising quickness. His fingers lingered on the skin exposed at the nape of my neck for a second before he pulled away, clearing his throat as he did so.

I turned on the spot, looking up at him and smiling lightly when I met his eyes. His usual easy demeanour had been replaced by something I had never seen on him before, but he smiled at me nonetheless as he held out his arm for me to take. I slipped my hand around the crook of his elbow, using my other to hold up the skirt of my dress so I could walk easier.

The halls of the castle were a flurry of activity around Maeteo and I as we walked to the Queen's balcony. It was up two flights of stairs and down so many corridors that I lost count, but when we arrived at a set of open double doors that led to a large, extravagantly decorated sitting room, I knew we were in the right place. Eyvlin hurried forward from where she had been standing, her face flushed red and her eyes wide with anger. Maeteo shook with silent laughter beside me, and I had to swallow my own.

Fussing over my skirt, Eyvlin shooed Maeteo away. He rolled his eyes but slid my hand out of his arm and stepped away, winking quickly before he strolled over to the balcony doors. Two more guards stood there already, and thankfully I recognized them both. Hollis, the small woman who had been with us on our first ride to the castle, and to her left stood a man, taller than she was, but with the same facial features and striking blue eyes and dark hair. I did not have to speak to them to know they were siblings.

I let my eyes run over the rest of the room while Eyvlin fluffed and re-fluffed the skirt of my dress, tutting and muttering as she did so. The high ceilings were lined with dark wooden beams; a large, candlelit chandelier hung from the middle despite the fact it was nearly midday. The flooring, I realised, was the same, dull, red carpet that had been in almost every room of the castle so far. I crinkled my nose, wondering how long it would take to get rid of it all and replace it with something brighter.

From outside, the sounds of cheering and partying drew closer, and I was assuming the gates had been opened to the public. My suspicions were confirmed when the balcony doors opened, and the cheering grew louder, and even from where I stood in the middle of the room, I could see the ocean of people gathered in the courtyard. Some were climbing onto the walls, some were waving flags, and some were singing and dancing in the middle of the crowded space.

I swallowed hard, my stomach fluttering with nerves at the sight. Placing my hands onto the bodice of my dress, I smoothed down the already perfect fabric and flicked my eyes over to Maeteo. He had stepped out onto the balcony, but was looking over at Hollis, laughing at whatever she was saying to him. She had to stand on her tiptoes to speak to him, a hand on his shoulder to keep her steady as she leaned up to speak into his ear. Her brother stood over to the other side, his head turned towards the crowd, so I could only see the back of his hair. He was tall, not quite as tall as Maeteo, and he was skinnier, but the definition of his muscles still came through his armour, and I wondered how dangerous he really was.

Emily burst through the doors behind me, her breath coming in quick pants as she straightened herself up.

"Sorry I'm late." She wheezed, holding up a finger and picking up a glass of water from the table, drinking half of it in one gulp, "I hate running."

I laughed loud, my head falling back against my shoulders as I did so. Emily had always been the same;

her main enemy in life had always been physical exercise.

Gracie followed close behind her, much calmer and dressed in the most beautiful shade of blue. I grinned at her, gesturing for her to come over to me while Eyvlin continued her fussing. She had moved away from my skirt and was focusing most of her attention on the cape-like sleeves now, making sure they were pulled out behind me properly, that they flowed nicely, and that the light was hitting them properly.

"Is this necessary, Eyvie?" Maeteo's voice drew my attention away from Gracie, and I looked up at him again. He had come inside from the balcony and made his way over to where we still stood without me even noticing. He tilted his head sideways and was looking at Eyvlin with a look of amusement on his face.

Eyvlin stood up, thunder evident in her eyes as she glared at Maeteo.

"How many times must I ask you not to call me that, General Stroll?" She snapped, pushing her dishevelled hair off her face. "I am simply making sure the Princess looks acceptable for her people."

"The Princess looks beautiful, and you know it, Eyvie." Maeteo smirked, locking eyes with me for a second before turning his attention back to the flushed Eyvlin. "But her people are getting antsy, so shall we get this show on the road?"

Eyvlin huffed but nodded her head. She ran her hands over her tunic, flattening out the fabric before fixing her hair as quickly as she could. Maeteo chuckled as he stepped up beside me again, holding out his elbow for me again. I smile as I slipped my hand through, and he placed his other hand on top of mine, grinning down at me.

The roar of the crowd outside the window died down slightly when Eyvlin stepped onto the balcony, raising her hands into the air.

"Fourteen years ago, we were subject to a brutal attack." Eyvlin's voice sliced through the air, and I was shocked momentarily by how a voice that loud came from such a small woman. "We lost not only our King and Queen, but we lost their daughter, our dearest Princess.

"Today, on her eighteenth birthday, she is returning to us; Ready to take her mother and father's place on the throne. She will lead us into a new age — an age of light, and prosperity, and growth. She comes to us ready to be the ruler we have so desperately craved these last years."

Noise erupted through the crowd. Cheering and people clapping, and the stomping of feet almost shook the walls of the castle. My stomach flipped and I clung to Maeteo's arm a little tighter. His thumb rubbed small circles on the inside of my wrist, and I felt him look down at me again, but I kept my eyes locked on Eyvlin's back. She had raised her arms, and the noise of the crowd slowly settled down. I briefly wondered how many times Eyvlin was going to give this same speech.

Eyvlin looked over her shoulder, nodding her head slightly at Maeteo.

He squeezed my hand one more time before he let his arm fall back against his side, my hand still tucked into the crook of his elbow. He took a step forward, and I jolted at the sudden movement. Eyvlin's voice was drowned out by the thundering of my heart in my ears. The balcony doors drew closer, and I briefly heard Eyvlin announcing me before Maeteo, and I stepped out into the midday sunshine.

The crowd in front of me stretched from right below the balcony to up against the far wall — people packed tight against each other like cattle heading to market, all waving flags or cheering up at me. Children sat on their parent's shoulders, and teenagers climbed to sit on the stone walls surrounding the gardens. My heart stopped in my chest for a beat, and my mouth opened in surprise.

Letting my eyes scan over the many faces in the crowd below, I caught myself searching for Dane. Or even Poppy. Some sign that my life outside of the castle was real. Disappointment sank deeply into me when I realised, they were not going to be easily spotted.

Maeteo nudged my ribs slightly with his elbow, and I snapped out of my daze for long enough to look up at him. He was watching me closely, a bemused look on his face.

"Wave," He whispered, his mouth barely moving. I felt the deep blush rise on my neck, and I snapped my head back around.

Slipping my hand out of Maeteo's arm, I stepped forwards towards the edge of the balcony, trying to keep myself from looking down at the drop from the edge. Squaring my shoulders and breathing deep, I let myself relax and smiled out at the crowd gathered. The cheers grew louder, and the crowd began to move as people rushed forward, as if they wanted to get closer to where I was stood nearly thirty feet above them.

Out of the corner of my eyes I could see Hollis and her brother standing close by, their hands behind their backs and their heads facing forward, but I could see Hollis's smile from here. On my other side, Maeteo came up beside me. Eyvlin and Emily were on his other side.

Raising one hand, I waved out at the crowd.

Feeling myself slip into the role, my smile became more genuine as people waved back at me. Little girls waved frantically, older women cried into hankies and waved them in the air, their husbands laughing at them as they did so.

Everything happened so quickly after that.

The crowd started to shift again, people falling to the ground as someone pushed their way through to the middle. Cheers turned to screams, and by the time I spotted what was going on, I was already being taken to the ground.

An arrow flew by where my head had been seconds before, and a small scream left me as I hit the stone floor of the balcony. Hollis's brother was crouched over me, a frenzied look in his eyes and his hands on either side of my head as he looked me over quickly. I just blinked at him, my breaths coming in short pants. Maeteo's shouting caught my attention and I twisted myself to look back at him. He was stood on the balcony railing, Hollis perched next to him, and I barely got to register the arrow she had nocked before she released it into the crowd.

Screams filled the air, and before I could register the movement, I was being hauled off the floor and dragged back inside.

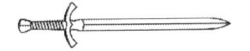

12
Maeteo

By the time Hollis and I reached the courtyard, the man that had shot the arrow was bleeding out on the ground.

Thankfully, most of the crowd had scattered the second they spotted him, so the grounds were nearly empty. I kicked his side, watching his eyes flutter slightly before he looked up at me, a sick, twisted smile on his face. My insides bubbled with anger.

Squatting down next to him, I flicked the arrow sticking out of his stomach quickly, making him yelp in pain. Hollis stood on his other side, her head tilted to the side, the braid she wore falling down her back.

"Who sent you?" I asked, my voice dark as I held onto the end of the arrow again, glaring at him.

His silence made me shrug, and I tugged at the arrow — enough to make it pull out slightly, before pushing it down again, driving it deeper. He roared in pain, his hands clawing desperately at my boots. I watched as his face contorted in pain and stilled the arrow again, his breathing coming fast and shallow.

"I'll ask you again," I cleared my throat, his eyes flicked to mine, "Who sent you?"

A cough racked his chest, and he gasped for breath. The way he was going, he would be dead before I had an answer. I looked up at Hollis, who was now inspecting the bow the man had brought with him closely. Her fingers were running along the solid wood, plucking the string, bending the spare arrow she had found in the man's belt.

When her eyes lifted to meet mine, I had my answer. He was from Fire.

Nodding my head slowly, I ran my tongue along my teeth, slapped a hand on his chest, and stood from where I had been squatting. He stared up at me from the ground, and slowly, slower than I would have liked, I watched the life leave his eyes and his chest huff its last breath.

Hollis moved to stand beside me, her small form almost vibrating with anger as she stared down at the body bleeding out on the stone.

My brain momentarily wondered how many more were hurt as everyone had tried to flee the grounds. I looked up from the body and quickly scanned the quad where we were stood, thanking the Lides that there did not seem to be any more casualties. A small group of teenagers hung around inside the gates, staring over at where we stood. I nodded at them, and they scattered, running through the gates faster than their legs could probably carry them.

"Tarian got Kira out of the way." Hollis said, her voice crisp and clear despite the circumstances. It was the same voice she had when she was going sword to sword in battle training, and she was trying to get inside someone's head. Full of confidence. I nodded at her words, running a hand over my chin and looking back at the body in front of me.

"Will I get one of the staff to clean it up?" Hollis asked, tilting her head and nudging him with her boot. I shook my head.

"No, no, they don't need to see this." I cleared my throat, looking over at the group of armoured up soldiers by the gates. "Get Cooper to do it."

Hollis's laugh was light and jovial, and I smiled at her before clapping her shoulder and nodding towards the group of soldiers.

Watching as she walked over to them, I almost laughed at their jump when Hollis's voice rang through the quad, calling them all to attention and making them scatter into position.

Turning on my heel, I headed back towards the castle. The double doors to the ballroom had been thrown open when Hollis and I had run down from the Queen's balcony, and the curtains were moving softly in the summer breeze. Staff still moved around inside the castle, but they seemed more urgent; more frenzied.

Essie ran up to me as I reached the ballroom door, her eyes wide and her blonde hair pushed over her shoulder. I raised an eyebrow at her, gesturing for her to go through the door first and following her into the open hallway. Her cheeks were stained pink and her breaths coming quick as she tried to keep up pace with me.

"Is it true?" She asked finally, her steps quiet on the staircase next to me. I looked down at her for a second before refocusing in front of me. All I cared about was getting to Kira, making sure she was okay, and then knocking seven bells out of whoever was on security at the gates today.

"Is what true?" I shot back, my tone sharp.

"That someone from the village shot a flaming arrow at Kira."

I snorted, my eyebrows shooting up to my hairline and my mouth dropping open. Of course, I knew people in the castle loved to gossip and come to their own conclusions, but Lides, that was fast, and ridiculous.

"Essie," I shook my head, running a hand over my jaw. "No, that's not true. The arrow wasn't flaming, and it wasn't a villager."

"But someone *did* shoot at her?"

I rolled my eyes, halting my steps and catching her arm in my hand. I knew I had caught her off guard by the small squeal she released when she was pulled to a stop.

"Essie, I'm not telling you what happened until *I* figure out *why* it happened." I said slowly, staring into her eyes as I did so, trying to make her hear the message loud and clear. "Go and tell your friends to mind their own business. I thought you were better than this."

Essie scoffed, shrugging her arm out of my grasp and turning on her heels to go back the way we had just came. I knew she had not been heading this way.

Shaking my head, I turned down the corridor towards Kira's quarters and rattled the door with my knuckles. When no reply came, I tried again, but it was to no avail. Sighing through my nose, I backtracked and went straight to the Queen's Balcony sitting room.

What met me there, was nothing short of bedlam.

Eyvlin was screaming some of the most colourful things I had ever heard. Emily was pacing back and forth in front of the — now closed — balcony doors. Tarian was stood outside of the bathroom door, a look of worry on his face as he knocked his knuckles on the wood. There was no sign of Kira, and my stomach flipped.

I crossed the room to Tarian, not even listening to Eyvlin as she tried to call to me. Something about setting up a council meeting as soon as possible, but I would get to that later. Tarian turned his head to look at me, a small look of relief crossing his features for a second.

"She won't open the door." Tarian said, his voice laced with anxiety. I clapped him on the shoulder and nodded towards the couch. He took the hint and moved slowly as he made his way over to it, flopping his entire body weight down onto the plush cushions.

I smiled lightly before I turned back to the locked door in front of me. I could hear shuffling from inside, and small, gasped sobs.

"Princess," I called, knocking my knuckles against the wood lightly, "Can you let me in?"

There was no answer, but the room around me had gone quiet. After no response I tried again, my knock slightly harsher.

"Your Majesty, you need to open the door." I tried, my voice taking on a more authoritative tone. "I can break it down easily, you know. Those are your only two options, darling."

Seconds passed before I heard the heavy lock turn on the other side of the door and it creaked open. I pushed it slightly farther with my hand and poked my head through the open space.

Kira was sat on the floor against the large bathtub, her head in her hands and her shoulders rising and falling as she gasped for breath. Her hair had been pulled out of it is complicated up-do and her tiara lay on the floor across the room from her. I slid myself through the small opening in the door and closed it behind me with a soft click, sliding the lock back into place to make sure Eyvlin didn't barge in with her demands.

She looked up at me, her cheeks stained with whatever Gracie had put on her eyes, and her hands shaking. My heart hurt in my chest as I moved to her slowly, my hands out in front of me. I sat myself down an arm's length away from her, my armour creaking uncomfortably as I lowered myself to the floor.

Kira looked at me through wary eyes, her lips pulled into a tight line. Her cheeks and chest were flushed a deep pink, and her dress was ripped at the sleeves slightly. Dirt from the balcony floor stained the white fabric of the skirt.

"He's dead." My voice started her, and she jumped away slightly, her eyes going wide. "Hollis shot him."

She nodded her head frantically, pushing herself off the floor and pacing the bathroom floor. She chewed on her nails as she walked, her eyes far away, as if she were not in the room with me anymore. I stood, putting out a hand and placing it on her shoulder lightly. She stopped.

"You're okay." I whispered, looking down at her. Her breath came out shakily, and her eyes started to fill again.

Before I knew what I was doing, I had pulled her into my chest, wrapping my arms around her tightly and was seriously considering going back outside to rip the limbs off the dead body lying out in the quad. Kira's sobs wracked into my chest, and I tried my hardest to rub comforting circles into her back.

We stood like that for longer than I could count, and she eventually pulled away from me, wiping her hands under her eyes and catching her tears.

"I can't do this." Her voice broke as she spoke, and I had to breathe through the sudden wave of emotions that came over me. "I can't be a *Queen*. I want to go home."

"This is your home, Princess." I said softly, reaching out and putting my hand onto her shoulder. "You have to do this."

"No! I don't!" She shouted, grasping at her hair. "I can abdicate, can't I? Would that work?"

"Not without a direct family member, no."

"Emily is my family!"

"Emily isn't your blood family, Princess." I kept my voice soft, running my hands up and down her arms. She looked so small, so…devastated, at the events of today. At the fact she had to stick this out.

A small shriek left her body, and she flopped back against my chest. I winced at the sound of her face hitting my armour, but she did not seem to notice. Carefully, I managed to move us down into a sitting position, my back against the wall and Kira curled into a ball on my lap.

The sounds of people talking in the room next to us filtered through the open space beneath the door, but none of what they were saying was easily understood. Outside the window, the afternoon sun had been covered by thick, dark clouds, and thunder rumbled ominously in the distance. I watched the clouds roll by slowly, until the small pattering of rain started to hit the windowpane.

Kira's breaths had slowed where she was sat on my lap, her hands wringing circles around each other. I tapped her shoulder lightly, gently moving her off my lap and helping her stand. Her face fell at the sight of the dirt coating the white fabric of her skirt, but I put a finger under her chin, pulling her attention back to me.

"You," I started, watching her closely, "are Kira Dagon. You are to be Queen of the Earth Kingdom. This whole thing today is not going to stop what is destined, do you understand?"

She nodded her head, her eyes dropping to the floor. I leaned forward, pressing a small kiss to her forehead.

"Please never forget that you are made for this — built for it. You are the first female born to our Kingdom in five-hundred years, people are going to want to hurt you, but I will not let them. We will not let them. I will set every one of them on fire and watch them burn for you."

13
Kira

My lungs burned as I crouched against the stone wall of the training ring.

After the calamity that was my first public appearance, Maeteo and Eyvlin decided my training had to begin before the sun had even risen. I had been dragged out of my bed at an ungodly hour, forced into the most uncomfortable armour I could imagine, and was now being subjected to seeing my breakfast in reverse.

Maeteo stood a few feet away, sweat barely starting to form on his hairline and sipping at water as he watched me closely; concern was written all over his face.

I had never done anything as excruciatingly painful as sword training. The pain in my shoulders, back, thighs, knees… even my thumbs were screaming at me in protest every time I picked up the heavy wooden sword Maeteo had given me to practice with. He had insisted that everyone, even him, had started with the clunky weapon currently lying discarded at my side.

A cold shiver ran down my back as the sight of dried blood staining the stones of the quad flashed in front of my eyes briefly, and I straightened up, pushing my hands on my knees and rolling my neck. I had barely managed to get to sleep last night, tossing and turning until I gave up and went down the kitchens. Whenever I had trouble sleeping in the cottage, Emily and I would make warm milk and eat slices of bread until we were full and sleepy. What I had not expected was the plump, whistling man to be sat on a stool in the corner of the room, peeling a barrel of potatoes with a pocketknife.

He had jumped up when he spotted me, knocking half of his un-peeled potatoes to the floor. After refusing to let me help him pick them up, he introduced himself as Declan, the night porter of the kitchens, and sat me at the large island in the stone kitchen and made me toast.

If yesterday was anything to go by, I was in for Hell trying to assert myself as Queen of these people.

Maeteo cleared his throat, snapping me back to the training ring and the still waiting sword. My muscles screamed at me as I reached down to pick it up, my knuckles turning white with the force I had to hold it with.

"Are you okay?" Maeteo asked as I made my way back to the centre of the ring. I nodded my head quickly, squaring my shoulders and standing in the position he had shown me earlier. I fixed my gaze on him, meeting his stare with much more confidence than I felt.

"I'm fine." I snapped sharply, "Let's go again."

Maeteo hesitated, his hand on his own tiny wooden sword before he sighed. He had been all too happy to leave his actual sword on the outside of the ring, and when I watched him, it was easy to see why. He could have killed me in one move, before I had even picked up any weapons myself.

Eventually, he nodded, moving to stand in front of me again and reminding me of proper stance, before the whole thing started again.

After sword training with Maeteo, Hollis took me out to an archery field on the other side of the castle grounds. The grass was trimmed to perfection, and a row of eight targets stood across from us.

Up close, Hollis appeared even smaller than she had when I first met her. Her hair was black and braided down her back, but her eyes were sharp, and I got the feeling she knew more about everything than I ever would. I wondered, briefly, if I'd ever be up to the same standards.

Hollis, thankfully, was a much kinder, more laid-back teacher than Maeteo had been. After he had shouted at me one too many times for letting my guard down, I had thrown my sword at his feet and walked away. Ignoring him calling after me and heading straight to my chambers to get changed. I'd barely gotten myself into a fresh set of leggings before Hollis came knocking at my door, a bow clutched in her hand and a smile on her face. It had been impossible to say no to her.

Now, as I stood beside her and watched her fire an arrow into the bullseye of each target with ease, I felt the nausea from earlier settle back into my stomach.

Hollis gestured for me to copy her; a reassuring looks on her face as she talked me through the proper technique again. The muscles in my arm screamed at me as I pulled the bow string back, a small grunt leaving me at just how much heavier it was than how it had looked when Hollis had done it.

Eventually I shot an arrow, and my chest deflated as it landed in the grass less than five feet away.

"Don't worry, the first time I shot an arrow I hit the wheel of a passing wagon." Hollis smiled, shrugging her shoulders, and placing a comforting hand on my arm. "It went right over the wall."

I laughed lightly, shaking my head and placing my bow down on the grass, sitting down next to it and stretching out my legs in front of me, wincing in pain. Hollis joined me, plopping herself down and crossing her legs under herself. She started to pluck grass from the ground, tearing out little bundles and then releasing them into the light wind.

"When Tarian and I turned eighteen," Hollis started, shocking me into looking at her, "The general before Maeteo came to our village. We lived right on the coast, in Bayshell, and he told us that Tarian had to go with him and enlist in the army immediately. We had only been awake an hour, maybe two, and he was being taken away. Mother and Father just... accepted it. They stood and waved him goodbye."

Her eyes were far away as she watched grass filter through the air.

"I was furious. I shouted and cried until I was sick. The thought of doing anything without Tarian made me feel like my world was crumbling, let alone living the rest of my life working as a seamstress like Mother while he was away at war, potentially getting murdered. I couldn't cope with it."

When I realised, she was opening up to me to get me to trust her more, I softened my features, listening to her intently.

"So, I waited until they went to bed that night, and I sneaked into their bathroom and used Father's razor to shave my head. It took *hours*, but when I had finished, I looked so much like Tarian no one would know the difference — I was so small, anyway, and I had absolutely nothing about me that screamed womanly." She laughed bitterly, shaking her head slightly, "Anyway, I left my parents a note and just... left. I walked for miles until an intake wagon passed on the road and I flagged them down, told them I had just turned eighteen and that I had been missed on intake. They didn't even question it."

A wry smile crossed over Hollis's face, her eyes slicing to meet mine.

"Tarian flipped when he saw me the next morning, lined up beside him and wearing the same uniform. He looked like he had seen a ghost, it was the best entertainment I could've asked for. But when he asked me why I was there, I told him exactly why. That never, in all our eighteen years, had there been a day in our lives where we hadn't done everything together, and it wasn't about to start then.

"Besides, why should he get to go and have all the fun, killing people and having adventures, and I had to stay at home and sew because I'm a woman?"

Hollis rolled her eyes, dusting her hands off on her trousers and smiling at me. I nodded at her words, completely understanding her point of view. I had never been one to let Dane do all the dirty work, we had always been hip deep in mud together.

Dane's face filtered through my mind briefly and I felt a pull of pain in my chest. His birthday was coming up soon, and he'd be turning eighteen, and after seeing the way Maeteo trained... I shut that thought out quickly.

"Do you think," I started, watching a butterfly fly past us and land on a nearby flower, "If your parents had stopped you, or if the guards hadn't let you on the wagon, that you would've stayed at home?"

Hollis looked like she was contemplating my question for a long minute, her lips pursed together, and her head tilted to the side.

"No. No, I don't think I would've." She said eventually, a small smile on her face, "I loved my parents, I really did, but I always knew that I was needed for something bigger."

I caught onto the way she said 'loved' and my heart tugged in my chest, and I reached out to place a hand on her arm.

Hollis and I spent hours out on the field, laughing and talking and working through her series of circuits to help me learn to shoot properly. And as the sun settled lower in the sky, I finally hit a target. Punching my fist into the air, Hollis cheered, running to grab the arrow and returning it to me. I took it from her with a smile on my face, letting the bow drop by my side.

We cleaned up the space, making sure everything was back in its place, and made our way back towards the castle. Shouts and the sound of boots hitting gravel came from behind us and Hollis tugged on my arm, pulling me as far to the side as she could manage on the narrow path, just in time for a band of soldiers to run past us, all dressed in full armour and carrying swords. I lifted an eyebrow as we watched them go by, followed by Tarian, his hands tucked into his pockets as he called out commands to the soldiers in front of him. He grinned at us as he passed, nodding his head at Hollis and bowing quickly to me.

"How do I stop people doing that?" I asked when he was out of earshot, and Hollis looked at me quizzically. "The bowing."

"Oh!" Hollis laughed loud, "Stop being royalty, I guess? I don't think it's going to stop anytime soon."

I rolled my eyes, pushing her arm lightly and laughing with her as we finally made our way through the door to the kitchen.

Hollis snatched a couple of bread rolls from the counters, calling out a thanks to chef before quickly ushering me out of the kitchens, chef's loud voice following her out into the hallways. We giggled all the way up to the second floor, where the council rooms were. This part of the castle, like everywhere else, had deep red carpets, high ceilings, and arched windows. It felt grand — far too grand for me to be wandering around eating freshly baked bread and trailing mud from the field into the carpet.

A yell from the end of the hallway made us pause. Hollis's eyebrows furrowed into a deep V, and I shrugged. Quietly, we both made our way down to the half open door. Hollis held out an arm, keeping me behind her as she peered into the open space. Maeteo's voice burst from the room, making my hear stop in my chest.

"This is ridiculous, Eyvlin!" He roared, the sound of hands hitting wood following his words, "She can't get *married*! She just got here!"

My eyes widened as I realised they were talking about me, but... married? Hollis looked at me quickly, the same look of confusion on her face as mine.

"What do you want me to do, General?" Eyvlin's voice sounded weary, "These papers are iron clad. Her father had been talking to King Conleth since before she was born."

"But it doesn't make sense!"

"It does, Maeteo." The sound of Eyvlin using Maeteo's name turned my stomach. "The Kings concreted the marriage pact the week Kira was born, and the attack... it was all planned."

Hollis's eyes went wide now, and she stepped forward, pushing the door open so fast it hit the wall with a loud smack.

Maeteo's head spun. He was stood leaning against the table, his hair falling into his face, his cheeks flushed, and his shirt untucked. Eyvlin sat across from him, her body slumped into one of the chairs, her long hair tied back into a ponytail. Her eyes met mine, and her lips pressed into a tight line.

The most surprising person in the room, however, was Emily. Stood against the window on the far wall, her arms crossed over her chest and her eyes focused on nothing in front of her.

Hollis stepped into the room, a deathly quiet settling over the three people around the table. I clung to the back of Hollis's shirt.

"I think," Hollis's voice carried through the room, making Maeteo wince slightly, "You three have a lot of explaining to do."

14

My father had promised my hand in marriage before I was even born.

I sat slumped back in a chair, my hands locked together in my lap, staring blankly at the scattered papers in front of me. Maeteo had been combing over them all afternoon looking for loopholes while I had been training with Hollis, while Eyvlin and Emily were trying to contact the Royal Family of our nearest allies — The Water Kingdom.

They had not been lucky yet. Apparently, their Queen was notoriously hard to get in contact with unless she wanted something from you.

Hollis sat to my left, her knee bouncing as she sat on her hands, her face the perfect mask of calm, composed rage.

"They arrived yesterday." Eyvlin sighed, pushing another stack of papers towards me. "Obviously with yesterdays… mishap, we didn't want to — "

"I would say being shot at is a bit more than a mishap." I muttered, cutting Eyvlin off in her tracks. Sitting forward, I took a hold of a stack of paper, eying them closely. My father's signature was scrawled in bright red ink, a matching one next to him in black ink — King Conleth, the ruler of the Fire Kingdom.

I swallowed uncomfortably. My stomach turning at the thought of my future being laid out in front of me in these sheets of paper, signed and sealed before I had even taken my first breath. A feeling of unease settled deep in my chest. Pushing the papers away from me, I looked out of the window to my right. The village square in the distance was packed with people, and a small family of birds flew past quickly, their tweets and calls filtering in through the open space.

Having no memories of my father made this feel worse. The way he spoke about me in the contracts, like I was a possession, not his daughter... like I was nothing more to him than something to be passed to the highest bidder. Like cattle at a Sunday market.

And now, years later, both Kings that had signed these papers were dead, and I was barely finding my feet in the castle. I had been ripped from everything I had ever known, forced into a role I did not want, and now was expected to marry a man I had never met.

A hand on my arm pulled me from my thoughts, and I looked to see Hollis, her face remaining unchanged, but her eyes burning with fire.

"We can get you out of this." She reassured me, her face certain; stubborn.

"How do you propose we do that?" Eyvlin sighed, rubbing a hand over her eyes. It was the most crumpled I had ever seen the woman, her hair dishevelled, and her robes creased. She looked like she had not slept a wink. Which, honestly, would not have surprised me.

"We fight them." My voice surprised even myself as it filled the room. Four sets of eyes rested on me now, and I sat up straighter in my chair. "We fight them. Tell them that I'm not marrying him."

"It doesn't work like that, Your Highness." Eyvlin sighed again, growing wearier by the second.

Maeteo cleared his throat, his hands resting on the table as he leaned forward slightly and locked eyes with me. My heart fluttered in my chest, and I watched as he smirked at the blush I could feel on my chest.

"Actually, Eyvie, Kira has a point." Maeteo looked away from me, nodding at Eyvlin, "Why shouldn't we fight them on this? They have no right to her."

"Except the rights her father signed over eighteen years ago."

"Before she was even alive!" Maeteo slapped a hand on the table, making Hollis and myself jump. "It is ancient nonsense that has no place in our Kingdom now."

Maeteo's words sat heavy in the air. He was breathing heavy, eyes boring into Eyvlin's as the older woman glared back at him, her lips pursed unhappily.

"It would mean war." Eyvlin said slowly.

"We have an army."

"It is nowhere near large enough."

"So, we bring in more troops."

Every argument that Eyvlin shot out, Maeteo managed to counter with one of his own, until the pair stood at opposite sides of the table, both leaning towards each other snarling.

I stood from my chair, the scrape of the legs on the wooden floor making Eyvlin tear her eyes away from Maeteo and stand up straight. She smoothed her hair at the root and clasped her hands together in front of herself, looking down at the scattered mess on the table. Maeteo almost looked smug as he stood up straighter, towering over us all in the room. Hollis had gone to his side, and the difference between the two in height was almost comical.

Excusing myself, I turned on my heel and stepped out of the council room, closing the door with a soft click behind myself.

I could have gone straight to my quarters, locked myself in and paced back and forth until there was a groove in the carpet, but instead I walked myself through the many halls of the castle. Past the portraits of Kings and Queens long gone, past depictions of bloody battles and farmlands, and men that looked incredibly uncomfortable in stuffy armour.

Without any intention to, I found myself walking through the kitchens, waving a quick hello to a few of the staff I had gotten to know a little better, and exiting into the large gardens.

The sun had barely started to set on the horizon, and the air still held onto the stifling heat of the day; humid and clinging to my skin. I wiped an arm over my brow as I wandered over the stone pathways, the gravel crunching under my feet softly. My mind spun with thoughts of everything I had learned in the last few hours. Everything from sword techniques, to how to hold a bow correctly, and Hollis's reasoning behind joining the ranks like she did. All of it swam in my head like hungry animals around an injured bird.

Right at the front, demanding more of my attention than anything else, was the marriage.

Nausea swam in my stomach as I made my way around one of the many stone fountains that decorated the gardens, and through the large iron gates to the quad. The absolute absurdity of marrying someone at eighteen years old, never mind marrying someone I had never met before, was completely devouring the inside of my brain as I made my way to what I wanted to see.

Still there in the middle of the stone, was the blood stain. It had faded now, like someone had scrubbed at it, but it was still angry enough that my heart dropped at the sight of it.

Crossing my arms over my chest, I forced myself to stand there and stare at it. Stare at the way it had seeped between some stones and spread through the cracks in others. Stare at how the small, green weeds that were growing in the dirt between stones were now dark and crumbling. Stare at the spot where someone had died. Someone who had tried to kill me first, granted, but still someone.

A thought, wild and worse than any I had ever entered my head, and I swayed slightly at the force of it.

I could…

A hand on my arm made me jump, and I spun around on the spot, throwing an elbow out instinctively.

Maeteo didn't even flinch at the force I hit him with, his eyebrows raised slightly and a bemused look on his face.

"Are you alright?" He asked, his voice soft, his hands moving slowly up and down my arms.

I swallowed quickly, schooling my face into a neutral expression, the fear that he could read my mind suddenly making me panic.

"I'm fine." I lied, smiling up at him, "Just a bit… shocked?"

"Naturally," He nodded, letting his arms drop by his side and studying my face as he looked at me.

I stood still, staring straight back at him and watching as his eyes moved from mine to my lips, and back again. He reached out, tucking a stray strand of hair away from my face, his fingers lingering on my cheekbone. Instinctively, I leaned my head into the palm of his hand, his eyes snapping back to mine. His pupils had blown wide, and I could hear his breathing starting to come faster. He shifted his body slightly, angling himself a little closer to me, the handle of his sword bumping against my hip.

A deafening roar caught us both by surprise. Maeteo threw out an arm to pull me behind him, and my hands flew up to cover my ears from the sudden noise. Maeteo turned us on the spot, his head whipping back and forth as he looked around for whatever had made the noise. He finally came to a halt, facing over towards the Lides mountain, and my eyes went wide.

There, atop the highest peak of the mountain, a dark figure loomed, rising into the sky above the clouds.

Silence fell before the figure dropped back through the clouds, spreading its wings and letting out another one of those bone-chilling roars. Maeteo stiffened, his arm dropping away from in front of me.

"Aepein," he breathed, watching the dragon fly across the sky and towards the castle with wide eyes. "She's awake."

15

The great beast landed in front of us with an earth-shaking crash.

Maeteo had dragged me across the quad to the back wall when he realised, we were not going to make it back inside before she landed. Her great, white wings curled in against her side, the scales iridescent in the setting sunlight. My mouth fell open at the size of her, her giant eyes easily bigger than my head. The white of her scales carried on over her body, fading to a grey at the tip of her tail, which she swished across the ground, casting dust around herself.

A huff came from her nose as she eyed Maeteo and me. Maeteo's arm across my stomach pushing me into the wall and making it hard for me to catch a proper breath, while his other hand was on the hilt of his sword. I had faith in his skills of course but looking at the size of the beast in front of me, I seriously doubted it would do much.

Shouts and screams came from beyond the quad wall, the sounds of several sets of heavy boots against the stone pathways as they came running towards where we were. Like lightning, Aepein's head shot up, her eyes turning panicked and her tail halting its lazy swishing. I grabbed Maeteo's arm, prompting him to look down at me.

"Tell them to stop." I said softly, pleading.

"What?"

"Whoever is coming, tell them to stop. They're scaring her."

Maeteo looked at me like I had two heads, and I pushed his arm away from me and stepped forward. His hand gripped at my sleeve, his knuckles turning white with the force. I snapped my head around to look at him, and for the first time, he looked scared.

"Have you lost your mind?!" He hissed, his eyes flitting from me to Aepein, her enormous form filling the quad as she panicked, knocking over a stone pillar that clattered to the ground. "Kira, listen to me — "

"No, General, you listen to me." I snapped, Maeteo's eyes widening at my tone. "She is scared. She is confused. She's just woken up from a fourteen-year sleep and now they are all coming running. Make them *stop*."

Maeteo searched my face for a second before he realised, I was serious, and he swallowed sharply before he nodded. Keeping his back to the wall, he slid along to the gate, keeping his eyes on Aepein as he did so. He slid through the smallest gap possible, his voice carrying over the commotion of the oncoming soldiers, telling them all to halt. If I did not know him, I would never have picked up the slight shake of nerves in his tone.

I turned back towards Aepein, my hands balling into fists repeatedly. Her breathing came in hurried pants, but her eyes were clear and striking, the icy blue of them cutting into my soul. Taking a slow step forward, I raised my hands to show her my palms; to try and show her that I was not going to harm her. She kept her eyes on me as I inched my way across the quad towards her. Her shoulders had dropped into a more relaxed stance, and her breathing had slowed, and the closer I got, the more her tail slowed its frenzied swaying.

I could hear the muttering and uncomfortable shuffling of Maeteo and all the gathered soldiers on the other side of the gate, and the clang of a sword hitting the ground made Aepein jump, her head shooting up and an angry scream ripping from her throat. I scrunched my face up against the noise, but I kept my palms raised and stood my ground.

"Kira," Maeteo's voice carried over the quad, a warning in his tone.

"Be quiet, Maeteo." I called back over my shoulder, not looking away from the great dragon in front of me.

Her head lowered again, her chin resting on the stone of the quad and her eyes flickering back to me. Eventually, after an agonisingly slow trip over the quad, I was within touching distance of her snout.

Gently, gentler than I had ever done anything in my life, I placed my hand on the bridge of her nose. Her eyes closed, and a contented huff left her nostrils. I stared in awe, my heart hammering in my chest at the sight in front of me. Out of the corner of my eye I could see more people starting to gather outside of the iron gates, Hollis and Tarian coming to stand beside Maeteo. I am sure if I had looked properly, Hollis would have had a grin on her face.

Moving my hands over the scales of Aepein's head, I let my hand wander up to the two twisted, shimmering horns that stretched another foot in the air. Her scales, which had appeared white from across the way, had a very light blue tint to them, although they were hot to the touch. Sliding my hand down her neck, I frowned at the large, jagged scar that ran in a line from her jaw to her shoulder.

"What happened to you, huh?" I asked softly, letting a finger trace the scar. Aepein huffed, her head turning to look at me. The look in her eyes told me what I needed to know. She had been injured the night of the Fire attack, and suddenly my plan that had come earlier, after finding out about my father and his plans to arrange a marriage for me, cemented itself into my brain.

Aepein huffed through her nose, her head jerking towards her back. I paused, furrowing my eyebrows at her. When I didn't move for a second, she nudged me with her nose, pushing me slightly, and repeated the motion with her head.

"Do… do you want me to get on?" My voice was disbelieving as I stared at her. She simply blinked in reply, nudging me closer to her wing again with her nose. I hesitated.

Maeteo's voice carried over the quad again, but I couldn't make out what he was saying — I simply glanced in his direction, seeing him making his way through the gates cautiously. I shook my head at him, waving an arm to get him to stop. Thankfully, he did, and I eyed Aepein's back, wondering how exactly I was meant to climb up there.

As if she could hear my thoughts, Aepein dropped her shoulder slightly for me, and popped out her front leg in a makeshift step. Being cautious of how much of my weight I put on her, I held onto her tightly as I stepped onto the little platform she had created, pulling myself up until I was sat between her two shoulder blades. My breath left me in a small laugh, it felt so similar yet was so wildly different to sitting on Freya.

Running my hands along the mane of silver hair down the back of her neck, I grinned over at Maeteo, who had lost all colour in his face. If the situation had not been so bizarre, I would have laughed at the look on his face.

With a sudden jerk, Aepein was on her feet, and my hands tightened around her mane. Maeteo yelled out my name, but Aepein turned on the spot, and with a small jump over the quad wall, took off at a run across the adjoining field. Screams of the people who had been working in the field filled the air, and all the air left my body as Aepein leaped into the air, her wings unfurling behind my back, and suddenly we were soaring.

I looked over my shoulder, seeing the castle grow smaller and smaller as Aepein flew up towards the clouds. The wind whipped harshly at my cheeks, and an almost hysterical laugh left me at the sheer unbelievable situation I had found myself in. Aepein hit a height that she deemed acceptable for coasting and took a sharp left. If my grip had been any looser on her mane, I would have gone plummeting to the ground below.

Staring down at the ground beneath us, I marvelled at the yellows and greens of the farming fields, how they gave way to the dark, paved paths of the village, the square bustling with people who were all staring at the sky, yelling and pointing. It almost seemed like Aepein was trying to parade herself about. The village was gone as fast as it had appeared, giving way to the thick trees of the forest.

Jade trees gave way to orange, and orange gave way to trees lacking leaves completely. Green, thick grass became ashy grey, and I realised where Aepein was taking me. To the Lides mountains. To where she had been sleeping for the last fourteen years.

I watched as the mountains grew bigger, the air got colder, and Aepein started to climb upwards again. I hunched my shoulders in slightly, lowering myself against her back as she shot up towards the caves. The speed at which she flew was eye watering.

When she finally landed with a sharp thump, I stayed hunkered down for a second. The wind had died down and it almost felt warm again and sitting up I realised she had flown us directly into one of the caves. Dark and dingy with water dripping from the ceiling, but it was filled with straw, grass, and...

A goat bleated at me from the back corner.

Sliding down off her back, I held onto her side as my feet hit the ground, all the feeling in my legs going completely to mush. Aepein huffed at me over her shoulder, and I glared at her.

"You shush," I muttered, letting go of her and rubbing my hands on my thighs, willing feeling back into them as I peered around the cave.

Aepein moved, shaking her mane and wandering over to a spot towards the back wall. It took my eyes a minute to adjust to the dim light further into the cave, but when they had I realised where she had gone, what she was doing.

She was crouched beside a nest. The largest nest I had ever seen, full of sheep's wool, straw, and leaves, but she was not concerned with any of that. She was nudging at two large, white eggs. Each speckled with spots of blue and green, and as they bumped against each other, Aepein whined.

My heart broke in my chest. She had brought me to see her babies.

Stepping forward, I ran my hand up her neck, along the jagged scar and let my hand rest against her jaw.

Aepein continued to nudge the eggs with her nose for a few minutes, before she sighed a deep, rumbling sigh, and turned her large head to look at me. I met her eyes, a sad smile on my face.

"They took one of your eggs, didn't they?" I asked, and she blinked in response. "They won't hatch without the last one?"

Aepein shook her head slightly, resting her chin on the edge of the nest and staring longingly at the eggs in front of her.

Again, a plan brought itself to the forefront of my mind. I crouched down next to Aepein's head, letting myself rest against her.

"I'll get them back for you." I whispered, reaching out to touch one of the eggs in the nest. "I don't know how yet, but I'll get it."

16

"Tell me again," Gracie gushed, her hands pulling my hair into a tight ponytail.

"There is nothing more to tell, Gracie." I laughed wearily. After Aepein had returned me to the castle, I had not been left alone for a minute. Maeteo and Eyvlin had spent a good hour yesterday evening lecturing me on being so reckless, and then another hour questioning every second I spent in the caves with Aepein. By the time I made my way to my bed, it was nearing two in the morning, and I slept as soon as my head hit the pillow.

Now, as I stood in my bathroom, dressed for a day of emergency council meetings in a white button-down shirt and linen trousers, I recounted the experience to Gracie; who had burst into my room the second the sun rose into the sky, Callum trotting dutifully at her heels. He had left after fifteen minutes but had said he wanted to be there to see Gracie's reaction to my story.

Her eyes were wide, and her mouth agape as she took in every detail. She asked question after question, and my voice was growing hoarse. With a final tug on my hair, she placed a small tiara onto my head, and I furrowed my eyebrows. She laughed lightly.

"You have to wear it to meetings," She explained, pinning it in place, "Now you're eighteen and your coronation is coming up in a few weeks, you have to present as a Queen in training, rather than a Princess."

I rolled my eyes, but nodded and squared my shoulders, ready to face whatever was waiting for me down in the council rooms. Emily was sitting on one of the sofas in my living area, her legs crossed over one another. Tarian, the focus of Emily's attention stood near the doors, his eyes cast downward, and his hands shoved deep into his pockets.

Emily looked up when I entered, a smile breaking out on her face. I hadn't spoken to her properly in days now, only seeing her yesterday with Maeteo and Eyvlin and those damned papers, and my heart ached a little at how much I missed her comforting presence. I smiled at her, letting her envelope me in a tight, squeezing hug.

Tarian cleared his throat by the door, and I pulled away from Emily.

"Tarian, to what do I owe the pleasure?" I smiled, stepping towards him. He blushed a deep red, and I felt bad for putting him on the spot. Hollis had said how shy her brother was.

"Maeteo sent me to collect you, Your Highness," His deep voice surprised me, "He's been caught up at training."

"Oh," I nodded, flattening my hands over my shirt and making sure nothing had gone out of place when Emily had hugged me, "Lead the way, then."

Tarian nodded, his hand on the door handle in a flash and gesturing for me to step out into the hallway. I thanked him, looking over my shoulder to make sure Emily and Gracie were following us, and started towards the council rooms.

The way Tarian led us took us through a back corridor that I had yet to see. The wall was made of entirely glass, and the carpets had given way to plain stone floors. It felt cooler — thankfully — but the sun shining in through the glass wall made it so much brighter than the rest of the castle, and I wondered why they had not taken this choice of windows and put it through the whole castle.

Emily and Gracie were still talking quietly behind Tarian and I as we walked, but I didn't catch any of their conversation. My eyes were drawn to the wall, and I marvelled at how far I could see from here. The castle gardens stretched around in every direction, and while people worked on trimming the hedges and keeping the grass mowed, birds fluttered between trees, and across the way the horses from the stables grazed in the fields. It was beautiful.

As we turned another corner, the views of the gardens gave way to views of the training rings, and I paused mid-step. The ring nearest to us, with a brick wall and open gate, was full of soldiers. All of them were cheering on the two fighters in the middle. Neither of them wore shirts in the already heavy heat of the day, but they both wore helmets and carried their swords — not the wooden ones Maeteo had made me practice with, but proper, steel swords. They were circling each other, almost like they were taunting each other.

My breath caught in my throat as I watched them, Tarian stopping a few steps ahead of me and looking back questioningly.

The two soldiers in the ring lunged at each other, and the clang of sword on sword could be heard where we were in the corridor. A hand flew to my throat as I watched.

"They won't hurt each other," Tarian said beside me, his voice strangely comforting. "Maeteo never gets hit."

My eyes went wide at the realisation that it was Maeteo I was watching. His muscles gleamed in the sun as he moved so effortlessly away from his partner's sword. It was the first time I had seen him without a shirt on, and the sight made my throat dry. Swallowing harshly, I tried to drag my eyes away, but it was as if watching them put me in some kind of trance.

Dodging and weaving, Maeteo worked his way around the ring, completely avoiding his opponent until they started to get sloppy in their movements, their agitation showing in the way they let their stance change, their swings of their sword more erratic. Maeteo noticed, too, and took his chance. Swiping his sword low, he managed to get his opponents legs out from under them, sending them flying backwards in the ring. They landed on their back, and Maeteo was on top of them, his legs at either side of their waist, and his sword swinging dangerously close to their head.

I gasped, my hand covering my mouth as he swung down, missing their head by only an inch. Tarian chuckled beside me, shaking his head.

"He's always been one for dramatics." He rolled his eyes, smiling down at me. When he smiled, he looked exactly like Hollis, just a foot and a half taller.

Maeteo pulled off his helmet, laughing as he jumped up, offering a hand to his fallen opponent and pulling them up beside him. He spread his arms, soaking in the cheers from the surrounding soldiers. He lifted his sword from the ground and whirled it around in his hand, shouting something that I could not hear as he spun in a slow circle, using the sword to point to a soldier across from him now. The boy stepped forward, and my heart stopped in my chest. He couldn't have been any older than eighteen, and he was scrawny and terrified looking.

Tarian's hand on my arm brought my attention back to the task at hand, and I dragged myself away from the window, following him through the rest of his secret hallways until we reached the second floor.

The corridor of council rooms was dark and cold compared to the wonderful hallway upstairs. I frowned as we followed the sounds of voices in the farthest away room. It was the largest out of the meeting rooms I'd been in recently, which meant every member of the council would be there. *Great.*

Tarian pushed the door open, and the room fell into silence. Every council member around the table stood from their seats and bowed their heads, and I gritted my teeth against the rising blush on my face. Emily had said I would get used to everyone bowing eventually, but that could not come soon enough.

Making my way across the room to my seat at the top of the table, I locked eyes with Alexandre. He was sat in the same place he had been last time, and he smiled a warm smile at me and dipped his head slightly. I returned the gesture with a smile of my own, and as soon as I sat myself down, Emily to my right and Gracie to my left, everyone else sat down alongside me.

Brond cleared his throat, and stood from his seat again, his eyes boring straight into me, and I held in my sigh.

"Thank you for your audience, *Your Highness*," He mocked, "We know you've been busy, flying away on dragons and such."

"Brond," Emily warned, her tone of voice heavy, "If you're not going to be constructive, you can leave."

"You would like that very much, wouldn't you, Emily?"

"More than anything else, yes."

Brond glared so fiercely at Emily that I worried she would burst into flames if he did not start blinking soon. Eyvlin shifted in her seat, wrapping her fingers around Brond's wrist and pulling him back down into a sitting position. His face went red, and I heard Tarian chuckle quietly, covering it with a cough.

Eyvlin shook her head, placing her hand on the table and looking at everyone individually, finally landing her gaze on me. Squaring my shoulders, I sat myself up straight, holding her stare.

"Your Majesty," Eyvlin started, her tone much softer than I had expected it to be, "We're glad you're safe."

"Aepein was never going to hurt her." Alexandre grumbled from the end of the table. He was flicking small drops of water out of his glass with his finger, and I felt myself smile when I realised, he was aiming them towards Brond, who looked like someone had placed his head into a furnace; his cheeks were flushed a pure, angry red.

"Regardless, Alexandre, it is nice to see the Prin — Her Majesty in one piece."

Brond grumbled something under his breath, and then he yelped in pain, as if someone had kicked him under the table. I looked to my left, seeing Gracie giggling into her hand, and Tarian on her left looking at me with an expression of faux innocence.

Eyvlin rolled her eyes, her patience already seeming to wear thin.

"We have several… delicate, matters we must discuss today." Eyvlin continued, shuffling the papers on the desk in front of her and casting her eyes downwards. "And, in a break from tradition, Her Majesty is getting word on all of them."

I blinked, my head whipping to look at Emily, who simply nodded, a small smile on her face. Several of the elder men around the table started to protest, raising their voices and shaking their heads, but Eyvlin simply held up her hand, silencing them without looking up from her papers.

"If you could all look at your minutes from last council, we can get started."

Once we had passed the usual subjects like meal plans for the week, training schedules for the soldiers, the issue of several of the wash house staff not managing to get blood out of cotton sheets, and of course after several unhelpful comments from Brond, Eyvlin looked like she was starting to lose her mind.

I cleared my throat, taking a sip of the glass of water in front of me before I stood. Every set of eyes around the table fell to me, and I could feel my heartbeat in my ears.

"I wanted to touch quickly on something I learned yesterday," I locked eyes with Alexandre, and the comforting smile on his face helped settle the nerves in my stomach, "Aepein took me to her nest."

Several mumbled around the table.

"She showed me where she and her eggs have been sleeping for the last fourteen years. She has *babies,* and they won't hatch, because their sibling was taken."

"Taken? What do you mean taken?" Brond spat the question at me, his eyebrows furrowed in the middle making him look older than he was.

"I mean that one of her eggs was taken the night of the attack." I looked Brond in the eyes as I spoke, "And the ones she still has cannot hatch until it has been returned."

"And how do you propose we do that, girl?" Brond's tone made anger bubble in my stomach, and I had to close my eyes and breathe deeply. I could hear people around the table mumbling again, several of them on my side. A surprise on its own.

"If we can get someone on the inside over on Fire's lands — "

I was cut off by a scoff, and Brond stood from the table, knocking his papers away from himself as he did so.

"She has no place as Queen!" He bellowed, "Look at her! She knows nothing — she is scruffy, she is uneducated on our protocols, and now she wants to send our people into their lands!"

Shock rippled around the room at Brond's outburst. He knocked over his water, sending it splashing across the table, and turned for the door. To everyone's surprise, the door opened just as Brond reached for the handle, and Maeteo stood there. Shirt on now, but sweat still glistening on his forehead, his hair pushed back off his face, and a bemused expression on his face.

"Have I missed something special?" He asked, amusement lacing his tone as he looked from Brond into the room, meeting my gaze. "Ruffling some feathers, Princess?"

A fiery blush spread across my cheeks, and I clenched my jaw, balling my hands into fists. Brond roared something I could not make out and stormed from the room, pushing his way past Maeteo. The silence that fell over the room was deafening, and Maeteo closed the door behind himself before he made his way right to Brond's seat and collapsed into it. He crossed his arms over his chest, grinning as he did so.

"Please, continue." He gestured towards me with his hand, and I sucked in a breath.

Everything in my body was screaming at me not to go ahead with this. People would protest, they would absolutely abhor the thought of their loved ones, their children going behind enemy lines... but surely, they must expect that when they are drafted?

I chewed my lip, looking around at the faces in the room. Whichever way they all voted; the Kingdom was going into a war we were not prepared for. Yes, we had soldiers and weapons and apparent allies to the West, but was it enough? If I kept my swords close to my chest, I could cut the war in half.

I cleared my throat, shaking my head at myself and smiling.

"It was a silly theory, Brond was right." The words burned my throat as I said them, and Maeteo's face fell, his eyebrows furrowing as he watched me closely. I sat back down in my seat and looked to Eyvlin, who looked just as confused as Maeteo. "Eyvlin, please, what's next?"

The meeting continued until every detail of my coronation and the accompanying ball was ironed out and perfect. Eyvlin had come prepared with a fourteen-page document detailing every minute of the procession, every person I had to speak to, when I could eat, drink, go to the bathroom. I looked over the list of names of noble men I was expected to share a dance with, and my heart skipped a beat when I saw Maeteo's name scrawled near the bottom of the list.

Looking up, I caught him watching me across the table. He winked quickly, smirking at me.

The sun had moved to the middle of the sky by the time the meeting had finished. The mid-afternoon sun beating down on the castle making the air hot and uncomfortable. I ran a hand across my forehead to catch the sweat that had beaded there and stepped out into the stuffy hallway.

Alexandre caught my arm with his hand, and I jumped, a hand flying to my chest in fright. The laugh that came out of him was rough and grumbled, like he had enjoyed too much tobacco.

"Sorry, Your Majesty." He chuckled, and I let out a breath, laughing alongside him.

"It's Kira, Alexandre, please." I smiled, clasping my hands together in front of me. Alexandre waved his hand, dismissing my plea.

"Have you read the book I gave you?" He asked, his face turning serious as we started walking towards the lower floor of the castle.

I had forgotten all about the book, and a flush of embarrassment crossed me when the realisation hit.

"Uh, no. Not yet. I've been quite busy." I stumbled over my words, stepping to the side so Alexandre could go through an open door before me.

"I suggest you get to it soon, Your Highness." Alexandre looked me in the eyes as he spoke now. He had stopped walking and blocked my way through the doorway. "The chapter about your father should be particularly interesting."

17

The red book sat on my bedside table.

After my chat with Alexandre in the hallways, I had to go to lunch with Emily, and a dress fitting with Gracie's mother, Anya.

Anya was the most soft-spoken, lovely woman I had ever met. But after multiple dresses that made me feel like I was supposed to be on top of my coronation cake, I had wanted nothing more than to return to my room and never look at tulle ever again.

Closing my door behind me, I let my back rest against the wood and let out a sigh. The quiet of the room made my ears feel like they were ringing. Someone had been in already and lit all my candles, and a fresh pot of steaming tea sat on my coffee table. I kicked off my shoes, letting them fall where they may and flopped my weight down onto one of the sofas.

Once I had a mug of tea in hand, I sipped at it as I wandered through to my bedroom, my eyes falling on the book. Its dark colour stood out against the whites and pinks and golds of my bedding and furniture, and my stomach dropped to my toes. Had Alexandre meant to scare me with what he had said about my father?

Placing my mug on top of my dresser, I picked it up and sat myself onto the edge of my bed and ran my hands over the leather cover. It felt old to touch, and I worried for a second that I would damage it. I let myself sit back against the pillows of the bed, and with Alexandre's words in my mind, I opened the book to the back.

My father's name — *King Petr Dagon, Bringer of Peace*, — greeted me in bold, red writing, taking up the whole page it had been written on. I ran my fingers over the letters, feeling how the pen had scratched into the paper.

Turning the page, I sat myself forward, my heart starting to hammer in my chest. Pages had been ripped out of the binding, and instead sat a scribbled piece of paper, crumpled and glued to the hard backing of the book.

Kira,

If you are reading this, it means Alexandre has done his job correctly. If you are not Kira, I ask that you put this book back where you found it.

My daughter, you have no clue how hard your mother and I tried for you. It took years before your mother fell with you. We had considered going to a healer for medicinal help, but as that thought entered our minds, the sickness started, and then there was you.

You may know by now that I have signed your marriage to Prince Cyrus Edward of Fire. If it comes as any consolation to you, my love, it was the hardest thing I have ever had to do. Your mother has no idea, but I know it would kill her if she did. Now, the bad part:

The attack was planned. I am writing this the morning before, and I will give it to Alexandre for safe keeping until you return to the castle. Please, do not think badly of me, my love, this is for the best. The best for you, and for the Kingdom.

You must marry Cyrus. You do not need to be happy about it, but you must do it. You marry him, you must go to Fire, and you take them down from the inside. You must kill him before he kills our Kingdom. I understand this is a big task, and hopefully it is one that goes against your morals, but if you are half the Queen your mother and I believe you will be, you will do what is right for your Kingdom.

Please know I never wanted it to come to this. I never wanted to leave this to you, but if it brings peace to our small corner of the world, what must be done will be.

Always remember you are loved.

Your father.

My eyes burned as I read the note from my father repeatedly. A lump formed in my throat, and I closed the book, placing it back in its place on my bedside table and climbing off my bed. I had not changed my clothes from my day of meetings, so it was only a matter of putting my shoes back on and heading out my door. Letting it thunk closed behind me, the noise echoed through the empty hallways.

I wasn't sure where I was going, but I let my legs carry me around the castle hallways for hours until my brain had grown sick of thinking about my father's words.

I had to marry him. I had to marry him, and then kill him.

It was strikingly like the plan that had been hatching inside my own mind. Though, that gave me little comfort. Alexandre had known that the note was in the book; He knew everything. If I went to him with my plan and my father's, would he be willing to help?

Chewing on my lip, I found myself heading towards the stables again. I knew most of the workers would be finished by now, so I would not be disturbed.

The hot summer air still clung to my skin as I stepped out onto the gravel path leading to the stables. I pulled my hair back off my face and back into an elastic, thankful for the small reprieve on the back of my neck. The bird songs from the day had given way to the sounds of owls and crickets in the grass, the gentle running of water from the fountains seemed so much louder, and the gravel crunching under my feet would have made me nervous if the castle had been smaller.

The clouds above blocked out any sign of the stars, and a part of me felt sad. The stars had always been my favourite thing to look at. Dane and I would spend our summers camping in the meadow by the cottage, lying in the grass and making pictures in the sky.

Briefly, I wondered if Dane missed me.

The stables sat in darkness, and only the noises of horses whinnying, and huffing came from inside. A smile came over my face as I slid the lock off the gate and pushed it open, making sure to lock it again behind myself. Freya's stable sat against the back wall, and her head lulled lazily over the half door.

I clicked my tongue at her, and her head lifted sharply. She shook her mane, huffing through her nose at me.

"Hi, girl." I smiled, running a hand up her nose and letting her nudge into my hand. I smiled lightly, pushing the small door open and edging into the stable.

Lighting the small lantern that hung at the top of her paddock, I checked her water bucket. It was full, of course, because the stable workers had only been gone an hour. Freya watched me closely, her mane falling down the side of her neck and over the front of her nose.

I picked up one of the soft brushes that sat on the shelves, testing the bristles against the back of my hand

and nodding to myself before I turned back to face Freya. She stood perfectly still as I ran the brush through her mane and tail, as if she knew I was thinking things through and needed to keep myself busy.

If I went through with my father's plan, was I a horrible person? Would the people of Earth end up hating me? Would I be seen as a traitor? The thoughts all came to me at once as I worked through a particularly tough knot in Freya's tail. Would I be forever marked as the one who abandoned her Kingdom to join another, regardless of if I murdered another Kingdom's ruler?

Would we still have allies in Water if I went through with this?

The sound of footsteps across the stable yard made my ears prick as I stood up straight. Frowning, I looked at Freya, who had hung her head over the door again. She let out a grunt, and I heard a deep laugh come from the yard. My heart stopped.

"Maeteo?" I asked before I could stop myself, putting the brush I was holding back on the shelf. Wiping off my hands on my trousers, I let myself out of Freya's stable.

Maeteo stood with his hands in his pockets, a shocked look on his face as he watched me emerge from the stable. He was dressed more casually than I had ever seen him, in loose, checked pyjama trousers and a fitted, white, short sleeve shirt.

"Princess? What are you doing out here?" He asked, a smile coming over his face.

"I had some things on my mind." I shrugged, crossing my arms over my chest, "Why are you out here?"

"Fenrir needs his nightly sugar cubes." Maeteo chuckled, digging into his pocket and producing a handful of pink cubes of sugar. I laughed lightly, shaking my head at him and watching as he opened Fenrir's stable door, pushing the great brute of a horse back so he could step inside beside him.

I let my arms rest on top of the door, a small smile on my face as I watched Maeteo fuss over Fenrir. He ran his hands over his horse's coat and spoke softly to him as he let him munch sugar cubes from his hand. The memory of him this afternoon, training in the sun without his shirt popped into my head, and I tried to shake it away as quickly as I could. Maeteo looked over to me, a strange expression on his face.

"Are you alright?" He asked, dusting his hand off on his pyjama trousers and standing up straight, "You look like you've seen a ghost."

I stepped back, letting him out of the stable.

"I'm fine," I lied, looking down at the ground, and then at the sky, and anywhere but at Maeteo. He chuckled, and his finger under my chin forced me to look up at him.

He was staring at me so closely that I forgot how to breathe for a second. His eyes, while they appeared a gorgeous, deep brown during the day, looked almost black in the low light of the stables. His hair had fallen over his forehead in waves that he normally had pushed back, and a shadow of stubble was starting to form across his jaw.

His expression softened, and he slid his thumb along the line of my jaw.

"Talk to me," He said softly, "I might not be much help, but I can listen."

I closed my eyes, laughing lightly. His skin was warm against mine and if I let myself forget who I was for a minute, he could have just been a man from the village.

"I'm just… worried." The words came out slowly as I opened my eyes again, and while it was not the whole truth, it was not a lie either. "Worried I'm not going to be the Queen everyone is expecting me to be."

Maeteo shook his head, his hand falling away from my face, and I caught myself quickly before I let myself pout at the loss of contact.

Instead, though, his arms wrapped around my shoulders, and he pulled me in tight against his chest. I let myself relax into him, the smell of soap and sugar cubes flooded my senses in an oddly comforting mix.

"You are going to be the greatest Queen our Kingdom has ever had." He said softly, his hands stroking through my hair, letting the strands fall against my back. "I have no doubt about that."

"Brond has a lot of doubt about it." I muttered into his chest, and his laugh rumbled through me in a burst.

"Brond doesn't know his ups from his downs most days, Princess. Take no notice of him."

I hummed in acknowledgment, letting my eyes close as Maeteo and I stood there together. His hands had moved from my hair to my back, and he was drawing small circles against the fabric. The only noises were those coming from inside the stables, horses' hooves knocking into buckets and the occasional whinny, and it was the calmest I had been in days.

When Maeteo loosened his grip on me, I stepped back, but his hands caught my wrists, and I looked up at him quizzically. His eyes flickered across my face, before he let out a sigh and stared up at the sky for a minute.

"To hell with it," He muttered, letting go of my wrists and sliding one of his hands to the back of my neck. I did not get the chance to ask him what he was doing before his lips crushed to mine.

His lips were soft and warm, and my eyes fluttered closed as he tangled his fingers in the hair at the nape of my neck. My fingers curled around the fabric of his shirt, keeping him close to me. The evening air still hung heavily around us, but my skin turned into goose-pimples at his touch.

All too quickly, he pulled away, resting his forehead against mine as he took shaky breaths. His fingers eased in my hair, and I felt myself smiling. My heart hammered heavily in my chest, and I untangled my fingers from his shirt to take a step back.

His hands fell by his sides as he stared at me, his eyes wide. Silence enveloped the pair of us as we looked at one another. Crickets sang somewhere nearby, and an owl flying overhead finally made me tear my eyes away from Maeteo. He cleared his throat.

"Sorry, Princess." He muttered; his eyes cast downwards.

"Why?" I asked, furrowing my eyebrows as I looked back down at him.

"I shouldn't have — "

"Please, don't." I stopped him, a small smile on my face as I took a step towards him. He flicked his eyes back up to mine, "Don't say you shouldn't have done that because I'm the Princess and you're just a General, because I don't care."

Maeteo smiled, reaching up to tuck a piece of hair behind my ear.

"You might not care, Princess, but plenty of other people will."

"Plenty of other people don't need to know." I shrugged, smiling and going onto my tiptoes to peck his cheek quickly. He closed his eyes, sucking a breath in through his nose. "I'll see you tomorrow, General."

18

Maeteo

Her coronation was less than a week away, and what was Kira doing?

She was doing handstands against the kitchen walls with one of Chef's daughters.

I watched her from where I was standing against the wall of the training ring, her hearty laugh reaching my ears a second after it happened. Her bright orange hair flowed down onto the grass as she flipped herself upside down again, and I smiled at the look of sheer glee on her face. It was nice to see her relaxed, and happy.

After a week of council meetings, coronation rehearsals, or training sessions — each of which had ended with Kira either frustrated or just plain upset, she deserved the break. I had not had the chance to be alone with her since our night in the stables, and my hands itched to feel her again.

A call of my name made me turn my head back around, my eyes scanning the packed space in front of me until they landed on Tarian, who was crossing toward me through the middle of the field as if there were not swords flying everywhere. I chuckled at the sight, pushing myself off the wall and meeting him at the edge of the field.

Tarian arched an eyebrow at me, a smirk on his face.

"Can you maybe pine on your own time?" He asked, and I frowned at him.

"Excuse me?"

"You're standing over here staring at her as if she put the sun in the sky this morning." He laughed, punching my arm. I acted wounded, but everyone knew Tarian was not the physical violence type. He was deadly with a sword and even more-so with a high ground advantage and a dagger, but he had always fallen short when it had come to a fist fight.

"Be quiet." I rolled my eyes, rubbing the spot he had hit on my arm and looking at him, "You're one to talk, anyway."

"I don't know what you — "

"How's Tristan?"

"You stop right there, Maeteo." Tarian's voice went hard, and I laughed loud at his reaction. He huffed, crossing his arms over his chest.

Tarian had been to the blacksmith four times this week, and while he said it was to make sure that they were getting the crown and sceptre right for Kira's coronation, Hollis and I knew it was also because he wanted to see Tristan, the blacksmith's apprentice and current infatuation of his.

Not that I could blame him, Tristan's muscles rivalled my own.

Shaking my head, I picked up my sword from where it was lying on the grass and nudged Tarian with my elbow. He looked up at me, still scowling. I gestured towards the field with my head, and his expression turned into a smile as he nodded.

I called all the sparring soldiers to the sides, all of them huffing and panting with exertion, and sent them all back to the barracks to rest. The summer heat was hard on us all at the best of times, and whilst I knew the fighting conditions on the battlefields would not let them take breaks for bathing or drinks of cool water, I did not want anyone dying on my training fields.

Stepping to the middle of the field with Tarian, I motioned for him to stand in front of me. He did, unsheathing his sword as he did so, the noise ringing through the air. I grinned, copying him and pointing it at him.

And then, we were dancing.

We moved around each other like a well-oiled machine, weaving and avoiding each other's moves like we had practiced a million times before now. The sun beat down on us as we moved, making beads of sweat run down my back.

Tarian laughed as he swiped at my legs with his sword, making me jump in the air with a yelp. It was a move he had used before, but it took me by surprise every time. Glaring at him, I lunged forward, swiping downwards towards his shoulder, but he blocked it in a second. I grunted, baring my teeth at him. He was the only person within the castle grounds that could make me sweat during a fight.

He grinned at me, whirling away from me and making me stumble forward, cursing as he all but danced across the field like he was taunting me.

"You're too distracted," He called, wiping his forehead with his arm, "Focus, General."

"I'll drown you, Tarian." I yelled back, "Next time you go for a bath, watch yourself."

His laugh was loud and echoed across the field, and I rolled my eyes as I grinned at him.

We carried on like that until the sun had moved across the sky and behind the trees, way past the dinner call and even after Hollis had come searching for us. She had laughed, seeing the pair of us with swords locked together and trying to out-do the other, and had left us to it. She knew from experience that we would tire ourselves out eventually, and we would end up sore the next day, but we would both feel better for it.

I held up my hands, my breaths coming hard and fast as I finally gave up. Tarian punched a fist into the air, whooping with delight at my surrender. Laughing, we both clapped each other on the shoulder, putting our swords back into their sheaths at our belts, and turned to head out of the training ring. There was not a single person within seeing distance, and we moved quickly through the quiet castle grounds.

We reached the gardens, the only sound being the water still running in the fountains, and I stopped. Sighing, I sat on the edge of the fountain, my elbows resting on my knees. Tarian didn't question my sudden stop, simply placed himself beside me and leaned back against the side of the fountain, no doubt enjoying the cooling spray of the water.

"How is Anders?" I asked, turning my head to see Tarian with his eyes closed. I had not seen the kid

Cooper had hurt back in the barracks yet, but between meetings with Eyvlin and training Kira, I had not had the time.

"He's fine," Tarian nodded. "He was moved to the bottom floor of the hospital wing. His wounds are healing, and he is feeling upbeat, as far as I know." He looked at me then, his eyebrows furrowing slightly. "He still won't be able to come back any time soon."

"Merethyl said he won't have full use of his arm again, do you know…"

"What do you really want to talk about, Maeteo?" Tarian cut me off, his arms crossed over his chest and a puzzled look on his face. I sighed, rolling my eyes inwardly at his uncanny ability to always tell when I needed to talk.

I sat back, copying his position and leaning back against the fountain with crossed arms. Tilting my head back I stared at the quickly darkening sky.

"I kissed Kira." I mumbled, watching an owl fly overhead. "A week or so ago, in the stables."

Tarian let out a low whistle but did not say anything. He sat in almost infuriating silence as I stared at the sky, my own thoughts racing. Had she told anyone what had happened? Would she? Was she still thinking about it like I was?

Groaning, I ran a hand over my face and huffed out a sigh.

"You regret it?" Tarian asked, his tone unusual. I peered out the side of my eyes at him, but he was staring straight ahead.

"No," I sighed, "I want it to happen again, really. She's driving me crazy."

Tarian laughed, and I glared at him. He shook his head, slapping a hand onto my shoulder and grinning at me.

"You're in trouble." He laughed, standing up from where he was sat. My mouth fell open as I stared after him, disbelief clouding me at his reaction. I scrambled to stand, following him at a jog. He was still laughing quietly to himself.

"Is that all you have to say?" I asked, my tone incredulous as I fell into step beside him.

"What else can I say?" He laughed, "I'm not judging you, not in the slightest, but I am saying that it's a dangerous game to fall in love with the soon to be Queen."

"I'm not *in love* with her!" I stumbled over my words, "I just..."

"Can't stop thinking about her." Tarian grinned, and I glared at him.

"Oh, go away." I grumbled as I pushed open the door to the barracks. The sounds of hundreds of men laughing and relaxing in their downtime greeted us, and Tarian patted me on the back with a laugh, before he turned to the left and disappeared towards the communal bathrooms.

I grumbled to myself as I walked down to my private room, my boots heavy against the wooden staircase. Several of the younger soldiers stopped and moved out of the way for me to storm past them. One of them even wished me a goodnight, but it did not register in my head until I was already past them and halfway to my room. Cursing myself, I made a mental note not to take it too hard on the kid the next day at training.

The door of my room opened easily, and I closed it behind myself with a sigh. I had grown so used to this room over the years, that simply stepping inside brought me a sense of comfort and relaxation. Slipping my boots off my feet, I stored them under the desk beside the door, and threw my sword down beside them.

Someone had already been in to light the candles next to my bed, and the smells of essential oils drifted through from the bathroom to my left. Groaning to myself, I turned and followed the smells, shedding clothes as I went.

The claw-footed bath stood in the middle of the room and was full of steaming hot water. I did not even test it before I stepped in, and I hissed as the water burned my skin, but I sat down anyway. Letting the water cover me up to my neck, I let out a sigh. The sounds from the barracks floated in from under my main door, but they were muffled enough that they were easy to ignore.

Tarian's words filtered through my head as I steeped in the water, and I found myself frowning at the clouds of steam that filtered up into the air.

I could not be in love with her. I had meant what I said to her about plenty of other people having an opinion about us if anything happened, and I could not let that happen.

I could not risk letting anyone not take her seriously because of me.

19
Kira

I jumped at the sharp pain of a sewing pin jabbing into my shoulder.

Anya, Gracie's mother and the castle seamstress, stood behind me. She had a serious look on her face and a dozen pins hanging from her mouth. Her eyebrows creased in the middle, and she flicked her eyes up to mine, a sign that, as I had gathered quickly, meant for me to stand still.

Looking at Anya was like looking at Gracie in thirty-years' time. Her hair, curly and dark brown like Gracie's, was greying at the roots, but her eyes were the same sharp, analytical brown that made it feel all too easy to spill all your secrets to her. She was currently stood behind me, pulling the shoulders of my communion dress tight against my skin and pinning them into place for last minute alterations.

The crowds were already gathering outside the castle walls. When I woke this morning, all I could see from my bedroom window was thousands of people gathered for miles and my heart had dropped into my stomach. The village bells rang loudly, reaching me even through the closed doors of my patio.

My breakfast sat untouched on my coffee table, having gone cold hours ago. Part of me knew I should have at least tried to eat it, but the thought of bringing it all back up in the middle of my coronation was enough to put me against it.

Now, standing in front of the triple mirror Anya had dragged in with her, I stared at myself. My hair had been washed and brushed and twisted into a style that resembled the ivy that climbed the castle walls, with fresh flowers woven through the braids and a tiara that took my breath away. It looked like the night sky, with diamonds and sapphires sparkling against the light coming into the room.

My dress hung around me in a curtain of dark green velvet. Black lace roses covered my chest and arms, and the bodice was a corset that had been tied so tightly I could not catch a full breath. The straps Anya worked on were the same dark, rich green as the rest of the skirt, and while she pulled at them, I ran my hands over the material of the skirt, the soft velvet sliding away under my fingers.

Anya finally took a step back, nodding her head to herself as she took in her handiwork. It had only been the two of us in the room for the last hour, and I could hear people's voices starting to float down the hallway towards my doors. I swallowed, my heart hammering in my chest and turned away from the mirror, looking at Anya.

"How do I look?" I asked, my voice shaking as I tried to smile at her. She took me in for a second before her face broke into a smile.

"Absolutely beautiful, darling." She reassured me, reaching out to put her hand on my shoulder. I let out a breath, smiling a little easier.

The door burst open then, and people flooded into the room. Emily, Gracie, and Eyvlin were all talking at once, and the tranquil peace of the room was shattered. I laughed at them all as they fluttered around the room. Gracie went straight to the patio, throwing the doors open and letting the sounds of people singing float into the room. She turned to me with a grin on her face.

Emily took my hand, turning me to face her. Her eyes were filled with tears and her smile was bright as she pulled me into a tight hug.

"You look…" Her voice caught in her throat as she tried to talk, and I raised my eyebrows at her. Emily had never been one to struggle with words, she always had something to say, but as she looked me up and down, she could not seem to get anymore words out.

I laughed, leaning forward to place a kiss on her cheek.

Eyvlin tapped me on the shoulder, and I turned again to face her, and blinked in surprise. She looked younger, with her long white hair tied up into an intricate style, and her face powdered and creamed, and a smile on her face that rivalled Gracie's.

"Are you ready, Your Highness?" She asked, squeezing my shoulder reassuringly. I hesitated but nodded my head anyway. It was not like I had any choice in the matter.

Eyvlin clapped her hands, and Emily slid her arm through mine as she led me from my room.

As far as I knew, the coronation would take place in the Green Haven Village church, and we would travel there in a horse drawn carriage that was both led and followed by members of our army. Word had reached me yesterday that the royal family from the Water Kingdom had arrived and were staying somewhere nearby, protected with a spell from Alexandre, of course.

Nobel men and women from the surrounding villages and towns had been arriving all week, and I wondered if the church was big enough to fit everyone in it. I knew a lot of the village people would have to wait outside and would only see me before or afterwards, which made me feel a pang of guilt. It was their church; they should be inside.

Thoughts whirled around in my head as we made our way through the castle to the main lobby. Staff lined the hallways, all cheering and applauding as I walked by, and I was glad that Gracie had put enough powder on my face to cover the deep red blush that I could feel working its way across my cheeks.

Maeteo stood at the open front doors, and my heart stopped beating for a minute. He was in full formal dress, with his sword sheathed at his hip and his hands behind his back. His hair had been combed back off his face and he had shaved, and the smile on his face when he saw me was blinding. Memories of his hands in my hair and his lips on mine flooded my brain.

Emily led me through the open front doors, right past where Maeteo stood and outside to the waiting carriage. The dark wood was brightened up by the shining gold of the door handles and windows, which were lined with deep red curtains. Four horses stood in formation, their manes and tails braided and knotted, and the driver sat atop of the carriage, his head bowing as he saw us coming.

The sounds of the crowds gathered reached over the gate, people cheering and singing and yelling, and my legs turned to jelly as I stepped up into the carriage, my dress gathered onto my arm. Emily climbed in after me, the door closing with a soft click behind her as she sat across from me. Her eyes were still misty as she watched me closely.

Maeteo's voice carried in from outside as he called out to everyone on horseback, and the carriage shuddered as it started to move forwards. The heavy groaning of the gate let me know that it was open, and we made our way out of the castle grounds.

I peered out of the window and my breath left me in a gasp. Thousands of people lined the road from the castle to the village, banners and flags waving above their heads, and red roses flying as they threw them to the carriage. People were waving, and crying, and singing, and I could not believe it was all because of me.

Sitting back in my seat, I looked at Emily, who had a sad smile on her face.

"Are you alright?" I asked, reaching forward to take her hand. She laughed, wiping under her eyes with her free hand.

"I should be asking you that question," She smiled, "I am so very proud of you."

"I haven't done anything yet." I laughed, squeezing her hand. She waved me away, a laugh leaving her as she did so.

"I wasn't born in Earth, Kira." She said suddenly, and my brows furrowed in the middle. "I was born in Fire. My mother... she was one of the King's mistresses. She fell pregnant with me after a year or so, and he wanted nothing to do with me, so mother said nothing.

"She fell ill when I was thirteen, and she told me everything. I was an accident, a mistake, but she loved me and wanted what was best for me. She took me to the Queen and told her everything. Queen Clarissa... she was beautiful. Truly, and devastatingly, but she was vicious. She was nearly twenty years younger than the King had been, but she hated the thought of him being interested in anyone but her, so she had my mother killed. Right in front of me." Emily's voice caught in her throat, but she shook her head, looking down and away from me. My heart was ringing in my ears as I listened to her story. I realised quickly why she had never told me this before.

"She gave me a choice. She told me I could either suffer the same fate as my mother or run for as long as I could until her men caught me. I... I ran. I ran out of the castle and into the woods, and I ran for days, until I reached the coast. I managed to get passage on a trade ship, and a week later I was in Earth. I didn't know where to go, or what to do... I was only thirteen.

"There was one night as I tried to find my feet here that I was working in a tavern in a village not too far south of here, and a man... a man tried to take me to the alley with him. I fought him, of course, but he was so much bigger and stronger than I was. My boss found us, thankfully, and beat the poor bastard into a pulp, but he had managed to break my wrist and give me a black eye in the process.

"A few of your father's guards were drinking in that tavern that night and they brought me to the castle. Your mother, bless her soul, took one look at me and told your father that I was staying, regardless of if he liked it or not." A laugh left Emily as she smiled at me, her tears finally having spilled over and running down her cheeks.

I swallowed back the sob that wanted to leave my throat.

"She put me to work in the kitchens at first. Then I would help her get dressed, and then… she had you. And you were the cutest baby I had ever seen, but you were a brat. You would cry if anyone put you down, or your mother had to leave the room, or if your apple sauce was too warm. So, she brought me up to her room and asked if I would help her with you… and you've been with me ever since."

"Emily…" I said softly, moving so that I was sitting next to her rather than across from her now. "Why are you telling me this now?"

"Because" She swallowed, squaring her shoulders and sitting up straighter, "I was not born in Earth, but this is my home, and I could not ask for anyone better to lead it than you."

I grinned at her, pulling her into a tight hug. She laughed as she hugged me back and wiped her eyes again.

As we drew closer to the village, the crowds outside of the carriage got thicker, and rowdier. The carriage shook as it hit the cobblestones of the village streets, and my heart leaped in my chest.

The familiar streets that passed by the windows brought a sense of comfort to me as we passed through them. People who hadn't joined the crowds outside hung from their upstairs windows, waving handkerchiefs and throwing flowers that landed on the carriage roof with soft thuds.

The sun was reaching the middle of the sky as we pulled into the church yard, and it beat down heavily. My dress, while stunning, was thirty pounds of velvet, and I was already starting to sweat. A barrier had been set up by the village mayor, and people were pushing against it already. The carriage came to a stop, and my palms started to sweat against my skirt.

Emily grinned at me as the carriage door was pulled open, and she stepped out first, the door closing behind her and leaving me alone in the cab for a minute. I took several deep breaths, my heart hammering so quickly in my chest that I would not have been surprised if it burst.

The door opened again, and the deafening cheers reached my ears. Maeteo grinned at me from outside, holding his hand out to me. I took it, clinging to it tightly as I stepped down from the carriage.

Flowers and stuffed bears were thrown over the barrier at me, and I lifted my head to look at the people gathered. There must have been thousands, from all over the Kingdom, gathered into this one village square. I stood up straight, letting Eyvlin and Emily sort the skirt of my dress as I waved to the crowd, meeting the eyes of as many of them as I could.

"Kira!" A voice called, and I turned, frowning as I searched the crowd.

It was a pair of blue eyes that caught my attention, with his dirty orange hair tied onto the top of his head, and the grin on his face that used to make my knees weak.

"Dane," I breathed, grinning. I stepped away from where Eyvlin and Emily were, and despite the calls from the guards, I made my way over to him. He grinned at me, holding out a bright red rose for me to take from him.

"You look good, Ki." He winked, his fingers lingering on mine slightly too long.

"You don't look so bad yourself." I grinned back at him, listening to the mumbles and gasps from the crowd around him. Poppy stood next to him, her eyes wide and her mouth opening and closing like a fish. I smiled at her, "If you'll excuse me, I have a... thing, to get to."

"On your way, Your Majesty." Dane winked again, his grin lighting up his entire face. I turned away from them, still smiling to myself as I smelled the rose he had handed me.

Eyvlin looked as though she were going to explode as I made my way back over to her. I would have laughed if Emily had not moved her away and towards the church entrance. Maeteo came to stand beside me, a smile on his face as he held out his arm for me.

I slipped my hand into the crook of his elbow, handing the rose I was holding to a nearby guard and took the large bouquet of white lilies that was being held out to me. It felt almost like a wedding bouquet, and I smiled as I took in the calming scent of them.

Taking a breath to centre myself, I squared my shoulder and rolled my neck. Maeteo chuckled from beside me, his free hand reaching over to squeeze mine reassuringly. I looked up at him, his dark eyes already watching me.

"Are you ready for this?" He asked, leaning down so his voice could be heard over the roar of the crowd.

"Not at all." I called back, and he laughed loudly as he started to lead me up the church steps.

The music from an old organ filled the church, echoing off the wooden ceilings and into the packed upper levels. Stain glass windows let in streams of different coloured sunlight, and the dust dancing in the bright light made me catch my breath. The pews were packed with people in their best clothes, women in hats and men in brightly coloured suits.

We paused at the door, and Maeteo squeezed my hand. I looked up at him quickly, but he was focusing ahead, his face set like stone in an expression I had only seen once before, the day he had come for me in the village square.

The organ stopped playing its upbeat melody and started a new song, one that was slower and heavier in tone, but every person in the church stood from their seats.

It took me an embarrassing amount of time to realise it was the Earth Kingdom anthem.

Maeteo moved before I did, stepping into the church first and almost tugging me off my feet. I sorted myself as quickly as I could, keeping my shoulders squared and my flowers clutched tightly in front of me.

My heart hammered, my palms were sweating, and my ears rang with the volume of the music playing, but I walked.

I kept my eyes trained on the priest at the bottom of the church, a smile on his face as he watched us walking towards him. However, halfway down the aisle, Maeteo stopped and gently removed my hand from his arm. I faltered, looking at him as I panicked. He just smiled at me, falling into a deep bow.

"You have to do this bit yourself, remember?" He said softly as he stood up straight again, his fingers tracing the lace of my sleeve at my wrist lightly, "Just like we practiced."

The practice that had ended in tears two days ago popped back into my head and I had to work hard not to grimace in public. Nodding my head, I turned my gaze back to the front of the church and swallowed the bile in my throat. I could do this. I had to do this.

Stepping forward by myself, I fought not to look at the people surrounding me as I continued the slow pace down the aisle of the church.

Emily was standing at the very end of the first pew, a wide smile on her face despite the tears that ran down her cheeks. I smiled at her, holding out the bouquet of flowers for her to take just like I had been told to beforehand. She gripped them tightly, and I turned to face the priest in front of me.

His hair was dark, spattered with grey, and his smile was kind. He gestured for everyone in the room to sit, and the room fell into silence. My eyes drifted to the throne on the left of the priest. The golden chair sparkled in the light, and the seat was cushioned in velvet. Next to it, a golden crown that made my stomach flutter nervously. Golden and intricately carved, with dark green velvet that matched my dress and deep, dark purple diamonds along the brim, it was something out of a dream.

"Each day is a new beginning." The priest began, "Each day of the last fourteen years we have prayed, and wished, and hoped for the new beginning that this coronation brings."

People in the crowd mumbled their agreement, and I swallowed harshly, a bead of sweat already starting to form on my back. The heat of the many bodies packed in so tightly, paired with the sun outside made the church feel like an oven, and my dress was just an added layer of warmth.

The priest started a prayer in a language Eyvlin had tried to teach me the basics of, but I had failed miserably, so I just bowed my head when I was expected to.

Two hours passed before we got close to finished, and I was having a hard time staying upright. My stomach was growling, my head felt like it was full of cotton, and if I didn't get a drink of water anytime soon, I was certain I would shrivel up into a prune.

Thankfully, the priest stopped his chanting and blessings, and turned to put his book of readings onto the table to his right. He almost looked thankful to be done speaking, with sweat dripping down the sides of his face and his cheeks flushed red. When he turned back to me, he smiled, reaching up to take the tiara from my hair. I dipped slightly to make it easier for him.

He turned again to his left this time and picked up the crown from its cushioned table. He lifted it high in the air, so everyone in the crowd could see it, and returned to his place in front of me.

"Do you, Kira Dagon, Princess of Earth, promise your life to your people? Do you promise to take their responsibilities on as your own and find their solutions? Will you fight for your Kingdom, protect them and feed them? Will you help them into this new age with strength and dignity?"

"I will." I said, my voice confident and carrying through the church.

"I here present to you, the people gathered with us today, Her Majesty Kira Dagon, Queen of Earth."

The church erupted into applause as the priest placed the crown on my head.

20

Air filled my lungs as I stepped out of my coronation dress.

We had returned to the castle just in time to be taken to the overwhelming seven course meal, and now as people filed into the ballroom, I finally got the chance to breath. The velvet of my dress pooled around my ankles as I stepped over it, and I rubbed at the pinched skin of my waist. Red welts from my corset stung as they finally got blood-flow back to them. My crown sparkled at me from where it sat on its holder in the corner of my bedroom. Eyvlin had explained to me that it was only to be worn on special or public occasions, and for the most part, I would be wearing the much smaller, much lighter, silver crown.

Not that I minded that, as I eyed the small crown on my dresser. The silver was twisted into two horns not unlike Aepein's, and they held a large jewel between them. It was simple, understated, and I felt more comfortable with wearing that.

Gracie had hung my ball gown on the front of my wardrobe. The fabric was the same dark green as my coronation gown, but the sleeves sat on the shoulder, and the skirt flared out much farther. The dark lace remained, but where it had covered my chest during the coronation, it was now snaked down throughout the skirt in patterns of flowers, sharp edged roses and soft lilies. The bodice was delicately beaded and shimmered in the low candlelight of my room.

I could hear Emily and Gracie chatting in the living room, and I quickly pulled the dress down off its hanger, slipping the material over my head. Gracie popped her head into the room just in time to help me tighten the bodice into a much more comfortable fit than I'd been in all day.

Slipping the smaller crown onto my head, I let out a sigh. My stomach still felt uneasy, despite the enormity of the meal we had just eaten, and the feeling that something was going to go wrong had settled itself so deeply into my chest that I could not shake it.

The ballroom had been shut off to everyone for the past two days. Eyvlin had made sure no one had gone in that was not meant to, and the decorations and preparations had been kept top secret. The drone of voices and music filtered through the castle hallways as I made my way to the upper floor entrance, the doors lay open, and I peered through into the lit-up room.

My breath caught in my chest as I finally got to see everything Eyvlin had been working on. From my height at the top of the double staircase, I could see it all — from the shimmering chandelier spinning in slow, delicate circles, spreading glittering light across the room, to the pillars that had been painted gold, and the floor that had been refinished in a dark stain. Small, paper dragons floated through the air on a magical wind, swooping down around people's heads and making them laugh.

Waiters dressed in the same dark green velvet weaved around the guests, stopping for them to pick up glasses of champagne and whatever small snacks lined their trays. The music playing was rich and soulful, and the floor was already full of dancing couples.

Emily stepped up beside me, placing a hand on my arm before she started to descend the stairs. The music stopped abruptly, and Emily clapped her hands above her head. Everyone in the room stopped moving, turning their attention to where she was. Her voice came out loud and carried around the room with ease.

"Welcome, all of you! We are delighted you could all join us on this most joyous of evenings." Emily stopped four stairs from the bottom of the staircase, and I took a deep breath to steady myself for what was to come.

"I won't bore you all with the long speech, that's Eyvlin's job," A flurry of laughter spread around the room, and even I felt a smile spread across my face. "So, without further ado, I would like you all to join me in welcoming our new Queen! Her Majesty Kira Dagon, Queen of the Earth Kingdom."

Applause erupted in the room, and I stepped out from the dark corridor I had been hiding in onto the small balcony at the top of the staircase. The light was almost blinding, but I kept my head high as I waved.

Descending the stairs, I let my eyes float around the room, taking in all the beautiful details. The patio doors were open wide, letting in what little breeze the summer evening allowed us, and I noted the four guards all standing on the back patio, their backs to the ballroom and their arms crossed over their chests.

The music started up again, and I was whisked away by Eyvlin who had, of course, already lined up several people for me to talk to.

First on the list was the King and Queen of Water. Both stood at least a foot taller than I did, their dark skin shining as though someone had dusted them with gold, and their outfits the most stunning of light blue. King Eoghan stood with his hand on the bottom of his wife's back. He had his white hair braided away from his face, which was plump and soft. His eyes were kind, and he smiled as I approached them.

His wife, Queen Saoirse, was the embodiment of elegant. Her dress floated all the way to the floor and her neck was dripping with white diamonds. Her hair was the same white tone as her husbands, but it was left to flow long and waving down her back to her waist. She sipped at her champagne and watched me closely.

"Your Majesty," Eoghan bowed his head, his voice was deep and comforting, "You look radiant."

I smiled, reaching out a hand to shake his, but he caught my wrist and pulled me into a tight, one-armed hug. I laughed, patting his back and stepping back as quickly as I could.

"We have waited a long time for you, dear." Saoirse said, leaning forward to place a kiss on my cheek.

"As has everyone, my love." Eoghan laughed, rubbing his wife's back. She smiled at him, and as they looked at each other it felt as though no one else in the room, including myself, existed. Eyvlin excused us and marched me to the next people on the never-ending list I had to meet.

Hours passed, the sun set low behind the trees, and my feet were screaming at me in my shoes. I had met, shaken hands with, and danced with what must have been upwards of a hundred people, and as I finally had time to stop at the buffet table along the far wall of the ballroom, I slumped slightly. My shoulders curled in on themselves, and I let out a heavy sigh as I picked up a small bread roll full of cheese and butter and bit into it, nearly groaning aloud at the taste. It was not the best thing I had ever eaten, but the meal from earlier had been burned off, and I was starving.

A throat cleared behind me and I snapped back upright, spinning on the spot with my mouth still full of bread and cheese.

Maeteo tilted his head to the side, a smirk on his face, and I let my shoulders slump again. I had not seen him since this morning when he had walked me into the church, but he still looked as wonderful as he had then. His hair was still perfectly combed back, his formal wear still perfectly creased and pressed, and my heart skipped a beat in my chest.

"Did I catch you off guard?" He laughed, leaning on the buffet table with his hand and smiling at me. I rolled my eyes, swallowing what I was eating.

"Obviously," I replied, wiping my mouth carefully with a napkin, "I was worried you were Eyvlin, I'm sure I'm not meant to be eating yet."

Maeteo laughed loud, the sound of it vibrating through my chest and warming me from the inside out. I smiled up at him, dusting the crumbs off my hands and turning back towards the room of people. As the sun had lowered, people had begun to drink more, and a lot of the noble guests had started to lower their inhibitions. It had gone from a put together, formal ball, to something you might see in the village tavern.

I preferred it this way.

Clearing his throat, Maeteo stood up straight and dropped into a bow at his waist. I frowned at him, watching as he held out a hand and grinned up at me.

"Will Her Majesty join me for a dance?"

I grinned, slipping my hand into his and letting him lead me onto the dance floor. My dress flowed behind me like jade green water, and people drifted away from the middle of the floor as Maeteo and I neared. He placed one hand on my waist, keeping the other clutched in his as he pulled me close to him. I hoped he thought the blush on my chest was from having one too many glasses of cherry wine.

The music in the room swelled to a volume that made my ears ring, but as Maeteo and I whirled around the room at dizzying speeds, I did not mind it.

A squeal left me as Maeteo swept me up into the air and spun me around, my dress flowing out behind us. Maeteo grinned wide as he let me back onto my feet softly, his fingers tangling in the fabric at the back of my dress again. If we had not been surrounded by people, I would have kissed him right there.

"You look deep in thought," he said into my ear, his breath flushing over my cheek. I laughed, shaking my head.

"No, no. I'm just enjoying your company." I grinned, and Maeteo laughed as we swept past Emily and Eyvlin, who were watching us closely. If I thought about it, it felt like every pair of eyes in the room were watching us. Maeteo bent his head again, his mouth dragging across the skin of my cheek to my ear.

"I want to kiss you again, too, y'know."

My stomach erupted into butterflies as he stood up straight again, his eyes watching my face closely, and a small smirk on his face. The music reached its peak, but Maeteo stopped our dance. I stumbled over my feet, not expecting him to stop so abruptly.

Maeteo's hand stilled on my waist, his fingers digging into the fabric of my dress.

I look up at him, my eyebrows furrowed together at the sudden stop in our dancing. He wasn't looking at me, though, instead his gaze was focused on something over the top of my head. The flames dancing in his eyes makes my back stiffen, and I gently free my hand from his, turning on the spot to see what has caused our dance to stop.

My breath caught in my throat as my eyes lock with a pair of icy blue ones. Black, slicked back hair wearing a glistening golden crown, and a jawline so sharp it looked like it would cut through diamonds — it took my brain a second to catch up with what I was seeing.

Prince Cyrus stood in the open patio doors. He had his hands shoved deep into his pockets with a smirk on his face and two guards stood directly behind him, their swords dripping blood onto the white stone of the patio.

The music that had been flowing through the room came to a sudden halt, the room falling into complete silence as all eyes turned to the uninvited Prince standing there, his tall, muscled form backlit by the mid-summer moon behind him.

Maeteo's hand returned to my waist, pulling me towards him again, but instead of holding me like he did while we were dancing, he moved me slightly behind him, placing himself between me and Cyrus.

"Am I interrupting?" Cyrus's voice was smooth, like honey slipping over a sore throat, "Sorry, I think my invite must have gotten lost before it was delivered."

I swallowed, my heart pounding in my chest. The blood dripping from his guard's swords was starting to pool around their feet, slowly spreading towards the thresholds of the doors. A muscle in Maeteo's jaw feathered.

"I don't believe an invite was sent your way, Your Highness." Emily's voice came from my left, and I looked over in time to see her breaking through the crowd. Her floor length, black gown swept across the ground as she walked, the only noise in the room being her heels clicking against the marble. Emily's words from earlier, about how she was born in Fire, how her mother was one of the King's mistresses, floated into my mind, and as I eyed the two of them in the same room, the familial similarities were easy to spot.

Cyrus eyed her, his smirk turning into a full-blown grin as he looked her up and down. My skin crawled at the way he was looking at her — like she was something to be won.

"Oh, Emily, that breaks my heart, don't you know?" He drawled, picking an invisible bit of lint off his shoulder and stepping away from the blood at his feet before it got on his shoes.

"You have one of those?" Emily asked, tilting her head and stopping a few feet in front of where Maeteo and I stood. "Nonetheless, you weren't invited. Please show yourself out, before we call for our guards. We don't want to ruin their evening."

Cyrus laughed; a harsh, bitter sound that made the hair on the back of my neck stand up uncomfortably. His eyes moved from Emily to Maeteo.

"I'm afraid their evening has already been ruined," Cyrus shrugged, "You really need to work on your security detailing, General, the children you had posted at the southern wall were all too easy to dispose of."

Maeteo's shoulders tensed, and I heard his jaw physically lock as he slammed his teeth together. He had deliberately put the youngest, less trained of his troops at the back of the castle, thinking that no one would be interested in the back walls, knowing all that was back there were the kitchens and servants' quarters.

I reached forward, placing my hand against the back of Maeteo's jacket in, what I hoped was, a comforting gesture.

The guards at Cyrus's back both had grins on their faces, their eyes wide and wild and dirt smeared on their leathers. Cyrus stepped into the ballroom, fixing the sleeves of his jacket as he took long strides towards where Maeteo and I were standing. Emily stood her ground, her chin held high as he drew closer to her, but he simply side stepped around her like she was a child in his way in the street, his eyes locked on me the whole time.

I tried to take a step back, but my back was met with a solid chest. I gasped, spinning around quickly only to find Tarian. His sword already drawn and his face ferocious, he looked at me for the briefest of seconds before he focused back on Cyrus, who was now standing almost chest to chest with Maeteo.
Cyrus looked Maeteo up and down, his arrogant smirk returning to his face as he did so.

"If you don't mind moving out of my way, General, I would like to speak with the Queen."

Cyrus's words made me feel like I was going to vomit on the spot, and I could've sworn I heard Maeteo growl, but he stepped slightly to the side. Not far enough for Cyrus to get to me, but enough that he could see me past Maeteo's broad shoulders.

"Hello, Kira." Cyrus grinned, "You definitely know how to throw a party, Sweetheart, that's going to come in handy."

My stomach dropped into my toes as he spoke to me, his eyes roaming over my dress, lingering uncomfortably on my chest.

Maeteo turned his head slightly, so he could see both Cyrus and I at the same time. His jaw was clenched shut, and I almost gasped at the murderous look on his face. The feeling of more bodies joining behind me had the hair raising on my arms, but from Tarian's quiet murmurs I gathered it was only Hollis coming to stand by his side. I was sure if I looked, I would have seen Hollis itching for a fight, her small frame vibrating with the potential to send her sword swinging, but I kept my eyes focused on the Prince in front of me.

Cyrus eyed the new arrival behind me with a look of amusement, an eyebrow raising upwards. He only took her in for a second before his attention returned to me, and he reached out past Maeteo, extending his hand to me with a grin.

"Dance with me, Sweetheart." He drawled, his voice carrying around the silent room.

I stayed where I was standing, my palms sweating where they pressed against the skirt of my dress.

Maeteo turned his head more, looking directly at me with wide eyes.

"You don't have to do anything with him." He growled, and Cyrus rolled his eyes.

"Possessive, isn't he?" Cyrus smirked, his hand wrapping around my wrist and pulling me past Maeteo. His fingers tight enough that they felt almost bruising, I looked over my shoulder at Maeteo and Tarian as Cyrus dragged me into the middle of the ballroom floor. Their faces were stoic, not a flicker of emotion on either of them, but the way Maeteo's hand fisted around the hilt of his sword, and the way Tarian's fingers curled and uncurled showed how unhappy they were about the current situation.

Quiet murmurs moved through the crowds of people gathered around the edges of the room. Cyrus let go of my wrist, only for his hand to move straight to my waist, pulling me flush against his chest. My cheeks turned warm again, but unlike with Maeteo, this was not from excitement, or nerves. The colour that brushed my cheeks this time came from an almost painful surge of anger.

Cyrus shot a look to the band hidden at the back of the ballroom, and instruments clattered and groaned in a second of panic before they started playing again. The music had turned from the upbeat, bouncy arrangements from before into a much more reserved composition. Cyrus nodded, a small smile gracing his face as he placed one of my hands on his shoulder, the hand on my waist holding tighter to me as he grasped the other. I sucked in a breath as he started to spin us.

I kept my eyes focused over his shoulder, not looking directly into his face as we danced in a wide circle around the room, like he wanted to flaunt to everyone and anyone that it was him that was dancing with me now, and not Maeteo. I caught flashes of Maeteo's hair as we passed him, but Cyrus spun me away quickly, making sure I could not get a good look at his face. I could feel his eyes boring into my back from across the room.

The wind blowing in from the open patio doors was warm, doing nothing to help the sweat beading across my back as Cyrus held me close to him, his hot breath washing across my cheek. He did not stumble or falter once as he led me around the ballroom. If it were not for his ridiculous show, I would have thought he was a wonderful dancer.

"You could smile, Sweetheart."

Cyrus's voice dragged my eyes to his face, my eyebrows drawing together as one of my feet slipped out of time a little with surprise. Cyrus barely noticed, correcting us without a second thought as he looked at me, his eyes roaming my face.

"Excuse me?" I asked, my voice polite.

"You could smile. Or, at least, try to look happy to be dancing with me."

"Why would I?" My words came out sharp, and Cyrus lifted an eyebrow, the music stopping momentarily before a new song began, but he did not stop our movements.

"I'm not a bad person, Kira." He said quietly, his features softening. "Our fathers signed that contract, not me."

I blinked, shock rippling through my body at his words.

If I did not know him, if I had not been listening to Emily and Eyvlin and everyone else in the castle tell me stories about Cyrus and his father, I might have believed him. His face was soft, his eyes almost boy-like.

I pressed my lips into a tight line, tightening the grip I had on his shoulder, so the fabric of his jacket crumpled under the pressure of my fingers.

"You want to force me to marry you." I started, looking directly into his eyes as I spoke, "You are not giving me a choice. You want to own me and turn my kingdom into workers for your people. You do not care for me, the people of my kingdom, or anything that doesn't benefit you. If that is your definition of 'good' then I am terrified of what you believe to be bad."

Cyrus did not react to my harsh words, but when the music stopped this time, so did he. He brought us to a graceful halt and stepped back, letting his hand fall from my waist to take hold of my hand. He brought it to his lips, pressing the softest of kisses to my knuckles, all the while his eyes still held mine. I sucked in a sharp breath, watching as he straightened up and let my hand drop back to my side.

I felt rather than saw Maeteo as he appeared behind me, his hands quickly gripping at my waist and pulling me back to his side. His anger was radiating off him in waves, his face and neck flushed an uncomfortable shade of pink. Cyrus smirked at him, bowing himself low to me.

"Congratulations, Sweetheart. When you come to Fire, it will be a party twice this size… with much better security."

With those words, Cyrus shot a look at Maeteo and turned. The crowd that had gathered around to watch us dance parted as he strode back towards the patio doors, where his guards still stood. The blood from their swords had now pooled enough to start to spread into the ballroom, the floor staining red as it spread.

I watched the outline of his figure retreat over the patio, his guards stayed behind for only a second before they turned and followed him down the stairs and across the open grass and over the back wall again.

Turning on the spot, I looked up at Maeteo's face. He was staring at the space where Cyrus and his guards had just hopped over the wall with his jaw locked tight. Something flickered in his eyes, and he sucked in a breath through his nose. Squaring his shoulders and rolling his neck, he turned to look at Tarian, muttering something to him that made his second nod and take off towards the patio doors, Hollis following close behind him.

Maeteo's eyes finally landed on me, his expression softening, almost looking apologetic. He reached out, taking my hand softly and moving us through the crowds of people towards the main doors of the ballroom. I swallowed, smiling at a few people and thanking them for coming as Maeteo took me from the room into the hallways. Guards were running back and forth, shouting at each other to get outside, find out if there were any of the Fire soldiers hanging around somewhere, and to find the bodies of the guards who had been stationed at the back wall.

I swallowed harshly, stopping walking in between two windows, the orange fire in the wall sconces the only thing illuminating the narrow hallway. Maeteo stumbled as he stopped walking, his eyes wide as he turned to look at me, searching my face.

"Are you okay?" He asked, his voice tight and panicked.

"Are *you*?" I replied, stepping closer to him. He nodded, but his hands shook as he wrapped his arms around me, pulling me tight against his chest. I closed my eyes, running my fingers in comforting circles on his back to try and ease his shaking. "It's not your fault, Maeteo."

I knew he would be blaming himself for it all. For Cyrus getting into the castle, for those guards harming two of the younger boys he had been training, for the jobs Tarian and Hollis now had to take care of — moving the boys' bodies and sending letters to their families.

He pressed his face into my hair at the top of my head, his breathing sharp and shallow, and we stood there like that; his face in my hair and my hands moving over his back until his shaking stopped.

21

"What do you suppose he meant, '*when you come to Fire*'?" Gracie asked around a mouthful of cake.

We were sat in my living room, on separate couches, with the coffee table full of different cakes. My coronation cake had been cut and a piece had been sent to every staff member of the castle, and thankfully Gracie had managed to steal two slices for us to enjoy this morning.

After Maeteo had calmed down last night, he had taken me back to my room, and I had not seen him since. He had barely spoken to me as he left, simply saying that, under no circumstances, was I to leave my room today. Gracie told me when she arrived that he had disappeared on horseback as soon as the sun was breaking the horizon this morning and had not been seen since. My stomach had been sitting uncomfortably since.

Thankfully, Eyvlin had cancelled all my lessons and meetings for the day, so for the first time since I arrived at the castle, I had a fully free day. My hair was still up in the intricate style from last night, there being too many pins pushed into it all for me to take out by myself, and I had black rings under my eyes from where I had not washed off my make-up correctly.

Sitting forward, I dusted crumbs off my fingers onto the silver plate in front of me and frowned. I knew I could trust Gracie; I could tell her everything right here and now and she would not think worse of me, but a small voice in the back of my brain told me it was a bad idea.

Would she think it a bad idea to go through with what my father had set up for me? Or would she want to come with me? For a second, I entertained the idea of her and I wreaking havoc on the Fire castle together, and a smile warmed my face.

Gracie cleared her throat, and I snapped my head up, looking away from the tray of crumbs in front of me and blinking a few times. She just laughed, placing her now empty teacup onto the table and scooting herself forward in her seat, her elbows resting on her knees.

"Are you alright? You seemed thousands of miles away." Gracie laughed, tilting her head to the side.

I laughed with her, waving a hand at her lightly.

"I was in a world of my own." I smiled, sitting back and resting against the cushions of my couch.

Gracie continued chatting away as I sat there, my mind wandering over the mountains and to the mid-sea. It would take a week, maybe slightly more if the weather was not on our side, to get to Fire. Everything I knew about Fire so far was from Eyvlin and her lessons, and while it sounded lovely - always sunny, always hot, the temperature never less than double figures, - the thought of living there made my skin crawl.

Looking at Gracie, I watched her as she inspected a small cake, sniffing at it before pushing nearly the whole thing into her mouth at once. I laughed, shaking my head.

"I have to tell you something," I said, my heart hammering in my chest. Gracie looked at me with wide eyes, her chewing slowing momentarily. She scooted forward in her chair, until she was barely sitting on the sofa at all and looked at me expectantly.

I could have laughed at the sight of her, but my heart was going faster than it ever had, and I felt nauseous.

"I — I kissed Maeteo." I blurted, the words I had intended to come out changing as they tumbled out of my mouth. Gracie's eyes widened even more, and her mouth fell agape, crumbs of her cake still coating her lips. That, I did laugh at.

"When?!" She shrieked, and I shushed her quickly, looking towards the open patio doors. She slapped a hand over her mouth, giggling into it as she moved over onto my sofa with me. "When did this happen? Why didn't you tell me?!"

"A week or so ago," I shrugged, scooting over so she could plop down beside me. She curled her legs up under herself, a grin bigger than any I had ever seen on her face. "I couldn't sleep after something Alexandre had told me, so I went for a walk, and I was in the stables with Freya when he came in. He said something about Fenrir needing his nightly sugar cubes, and we just... did."

Gracie squealed, clapping her hands in front of her like I had just told her she had won a slab of her favourite chocolate. I waited for her to be finished, which took longer than I expected, and laughed when she finally looked at me, her hands going to my arms.

"This is huge. Does he know you're telling me? Has *he* told anyone? Have you seen each other since?"

Gracie fired off question after question, barely giving me enough time between them to answer them.

"There's something else." I sighed after she had finished asking questions, and she flopped back dramatically on the sofa, covering her face with her arm.

"Please, I don't think I can take any more excitement." She dramatically fanned herself with her free hand, and I laughed as I pushed myself off the sofa and headed into my bedroom to find the red book Alexandre had given me.

I paused as I picked it up, the weight of it heavy in my hands as I stared at it. Was letting Gracie know the right thing to do? I knew I could trust her with most things, like what had happened with Maeteo, but this? Was this too much?

Swallowing hard, I turned and forced myself to walk back to where Gracie was now sitting up. She furrowed her brows in confusion when she saw the book in my hands. I place it on the coffee table in front of her and stepped back, my hands going behind my back as I watched her. She looked from me to the book, and back again.

"Is that…?"

"The history of my family, yes." I nodded, clearing my throat. "I need you to read the very last page and tell me what I should do."

Gracie tilted her head, but she picked up the book anyway, running her hands over the aged leather softly before she flipped it open. She turned the pages delicately, and my heart hammered in my chest.

I saw my father's scrawled handwriting and pressed my lips into a tight line. Every inch of me was screaming to take the book off her before she read too much, or before she got up and ran screaming to Eyvlin. Her face flickered with shock as she registered what she was reading, and she looked up at me. I nodded, gesturing for her to keep reading.

There was no going back. Gracie would know what my father had planned for me, and I would have to trust her not to tell anyone what my next step was. I wondered if I should have given her a choice in the matter.

"Your Majesty…"

"Oh, please. You and I both know you don't call me that."

"Kira," Gracie sighed, her body slumping as she closed the book. She sat with it on her lap for a minute before nearly throwing it back onto the table. "What are you going to do?"

"I… I think I'm going to marry Cyrus." I said, my voice shaking as I picked at my fingernails. Gracie's face fell, "Only because I have to."

"Surely Eyvlin could get you out of this? She must know people who can help!" Gracie stood from the sofa, her arms falling to her sides. "We have to tell her!"

"Eyvlin already knows." I shrugged, "So does Maeteo. And Emily. They… they are trying to get me out of it, but it is going to start a war."

Gracie visibly recoiled at the mention of war, her skin paling.

"They know about the marriage, but they do not know about this letter." I pointed to the book on the table, "The only people that know about that are me, you, and Alexandre."

"Alexandre?" Gracie gasped, her hand going to her chest.

"He gave me the book and told me that there was something interesting about my father in it." Gracie stepped forward at my words, rounding the sofa I was standing behind and wrapping her arms around my shoulders. I hugged her back as tightly as I could.

We stood in silence for a minute, before Gracie pulled back and held me at arm's length. She had a fierce look on her face unlike any I had ever seen on her before, and it shocked me.

"Whatever you do, I will be with you." She smiled, squeezing my shoulders reassuringly. I smiled weakly, a lump forming in my throat. "Just tell me when and where, and I will be there."

22

My muscles ached as I fell to my back in the middle of a training ring.

The sun beat down from the sky, making the sweat that clung to my skin turn sticky and itchy against my clothes. I groaned, turning myself onto my side and dry heaving slightly into the grass. I could hear Maeteo laughing somewhere nearby, and I lifted my hand in an obscene gesture towards him.

His laugh grew louder as he walked towards me.

"That wasn't very queen-like." He chuckled, dropping down into a squat in front of me, his elbows resting on his knees and his hands clasped together. I glared up at him, my ears ringing with my raised blood-pressure. We had been training outside for hours now. I had planned to go and see the Lides mountains today. To go and see where Aepein was, since no one had seen her in a week or so, but Maeteo had caught me as I was leaving my room this morning. Hollis and Tarian dropped by occasionally to take over when Maeteo had to go and deal with things inside the barracks.

My knees were bloodied and bruised from the number of times I had fallen onto them, and the palms of my hands had blistered against the handle of my sword. Tarian had arrived, with Tristan in tow, and presented me with my own sword this morning before training began.

It was a work of art. Solid steel, yet somehow still light enough for me to swing without pulling any muscles. The hilt was leather, with intricately carved steel vines working their way around and down to the large, shining gem embedded in the leather. The belt attached to the scabbard had gold chains falling from the edges, and the buckle was shaped like a dragon. It took my breath away every time I looked at it.

Tristan had blushed the brightest shade of red when I thanked him. I had caught Tarian staring at him as if he put the stars in the sky and the fish in the ocean, and my heart swelled slightly at the sight.

Maeteo chuckled softly beside me, a soft expression on his face as he watched his best friend with the person he liked. I nudged him with my shoulder, raising my eyebrows at him and turning away from the two men to give them some privacy.

"Tarian has been in love with Tristan for at least a year," Maeteo said quietly, smiling over his shoulder at his best friend, "Not that he'll do anything about it."

I looked back at the two men standing at the entrance to the training ring. Tarian had his hand on Tristan's shoulder and was grinning from ear to ear. Tristan was slightly shorter than Tarian, — his head only reaching Tarian's chin — so he had his head tilted back slightly to look up at him. My heart felt full at the sight of them, lost in their own conversation.

"Well, why not?" I asked Maeteo as he led me over to where his weapons were waiting.

"They're both stubborn, I guess." He shrugged, picking up his sword and swirling it around a couple of times. The action seemed effortless for him, and I had to bite the inside of my cheek to keep myself focused. "It's not for lack of trying. Hollis and I have been trying to get them together since they met."

I laughed, the image of Maeteo and Hollis trying to set up Tarian seeming so unusual in my head.

Maeteo had gestured for me to move back to the middle of the ring, a smile spreading on his face as he watched me experiment with my new sword for a second.

"Time to put those skills to good use, Princess."

He had pushed me to the point of vomiting, and my shirt and leggings were both full of holes from when I had not moved out of the way fast enough, and he had nicked me with his blade.

I growled at him as I pushed myself back up into a sitting position, my arms resting on my knees and my breaths coming in quick pants as he handed me my water flask. I gulped it down greedily, wiping my mouth on the back of my arm.

"I think you're a sadist." I grumbled, wincing as I stretched my legs out in front of me, my palms massaging the tense muscles in my thighs. Maeteo barked a laugh, moving so he was no longer squatting next to me and was instead sitting, his legs stretched out and leaning back on his hands. He looked the picture of relaxation.

"This is nothing. You should see some of the drills I put the intakes through." He grinned at me. The hair falling into his face was damp with sweat, and the sun glinting off his skin made him look like he had been painted, ready to hang on the walls of the castle hallways, immortalized in his beauty.

I flushed as I caught myself staring, and I was glad for the shade of red my skin turned when I exercised, because it was hidden under my already red cheeks. We sat in comfortable silence for a minute, listening to only the birds that flew by overhead, and the sound of Chef shouting in the kitchens.

Leaning back onto my elbows, I tilted my face back and closed my eyes, letting the sun seep into my skin as I enjoyed the welcome break in our training. I supposed that after vomiting for the third time, Maeteo took pity on me.

Cyrus's face popped into my head as I basked in the sunlight, and my stomach lurched uncomfortably. We had no idea where he or his soldiers were, or if they were even still in Earth at all, but the thought made me feel uneasy. The Fire army were much, much bigger than ours, and if they took us by surprise, it would be catastrophic.

We knew they were coming; we just did not know when.

Sighing, I let myself lie back fully, my arms spread wide as I flopped onto the grass. Maeteo's deep chuckle came from next to me, and I opened one eye in time to see him lie down on his side next to me, his head propped up on his hand.

"Why are you staring at me, General?" I asked, closing my eye again and turning my face back towards the sky.

"Because you're beautiful." He said casually, "And because I can."

"Behave," I laughed, turning onto my side and mimicking his position, resting my head on my hand, propped up on my elbow. "I bet you've said that to all the girls in this castle."

Maeteo rolled his eyes, but he smiled, reaching forward with his free hand to tuck some hair behind my ear.

"Hollis and I used to flirt a lot back and forth, but nothing ever came of it. She's more like a sister to me than anything else," He shrugged, letting his free hand fall onto the grass between us, "I had the biggest crush on Gracie for a long time."

"I don't blame you, she's beautiful." I grinned, and Maeteo nodded, running his fingers through the grass repeatedly.

"She is. She's still nothing compared to you." He looked up at me through his lashes, and my heart leaped at the vulnerability in his eyes. I lay my hand next to his on the grass, and instantly he slid his fingers through my own, locking our hands together.

"You're a smooth talker, General." I laughed, lifting our hands so I could examine them. His fingers dwarfed mine, making it look like he was holding hands with a child. His face split into a grin, and my stomach filled with butterflies. *Damn.*

A yell from the other side of the training ring made Maeteo strain his neck to see over my shoulder. Whatever he saw made him sigh, his hand dropping mine as he pushed himself up from our position. My heart ached for a second, but when I sat up, I saw why he had to move.

A band of soldiers, all in full armour, were filing into the training ring. They were all staring at us, and the back of my neck heated with embarrassment. I pushed myself up until I was standing, dusting myself off from grass and dirt, and picked up my sword. I had attached the belt and scabbard before we had starting training with it, and a bit uneasily, I sheathed the sword at my side.

Maeteo was a few steps ahead of me, so I had to run to reach his side. He grinned down at me, but his face turned back to that of the grumpy General when he looked to the soldiers mulling about the edge of the ring.

"Her Majesty will be joining us for today's training." He called, his voice carrying around the space easily. Every set of eyes in the ring moved to stare at me, and I fought my instinct to shy away from them, instead I lifted my chin slightly and smiled.

A sea of anxious eyes stared back at me, but Maeteo called them all into formation, and as they scurried to find their places, he took my hand. I grinned up at him and he squeezed my fingers tightly, just once, before he let me go and went off into the middle of the ring again.

23

I stood at the bottom of the Lides mountain, my hands on my hips and my breath coming in fast bursts.

No one had seen Aepein again since the day she had made her reappearance, and worry had started to settle itself into my stomach. I had woken up with the sun this morning, a shock to my system, and had hopped out of bed as soon as I remembered what I had planned to do today.

I had dressed quickly and took off towards the kitchens, planning to beg Chef to give me a goat carcass, or even a chicken if that was what he could spare, to take with me so I could entice her out of her cave. He had stared at me like I had two heads, but eventually he handed me over three dead chickens, tied together by their feet and plucked of their feathers. I had cringed, but attached the string to the belt of my trousers and thanked him, leaving the kitchens to the sound of mumbles.

My plan had nearly gone perfectly, and I was climbing into the saddle atop of Freya when I heard a throat clear outside of her stable. My head shot up, and there stood Tarian, his arms crossed over his chest and his shoulder leaning against the door frame. His eyebrows were raised, and he was smirking.

I had sighed, sinking into my saddle and muttering that I did not think I would get caught, and Tarian had laughed, before he had gone to get his own horse saddled up.

He followed me to the mountains, until both of our horses would go no farther. We had tied them to a wooden fence in the closest field and set off the rest of the way on foot.

"This really, really, does not feel like a good idea." Tarian grumbled, not even the slightest bit out of breath. I glared at him; he had been… less enthusiastic that my plan would work as we had ridden out here.

"Then go back to the castle." I snapped, stepping over a fallen branch and pushing my hair off my face.

"And risk the wrath of Eyvlin and Maeteo? No, thanks, I'll take the dragon."

I laughed, lifting my gaze to the top of the mountain. It looked intimidating from the castle, but up close it gave me full body chills. The grass was ashen and grey under my feet, and the birds had stopped chirping the closer we got. I swallowed down the dread I felt in my chest and pushed forward, holding a low hanging branch out of the way for Tarian to duck under. Tarian's hesitation to return to the castle mirrored my own. I knew I would be in trouble as soon as my feet touched the stone of the courtyard, but I hoped they had sense enough to notice Tarian's horse, Thor, was missing too.

The frigid wind felt like it was coming from the middle of winter, the opposite of the summer weather of the castle and the blue, shining sky had given way to dull, grey clouds that looked ready to pour rain onto us at any minute. Tarian walked ahead of me now, his pace slowing so I could keep up.

"Tell me," I started, looking over my shoulder at the sound of a twig cracking. I hoped it was just an animal I hadn't noticed. "Tell me about you."

"Me?" Tarian asked, his voice far away.

"Yeah," I nodded, "Maeteo hasn't told me much about anyone, and all Hollis told me is that the two of you have never spent more than a day apart."

Tarian laughed, shrugging his shoulders. He stayed quiet for a moment, placing a hand on top of a large boulder and hoisting himself up and over. He reached back for me, holding onto my hand tightly and helping me over it. I grinned at him in thanks, and we started walking once again.

"I guess there isn't much to tell." He said quietly, "I was enlisted when I was eighteen, and I've been here since."

"There has to be more than that," I sighed, checking that all three chickens were still attached to my belt. The smell of them had started to make my stomach turn, so I tried not to focus on them for longer than necessary.

"I'm pretty boring." Tarian smiled over his shoulder at me, "Sorry if that isn't what you wanted to hear."

I rolled my eyes but let us fall into silence again as we walked farther up the mountain.

We had been walking for hours when we reached a break in the path. One led towards the left of the mountain and was completely barren. No trees, no bushes, not even a twig lined the path curving around the mountain side. The other led to the right, and it looked the same as the path we had already been on — greying grass, and at least the ghost of trees. I paused, frowning at the fork in the road. I had not noticed it when Aepein brought me up here.

The castle gleamed in the distance, and I wondered just how much chaos Tarian and I had caused by disappearing.

Tarian's presence beside me warmed my side, and I looked up at him. His lips were pressed into a line and a small crease had appeared between his eyebrows. He was staring off to the left path, his shoulders slumped slightly.

"I hate to say it, but I think we have to go this way." He sighed, rubbing a hand over his face and frowning. "The stories always said nothing grew in a dragon's path…"

I nodded as he gestured towards the path in front of us. He sighed through his nose, but he started off down the path. I followed close behind him, eying the sword sheathed to his side and wishing I had one of my own.

Tarian walked slowly, keeping his steps light and silent as he worked his way along the mountain side.

The air shifted as we walked, turning thicker and smelling more like charred meat. I clung tightly to the chickens at my waist, and Tarian unsheathed his sword, holding it out in front of himself.

The sound of shuffling and a pig squealing came from around the bend in front of us, and Tarian froze. I held my breath, creeping up behind him. He hissed out the corner of his mouth when I squeezed past him, making my way slowly up the path until I could see what was waiting for us.

"Your Majesty!" Tarian whisper-hissed, his steps light as he followed me, "This is the stupidest thing I've ever — "

"Shh!" I shushed him, waving my hand at him as I peered around the corner.

My gasp caught in my throat.

Aepein was there, hunched over the body of a boar and blood spraying in every direction, but beside her is what made me truly feel scared.

Another dragon, bigger than even Aepein, and pure, inky black. Its scales were sharp and fierce looking, with jagged spikes all along its tail and back. Its wings were large, with jagged holes scattering the membrane between the bones. Sharp, green scales ran down the underside of its neck onto its stomach, and it stood protectively over Aepein as she ate, it's eyes sharp as it watched their surroundings.

My hand came up to cover my mouth as I realised what I was looking at.

Gavrun, Aepein's mate, was awake.

Tarian's body stiffened beside mine, and his hand gripped my wrist tightly.

"Okay, you've seen her, she's fine, can we *please* go before we become lunch?" He hissed, and Gavrun's large head turned towards where we were standing, his eyes narrowing. Tarian began to tremble. "Your Majesty, let's *go!*"

I shook my head at him, managing to free my wrist and stepping out from where we were hidden. I could practically hear the shriek Tarian had to hold inside, and as I stepped out into the path of Gavrun, I did not blame him.

The beast in front of me was, easily, taller than the church in the village. His breath blew my hair back from my face even from this distance, and I let out a shaky breath as I stood there.

Gavrun stared at me, blinking slowly, as if he could not believe what he was seeing, before he let out an ear-splitting roar. I cringed, lifting my hands to cover my ears, but I stood my ground.

Then, the unthinkable happened.

Aepein nudged her mate with her head, huffing through her nose at him as if she were scolding him, and stepped in front of him. Gavrun's roar cut off instantly, his giant head turning to look at his mate, blinking at her in curiosity.

Aepein stopped a few feet in front of me, crouching her front legs and lowering herself to the ground, her head now perfectly at my eye level. I let out a breath and smiled, closing the gap between myself and the beautiful, pearly white dragon in front of me.

"Hello, girl." I smiled, placing my hand on her snout and gently scratching the scales there. "You had me worried."

Aepein blinked, tilting her head to the side and starting to nudge my hip with her nose. I laughed, unhooking the chickens and placing one on the ground in front of her. She sniffed at it for a second before she picked it up in her mouth and swallowed it in one bite.

I looked over to where Gavrun stood, his eyes still narrow as he watched his mate and I interact. I held up a chicken, shaking it slightly before I tossed it over Aepein's back. It landed on the ground in front of Gavrun with a soft thunk, and he did not so much as look at it. Aepein nudged it forward with her tail, a huff coming from her nose.

I think if she were able, she would have been rolling her eyes.

24

Maeteo was waiting at the gates when Tarian and I got back to the castle.

We had spent another hour with Aepein and Gavrun. Tarian had eventually came closer to the two dragons, his whole body vibrating with nerves, but once Aepein had let him stroke her, he calmed down. He and Gavrun spent most of the time eying each other wearily, whilst Aepein had been content getting scratched and fussed over.

We had made our way down to the bottom of the mountain quicker now that we knew the way, and when we reached the horses, we looked up to the sky to see the two great beasts circling the sky around the mountain. Tarian had watched them in awe, his mouth hanging open.

Now, though, as we drew nearer to the castle grounds at galloping speed, Maeteo's figure loomed. He stood against the stone wall, his arms crossed and a murderous look on his face. I slowed Freya down to a walk, and Tarian copied, pulling up alongside me and shooting me a look that said, *"I told you so."*

I rolled my eyes, squaring my shoulders as we closed the distance between us and Maeteo. He stood up straight, pushing himself away from the wall and starting towards us.

"General," I smiled, tilting my head to the side, "To what do we owe this welcome party?"

He simply glared at me, stalking right past me and straight to Tarian. He grabbed Tarian by the arm, yanking him down off Thor's back and started to hiss into his ear. I frowned, getting down off Freya and turning towards the two men.

Tarian had his jaw locked tight, but his eyes flickered towards me. He smirked when he saw me watching them and winked quickly. Maeteo's grip on his arm tightened, and I heard some of what he was saying to him.

He was blaming Tarian for taking me from the castle.

I frowned, my eyebrows knotting together as I stepped forward again, my hands balling into fists.

"Don't get pissy at him, Maeteo." I said, and Maeteo's head snapped to look at me, his eyes blazing.

"It was my idea to leave. I was going to go myself, but Tarian caught me leaving."

"I'll deal with you in a minute." Maeteo growled, glaring at me. My eyebrows shot up to meet my hairline. He seemed to regret his tone instantly, as his face softened slightly and he sighed, letting go of Tarian's arm. "I didn't mean — "

"No, no, continue. How will you *deal with me*?"

"Princess, I didn't mean —" My eye twitched slightly at his nickname for me.

"Because here was me thinking I was your *Queen*, and I didn't need to ask permission to go on a morning trek with my horse."

Maeteo closed his eyes, breathing deeply through his nose and rolling his neck. Tarian was still smirking, and he stepped away from Maeteo slightly and took Thor's reins in his hand. He stepped forward, gesturing towards Freya and I nodded, slipping her own reins over her head and handing them to Tarian. She whinnied, trying to pull away from him, but Tarian's soft voice calmed her in seconds, and she walked with him through the castle gates and towards the stables, leaving Maeteo and I glaring at each other.

The summer breeze blew some of my hair into my face, breaking our intense eye contact as I tried to wrangle it back into the ponytail it had been up in until now. Maeteo sighed.

"Princess," He started, taking a step forward.

"Don't call me that." I snapped, crossing my arms over my chest. "What is wrong with you?"

Maeteo sighed, running a hand along the back of his neck and lifting his eyes to the sky. I waited, watching him closely as his posture changed from the angry one, he had when we arrived, to the one he had now. His shoulders curled inwards slightly; his hands shaky... he almost looked scared.

"I was... When I came to find you this morning for training and no one had seen you, I nearly ripped poor Gracie's head off — then when I found out you had run away at the crack of dawn with Tarian... I didn't know what was happening."

"I didn't *run away*," I rolled my eyes, sighing. "We went on a trek to the mountains."

"The mountains?"

"To see Aepein. I was worried about her."

"You were... worried? About a dragon?" Maeteo's tone was incredulous, a small smile on his face. I simply nodded, keeping my arms crossed.

Maeteo laughed, though it lacked any amusement, shaking his head and rubbing a hand over his face.

"Do you not realise how dangerous that was?" He asked, stepping closer to me again. I stepped back, determined to keep distance between us.

"She wouldn't hurt me." I lifted my chin, glaring at him, and he laughed again.

"She might not, but we still don't know where Cyrus is. We can't find him, or his troops, or even any sign that they were *here*." Maeteo's voice took an edge to it that I had never heard before. "We don't know what his next move is."

I frowned, my eyes searching his face. Under the anger, under the way his eyes were blazing fire, he looked scared. His hands were trembling by his side and his complexion had gone pale, and he had looked away from me to stare at the dirt under his boots. Stepping forward, I placed a hand on his cheek, waiting for him to look at me.

Here was this man, strong and capable, terrified because he did not know what was happening next. He was never out of control, and that scared him. I could tell by the way his shoulders curled in on themselves and his head hung low, his breaths slow as though he was focusing on keeping them steady. For the first time that day I wondered just how deeply my leaving this morning had affected him, and I felt a stab of guilt in my stomach.

His brown eyes finally met mine, and I smiled lightly.

"I'm okay, Maeteo." I reassured him, and he let out a sigh, wrapping his hand around my wrist and pulling me into a tight hug. He buried his face in my hair, and his chest expand as he breathed in deeply. I nuzzled my face into the fabric of his shirt, taking in the smell of him.

He smelled like citrus fruit and soap, with something that was distinctly Maeteo. I could not tell if it came from him naturally or if it was something his clothes were washed in, but it was comforting like nothing else I had ever smelled before.

"You scared me," he said softly, his voice muffled by my hair. I tightened my grip on him.

"I know, I'm sorry." I sighed, rubbing the base of his back in small circles.

My mind wandered as we stood there, just holding each other in the late-afternoon sunshine. The birds sang in the trees above us, and if I did not think about it too much, this whole situation almost felt normal. It felt like I was just Kira again, and Maeteo was not a General, and we had simply sneaked into the woods to be together in private, not because we had to keep moments like this to a minimum.

A shadow passed overhead, and I tilted my head back long enough to see a dragon's tail disappearing out of view above the trees. The white scales glistening in the sun made me smile slightly, and I felt a strange comfort at the fact that Aepein was near, keeping an eye on things from above, giving us an advantage.

Gasping, I pulled back from Maeteo, startling him. He held me at arm's length, his eyes wide as he peered down at me. I gripped his forearms, excitement lacing my features as I looked between him and the sky where Aepein had just disappeared.

"Princess?" He asked, his tone concerned.

"I need everyone in the council rooms." I said quickly, shaking his arms slightly, "As soon as you can possibly get them there."

Maeteo nodded, and together we took off at a run, back through the castle gates and over the pebbled paths. We split apart at the kitchen doors, me running through them and Maeteo turning to the left to go towards the barracks.

I squealed as I accidentally ran into Chef, apologizing profusely as I helped him pick up the vegetables he had dropped when we collided. He cursed and muttered, but he waved me away.

The halls of the castle were surprisingly empty as I jogged through them to my quarters, and any staff that I did see moved out of my way quickly. I pushed my doors open without stopping, letting them slam closed behind me as I went straight to my bedroom, ripping open the drawers and gathering clean clothes to change in to.

We had an advantage.

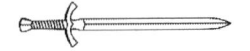

25
Maeteo

There was a buzz about the council rooms that had my skin tingling.

It had taken me an hour to get everyone into the room Kira was waiting in. She had changed her clothes from the ones she had been wearing earlier into a loose linen dress that floated behind her when she walked. Her hair had been braided and pushed to one side, and she wore the smallest crown she could get away with. She looked every bit a Queen, and my heart squeezed in my chest at the sight of her.

Voices echoed around the small space as chairs were pulled out and people sat down. I had brought Tarian and Hollis along this time in case someone decided they did not like whatever Kira was going to say, and they stood at either side of the door. Tarian watched everyone in the room closely, his eyes narrowed, and Hollis was bouncing on the balls of her feet, her hands patting against her thighs repeatedly.

Kira stood at the head of the table, her shoulders back and chin lifted high as she watched everyone file in and sit down. Her hands were clasped in front of her, but I could see them shaking from where I was sitting. The sun filtered in through the open windows, casting dust patterns in the air and stretching the shadow of the table over the floor.

Eyvlin entered the room last, her cheeks flushed and her eyes wild as she rushed in and to her seat. She had stacks of papers in her arms, overflowing and falling to the ground as she tried to manoeuvre around the table full of people. Kira waited for her to be seated before she stepped closer to the table, unclasping her hands.

"I know this is short notice and I apologise," Kira started, a smile on her face. People mumbled in reply, but by the way they all sat forward, their eyes on Kira, I could tell they were all just as intrigued as I was to hear what she was planning.

"I wanted to touch on a… sensitive topic. I believe we may have an advantage if, or should I say when, we go to war with Fire."

Brond scoffed loudly, and I sat forward in my chair to glare at him. Everyone in the room was silent at her words, including Emily, who simply looked shocked.

Kira visibly swallowed, her eyes flicking around the room quickly, trying to gage the reaction of the council members sat around the table. When her eyes settled on me, I gave her a small smile and nodded, encouraging her to continue. She placed both of her hands on the table, her fingers spread as she leaned forward, a twinkle in her eyes.

"We have dragons. Aepein and Gavrun are awake, and what better way to find out where, when, and *how* Fire is planning their attacks than being able to see everything from above? I believe that if we used these dragons to our fullest advantage, we would not need an army triple the size of the one we currently have. We could undercut and over-power Fire easily."

Silence.

Papers shuffled, and people averted their eyes from Kira's. I looked around the room, frowning at the older men who were smirking and looking away. The only person still staring at Kira was Brond, and the look on his face made my jaw lock tight.

Brond's sudden laugh made Kira, and several others, jump at the sudden break in the silence. He had put his head into his hands, and he laughed loudly into his lap. The two men on either side of him joined in with his laughter, and I had to restrain myself from leaping over the table at them.

"Something funny, gentlemen?" Kira asked, standing up straight again and tilting her head to the side. A chill went down my spine at how she was carrying herself. A few weeks ago, she would crack and cry under Brond's critical gaze and harsh words, but now here she stood, solid and sure of herself.

"You are a mad woman." Brond chortled, standing from his chair and wiping tears from laughter off his cheeks. "Dragons are beasts, not weapons of war. No one could get close enough to them."

"In case you have forgotten," Kira started, smoothing out the skirt of her dress as if she had nothing else to be doing "I have ridden Aepein, and she is completely tame. And Tarian was closer to Gavrun this morning than anyone else has been in the last fourteen years."

All eyes in the room shifted to Tarian, who's cheeks went red at the attention, but he nodded. Hollis grinned beside her brother, punching him in the arm and making him wince.

I shook my head at the pair of them, rolling my eyes and turning my attention to Kira. She was still standing strong, her eyes focused solely on Brond and his accomplices. Something sparked in her eyes that made me take a breath, my heart hammering uncomfortably in my chest.

Brond stopped his laughing, his face starting to take on the tell-tale pink of him getting angry.

"If you truly believe people are mad enough to jump on the back of a wild beast for your delusional —
"

The sneer on Brond's face made me rise from my chair, my hands balled into fists at my sides. Brond glared at me, but the hint of fear in his features made satisfaction swell inside. I was getting ready to tell him exactly what I thought of him when Kira's voice cut me off.

"Sit down, General."

I turned my head to look at her, my eyebrows raised. She stared back, her eyes unlike I had ever seen them; fire raging under the usual calm.

We stared at each other for a second before she spoke again, her voice firmer this time.

"I said sit down."

I raised both my hands, palms up and let my body flop into my chair. Relaxing back, I looked over to Brond with a grin.

"If you do not agree with my plans, Brond, that is fine. You can voice your opinion and we can take a vote, like a civilized council would." Kira smiled sweetly, though her voice was dripping with venom. "But I will tell you now — you *do not* disrespect me. You do not talk to me like a child in need of scolding. You do not throw yourself around my council chambers and make scenes just because you cannot handle a woman being in charge. You are not better than me because you are male. You are no better than anyone in this room, and you will not act as such."

Brond's face drained of all colour, and by the door, Hollis shrieked in delight. Emily had a hand over her mouth, her eyes wide, and Eyvlin looked as though she was going to faint. I pressed my lips into a tight line to suppress my smile, and beside me Gracie was shaking with silent laughter, barely contained by her fist pressed against her mouth. The younger members of the council all exhaled in relief, and while most other elderly members looked offended, Alexandre sat in his chair and looked proud.

Kira rolled her neck, squaring her shoulders and clasped her hands in front of her again. They had stopped shaking.

"Now, Brond, are you going to sit down and act like an adult, or are you going to leave? Please decide quickly because we have some important business to attend to."

Brond stumbled over his words, his face a picture of shock, before he pushed his chair away from behind himself and stormed out of the council room. He slammed the door behind him with enough force to shake the water glasses on the table, and Kira slumped slightly, her shoulders relaxing in the following silence.

Amazingly, after Brond made his exit, everyone in the room except for two agreed that Kira's plan would work. She had looked shocked when the vote had gone her way, but the smile on her face afterwards was enough to light up the room.

After the details had been laid bare and worked out, Kira slumped down into her chair, pushing her hair back over her shoulder and looking at everyone still sitting around the table. It had been decided that she and Tarian would return to Aepein and Gavrun tomorrow and try to ride them. I had protested, a mixture of worry and anger making me want to go with her instead, but Kira had simply shaken her head, claiming it would be better for Tarian to go, since Gavrun already somewhat knew him.

I had huffed, crossing my arms across my chest and Kira had laughed, rolling her eyes at me.

I waited outside the council room now, my shoulder leaning against the wall beside the door and a frown on my face. Everyone else had left fifteen minutes ago, but Kira was still inside talking to Alexandre, and it took every ounce of my self-control not to listen through the small crack in the door to their conversation.

My eyes had drifted to the small group of my soldiers that had gathered outside the nearest window; their heads all pressed together as they spoke. I frowned, tilting my head as I watched them. The sun was setting behind the trees, casting the gardens in a fiery orange glow.

I pushed away from the wall, letting my arms swing by my side as I moved across the hall to the window. Everyone knew that if they were not in the barracks by sundown, they would not get fed — and these kids were cutting it extremely close. Knocking my knuckles against the windowpane, I smirked as the four of them jumped apart, their faces falling when they saw me through the window.

I raised an eyebrow at them and lifted my hand to point in the direction of the barracks. They all nodded, sprinting away from me and across the grassy gardens. A piece of paper fluttered to the ground as they ran, and I frowned, straining my neck to try and see what it said, but it was too far away.

"Maeteo?" Kira's voice from behind me made me jump, turning on the spot to see her stood behind me with an amused look on her face, but her eyes were rimmed red and glassy, like she had been crying. Alexandre was walking down the corridor in the opposite direction to us, whistling to himself casually.

"Are you alright?" I asked without thinking, reaching forward to move her hair away from her face.

My stomach fluttered as I dipped my head and brushed a soft kiss against her lips.

A blush started to form on her cheeks as she quickly looked both ways down the corridor.

"I'm fine." She smiled, slipping her fingers into mine and squeezing lightly. "Why did you wait for me?"

"I wanted to tell you how well you have done today." I started us walking slowly, relishing the feeling of her small hand gripped in mine. She looked up at me with wide eyes, her mouth open slightly. "The way you stood up to Brond was the best thing I have seen in a long time."

She laughed loudly, shaking her head. I watched in wonder as the sound of her laugh made my stomach flip, the evening light coming through the corridor windows lit her up from the side and made her freckles stand out against her pale cheeks. I took a breath through my nose, tearing my eyes away from her and focusing on what was ahead of us.

Most of the castle staff would already be done for the night and retreated to their chambers or would still be in the staff dining rooms finishing dinner, so the chances of us getting caught together was slim, but the sound of footsteps coming from the corridor in front of us made me jump away from Kira. The loss of her hand in mine felt heavy, and I clenched my hand into a fist.

Hollis came around the corner to our left, her mouth still full of whatever she had scrounged from the kitchens and skipped over to us.

"Hello, you two." She smiled, slipping in between the two of us. I glared at her, and she only looked up at me with a wink in reply. She knew exactly what she was doing, and I was ready to bet that Tarian had put her up to it.

"Hollis," Kira's voice was kind, but her face was annoyed, and her hands were ringing the fabric of her skirt as she walked.

Silence enveloped the three of us as we kept walking through twisting corridor after twisting corridor. Hollis dug her elbow into my side, and I had to use every inch of my self-control not to push the little rat into the nearest open door and lock it behind her.

As we reached the corridor that led to Kira's quarters, she paused, her gaze flitting from Hollis to me with a strange look on her face. I ran a hand through my hair, sighing through my nose and hoping she did not think I had asked Hollis to join us.

She was going to get an earful as soon as Kira's door was closed.

Hollis bounced on her heels, her hands stuffed into her pockets and the same grin on her face that had been there for the entire time she had been with us.

"Well, I guess I'll see you both tomorrow." Kira smiled, waving one of her hands weakly and turning into her bright corridor. There was no other corridor in the castle that looked like this one, and it made me smile every time I saw it. It was so perfectly Kira.

"Goodnight, Your Majesty." I tipped my head slightly, and Kira stopped at her open door, her gaze coming back to me and Hollis. A small frown danced on her lips, but she nodded, closing the door behind her with a soft click.

Hollis giggled beside me, and I caught her by the wrist, glaring down at her.

"What. Was. That?" I forced out through gritted teeth. Hollis just laughed louder, patting my shoulder with her free hand and wriggling her wrist out of my grasp. She did not reply before she started off down the next corridor, and I followed close behind her, seething.

"Tarian said you were falling for her, but I didn't actually believe him." She laughed, pushing her hands into her pockets.

I rolled my eyes, wishing I had never opened my mouth to Tarian in the first place.

"I'm not — "

"Oh, be quiet, Maeteo." Hollis laughed, holding open a door for me to go outside first. I glared at her as I passed. "You might as well announce it to the entire Kingdom."

I deflated slightly, my shoulders slumping as I let out a sigh. Hollis walked slowly beside me as we crossed over the stone pathways and onto the dirt track that led to the barracks.

If I looked behind me now, I would be able to see the small balcony of Kira's quarters.

"I know," I muttered, "It might be the worst thing I've ever done."

"Definitely not the worst." Hollis smiled reassuringly, nudging me with her shoulder, "Not exactly your smartest move, either, but definitely not the worst."

I laughed without any humour in it, rolling my eyes and pushing through the door of the barracks. I held it open for Hollis to move past me and looked back towards the castle.

Kira's curtains were swinging closed.

26
Kira

Flying over the Kingdom on the back of Aepein was quickly becoming my favourite way to spend an afternoon.

Every day for the past week, Tarian and I had been coming to the mountains, climbing to the cave where Aepein and Gavrun were sleeping, and had been training them. The first day was total chaos, with Gavrun throwing Tarian off more than once, and Tarian losing his temper with the beast and threatening that the castle needed a new rug. I had laughed until my sides hurt.

It had been easier the next day, with Tarian only being knocked to the ground once, and every day since had been better. Now, as we soared across the valley and towards the coast — a three-day ride on horseback — with Tarian on the back of Gavrun and me settled between Aepein's shoulder blades, it felt like we had never struggled.

Gavrun swooped down beside us, as close as he could get to his mate given the span of his wings and huffed a breath out of his nose. Aepein replied with a grunt of her own, and once he was satisfied with her reply, Gavrun gave us a wider berth again. Tarian looked at me and rolled his eyes, and I laughed loudly, squeezing Aepein with my thigh to get her to turn slightly.

The sprawling greens and browns of fields gave way to the golden sand and azure blue of the sea. Gulls screeched loudly at the sight of the two dragons barrelling towards them and scattered. Aepein yelped in surprise at the sudden flurry of birds and dove out of the way.

I laughed, patting her neck reassuringly. Tarian and Gavrun came down beside us again, and Tarian waved his arm to get my attention, pointing to a sand dune. I nodded, manoeuvring Aepein downwards until her feet landed in the sand and I could slide off her back.

Gavrun landed beside us in a cloud of sand, and I shielded my eyes from it, a grin on my face. Tarian jumped down in front of me, a grin on his face as he landed.

"You doing okay?" He asked me, turning towards Gavrun's head and giving the great beast a scratch on the end of his snout, making his tail swish happily. Aepein caught it between her teeth, nipping lightly and making Gavrun jump.

"I'm fine," I smiled, stretching my arms above my head and relishing in the sound of my shoulder bones popping in happiness. "Grateful for the break, though, my legs feel like Chef's jelly."

Tarian laughed, nodding his head in agreement and stepping away from Gavrun, leaving him and Aepein to lie in the sand ditch together, their tails intertwined as we started to walk over the dunes.

We had flown South yesterday, towards the mid-sea that separated Earth and Fire, but found no signs of Cyrus or his army anywhere, much to Maeteo's annoyance. He had grumbled that maybe he should be coming with me instead today, but Tarian had rolled his eyes at him and climbed up Gavrun's lowered wing, settling himself into the space between the beast's shoulder blades while Maeteo grumped.

I braced myself against the sudden breeze as we reached the top of a dune. My hair whipped around my face, and my teeth clenched against the cold. It was hard to believe it was still summer with the bite in the air, but the wind coming from the North was always colder and more bitter than anywhere else.

My eyes scanned the horizon, taking in the point where the ocean met the sky. We knew Cyrus was here somewhere, it was just a matter of finding out *where*.

I let a sigh out through my nose, hugging my arms close to my chest and watching a flurry of birds fly overhead and towards the cliffs to our left. From here, the village that sat atop the cliff looked small enough to be mistaken for a children's toy. The wooden houses with thatched roofs looked like something from a painting, and the sounds of laughter floated across the beach on the wind.

Tarian's presence next to me was a comfort, and when I looked up at him, he was staring up at the village with a small smile on his face.

I bumped him with my elbow, raising an eyebrow.

"That's Bayshell. Where Hollis and I lived." He smiled softly. The village had only mentioned once sparked with familiarity. "I haven't seen it in a while."

"Shall we go and visit?" I asked, turning my attention back to the village, "It doesn't look like too far of a walk, and I'm sure your parents would love to see you."

Tarian thought about it for a second, his lips pursed together, and his head tilted, but a smile appeared on his face quickly.

"Hollis would kill me if she found out I saw them without her." He chuckled, pushing his hands into his pockets, "Let's go."

I laughed loudly, linking my arm through Tarian's and letting him guide us over the sand dunes and up to the grassy cliff-side path. The wind picked up even more as we made our way around the twisting path, and I shivered slightly at the bite of it. It was easy to forget that farther in land was still swelteringly hot, and I was glad that Tarian had insisted I wear warmer leggings today.

As we walked, Tarian was silent. I had let go of his arm once the path had gotten less rocky and more straight forward, and now as I watched him, he seemed far away in his own head. Not that I could blame him, with the views like the ones we were having right now, I could get lost in my own thoughts, too.

The noises of Bayshell grew louder as we got closer, and eventually we left the grassy path and found ourselves walking on cobblestoned streets. Lined with wooden houses and flower boxes, black steel streetlamps, and open doors.

Houses gave way to several bakeries, fish mongers, and merchants. Slowly, as we walked, I noticed a small crowd gathering behind us. I looked back over my shoulder, meeting the eyes of a young girl. She could not have been older than six, with wide eyes and light hair that was pulled back into a bun.

I put my hand on Tarian's arm and stopped walking. He stopped beside me; his eyebrows raised as he looked from me to the growing crowd behind us.

"What did you expect?" He laughed, "Their Queen just walked into their home without any notice or any of her guards."

I rolled my eyes at him and turned to face the crowd fully. The little girl in front of me grinned.

"Hello," I smiled, kneeling in front of her. "What's your name?"

"Willow." Her voice carried through the village street, and a woman behind her beamed with pride. I assumed she was her mother.

"That's a beautiful name." I nodded, standing up straight and dusting off the knees of my leggings, before reaching out to take the young girl's hand. "Would you like to walk with us, Willow?"

Willow looked back at her mother, who nodded her head and gestured for her to walk alongside us. And when she turned back to us, Willow grinned up at me, and my heart melted at the sight of her missing front tooth.

Tarian started to lead us through the twisting streets of Bayshell again, pointing out places he and Hollis used to play, which bakery made his eighth birthday cake, and where he first knocked out a kid that had been picking on Hollis for her size. I had laughed at that, shaking my head. Willow's small hand in mine was a comfort as the crowd behind us grew larger, until every single person in the small village was following us around, whispering and muttering.

We turned a final corner, and Tarian's face burst into a grin. A small cottage sat behind a wooden fence, with dug out gardens full of vegetables and a red painted front door. The windows were thrown open, and the smell of freshly baked bread floated towards us. My mouth watered at the wonderful smell, and as we stopped walking, the front door was thrown open from inside.

Tarian's mother looked exactly like the twins. Black hair curled down over her shoulders, pale skin, and the same wild, wide eyes. She stood there in an apron and a pair of slippers, staring at the two of us standing at the end of her garden path.

Tarian raised a hand, waving as he pushed open the gate. I let go of Willow's hand, smiling down at the girl who had bent down to pick a daisy. She placed it into the hand she had just been holding and turned on the spot, running back to her mother with a loud giggle.

I watched her as she ran, smiling and nodding at her mother when she caught Willow mid jump with a laugh.

Tarian tapped my shoulder, gesturing for me to go through the garden gate before him. I thanked him and stepped onto the brick path.

A man had joined Tarian's mother at the door, and I quickly gathered that he was Tarian's father, given the height and the sharp angle of his jaw. He had the same stubborn set of his features that Tarian did.

"What in Lides' name —" Tarian's mother's voice carried over the garden as we drew closer, and she stepped out of the house, her slippered feet carrying her down the path quickly and into Tarian's waiting arms. He squeezed her tightly, lifting the short woman off the ground as he hugged her.

"Surprise?" Tarian laughed, placing his mother back on the ground and stepping back. She grinned up at her son, and then turned her attention to me. Her face paled, and she quickly swiped a hand over her hair and tried to straighten out her apron.

"Oh! Oh, Tarian, some warning would have been nice!" She hissed, and I laughed lightly at the look Tarian gave her, "Your Majesty, what an honour!"

"It's lovely to meet you." I smiled, holding out a hand for her to shake. She gripped it tightly in both of hers, a smile spreading across her face and making her look exactly like Hollis.

"Kira, this is my mother, Cecilia," Tarian wrapped his arm around Cecilia's shoulders, squeezing her into his side, "And this is my father, Levi."

Levi had made his way down the path slowly, leaning on a wooden cane. His smile was wide as he took in his son and me.

"Your Majesty, welcome." He bowed his head, "I have to say this is a bit of a surprise."

"We were in the area." I smiled, clasping my hands together in front of myself and rocking back onto my heels. The sound of the crowd that had gathered behind us drew Levi's eyes towards it, and he blinked fast, as if he could not believe what he was seeing.

I looked over my shoulder in time to see the crowd starting to disperse, and Cecilia ushered both Tarian and I inside the small cottage. Tarian was staring at the cane his father was walking with, a frown on his face as he took in how slowly he moved.

Inside the cottage reminded me of being at home with Emily. The red checked curtains on the windows swayed in the breeze coming in through the window and the dining table was covered in a matching cloth and mismatched crockery. There was a stone fireplace in the corner of the room, loaded with wooden logs. I turned slowly, taking in the space. It was small, and cosy, and made my heart ache in my chest.

Cecilia gestured for me to sit down on one of the dark sofas. I thanked her as I sat, watching her flutter around the kitchen, opening the light blue cupboards and pulling out mugs and biscuits, and a teapot that was already boiling on the cooker.

Levi sat down across from me, groaning as he stretched out his leg and rubbed at his knee. Tarian sat himself on the arm of the sofa, his arms crossed over his chest and a frown on his face.

"What 's wrong with your knee?" He asked, nodding towards his father's leg. Levi just grunted, waving his hand in dismissal.

"Just the damp air playing havoc with my old joints." He smiled, winking at me and making me laugh lightly.

Cecilia placed a tray full of biscuits on the small table between the two sofas, her cheeks tinted pink and her hands shaking a little as she did so.

"Do you want tea, Your Majesty?" She asked, picking up a mug and starting to pour water into it.

"I can do it," I smiled, placing a hand on top of her shaking ones, "And please, just Kira is fine."

Cecilia giggled, making both Levi and Tarian roll their eyes as she sat down on the sofa next to Levi.

Tarian slipped down onto the sofa next to me, and after I had made my own mug of tea he took the pot off me, pouring one for both of his parents and himself. I watched as Cecilia stared at her son, completely awestruck at the sight of him in front of her.

Levi caught me staring and winked again.

"Tar has always been Ceci's favourite." Levi laughed, sipping at the mug Tarian handed him. Cecilia gasped, smacking her husband on the arm and making him jump, tea splashing over the rim of his mug.

"That is not true, Levi, don't you dare!" She hissed, making Levi chuckle, "I love both of my children equally."

"That's not what you said on their fifth birthday," Levi mumbled, dodging out the way of is wife again.

Tarian shook his head at the pair, but there was a loving smile on his face as he watched them. Cecilia sat back in her chair, crossing her legs over one another and straightening her back.

"Where is your sister, Tarian?"

"She's running the archery training today, but she doesn't know we're here." Tarian chuckled, slouching back into the sofa and making himself comfortable. "We were… in the area, so we figured we could come and say hello before we head back to the castle."

"In the area? What for?" Levi asked, and Tarian and I looked at each other.

I opened my mouth, ready to tell them, when Tarian cut me off.

"Just out on an adventure, Pa, nothing serious." He smiled, and his father nodded, turning his attention back to his wife.

I looked at Tarian, confusion written on my face, and he shook his head at me. I assumed he did not want to put a heavy cloud on the day, with how long it had been since he had seen them.

The afternoon passed without my realizing. Stories of Tarian and Hollis as children were shared, making me laugh until my sides ached, and I had drunk so much tea that I was sure I was going to burst. Levi and Cecilia were quickly becoming my favourite people I had ever met. The pair were warm, welcoming, and not afraid to talk their minds, and it was easy to see where Hollis and Tarian got their view of the world from.

Cecilia was taking the empty teapot back into the kitchen for the fourth time, and I had volunteered to help her, giving Tarian a minute alone with his father. He had been prodding at him for information on his leg, but Levi had been brushing him off every time, and I hoped giving them some privacy would make him feel more comfortable telling Tarian about it.

The small kitchen of the cottage was just off the living area, separated by a single half wall. The cupboards were painted a light blue, and there were yellow curtains hanging in the window. The view from the window took my breath away, as it looked right over the edge of the cliff and towards the horizon.

A black silhouette on the horizon caught my attention just as I looked away from the window. Snapping my head back around, I placed the mugs I was holding on the counter before leaning closer to the open window. The ocean air whipped my hair around my face as I stood there, eyes wide and mouth open in disbelief.

The shape on the horizon grew taller, and two more appeared at its sides, and two more after that. My heart dropped to my stomach as I realised what I was looking at; what was coming.

"Is everything alright, dear?" Cecilia's voice came from behind me, and I jumped back from the window, spinning on the spot to see the small woman looking at me worriedly. Tarian had stood from the sofa and was already crossing the room, his hand meeting the top of my arm as he leaned out the window himself.

I watched as his shoulders tensed and he sucked in a breath.

"We need to go," he said suddenly, turning away from the window and pulling his mother into another bone-crushing hug. "Everything is fine, don't worry. Stay inside, and close the windows, okay?"

Cecilia nodded, squeezing her son tightly and stepping away from him. Levi clapped Tarian on the shoulder as I hugged Cecilia goodbye. She smelled like tea and freshly baked bread, and it hurt my heart to let her go.

Levi leaned down to place a kiss on my cheek, his rough beard scratching my skin as he did so.

"Do what is right for our Kingdom, Your Majesty." He said softly so that only I could hear. I stepped back, a small smile on my face as I nodded.

Tarian and I took off at a brisk walk so as not to frighten any of Bayshell's villagers, but as we passed them, we gave quiet warnings; *get inside, close the windows, do not panic.*

"Why are they coming from the North?!" I hissed as we hurtled down the grassy cliff-side. Now that we were out of the village, we had picked up the pace, the two of us almost sprinting down the paths to reach Gavrun and Aepein. We had wondered yesterday why the South was so quiet, when it was closest to Fire.

"To take us by surprise." Tarian grumbled, holding out his hand to help me jump down onto the golden sand. "They've gone right around to throw us off."

Thankfully, Aepein and Gavrun were right where we left them. The two dragons dozing lazily, their tails swishing in the wind and their eyes closed. It felt like a shame to disturb them, but as the ships on the horizon started to grow in numbers, we needed to move quick.

I climbed up onto Aepein's back with ease now that I was used to it, and she lifted her head from the sand. She must have sensed the urgency in our movements, because she jumped up from her lying position and took off into the air without much prompting.

As we rose above the beach, I looked over my shoulder. The single ship that I had spotted from Cecilia's kitchen window had become at least fifty, and I felt the air leave my lungs.

Fire was here.

27

Maeteo stood with his hands on the table, his shoulders flexed in the low light of the war room.

As soon as we had returned to the castle, Tarian had dragged me straight to the barracks and into Maeteo's private chambers. He had been shocked, to say the least, to see the two of us burst into his bedroom with wild hair and panicked expressions.

Tarian had explained what we saw at the beach, and I watched as Maeteo's face went from one of shock, to one of anger. His jaw tensed, and his shoulders stiffened, and his hands balled into fists. He had sent Tarian to rally every soldier he could find, even the lesser trained ones, and had taken me by the hand and lead me to the small room we were in now.

The table in front of me was made of solid oak, with a map of the Earth and Fire Kingdoms spread across it, held in place at the corners by daggers and heavy figures. The walls were lined with armour, helmets, and weapons of every shape and size.

Hollis had appeared beside me, her face stern and her hands clasped behind her back. It was the most serious I had ever seen her, and it was terrifying.

"Tarian has gone to fetch Tristan and the Queen's armour." She said, her voice cold. Maeteo did not answer her, simply nodded his head and continued to stare at the map in front of him.

"If we cut them off before they reach Ebonfort," Maeteo pointed to a spot Northwest of where we were now on the map, a slight shake to his hand, "There shouldn't be too much damage to the villages farther inland."

"What about Bayshell?" Hollis asked, her tone clipped. Maeteo looked up at her, his shoulders still strained as he leaned on the table, but again he did not answer her, just pulling his lips into a tight line and looking back down at his map.

The sounds of Hollis' teeth crashing together made me wince in the silent room.

Maeteo pushed himself off the table, grunting as he stood up straight in the small room. He devoured the space, his head nearly touched the ceiling as he stood to his full height, blocking out any remaining light coming in from outside.

His eyes landed on me, and I felt smaller than I ever had as he stared.

"We leave for Ebonfort at first light." He nodded; his words aimed at Hollis though he was still staring right at me. Hollis simply nodded her head, turning on her heel and leaving the room, the door slamming behind her, shaking the small figurines on the table.

Maeteo moved as soon as the door was firmly shut. He was around the table and in front of me before I even had time to blink, his hands cupping my face and his lips crushing to mine.

I stumbled slightly at the force with which he kissed me, but he steadied me against the closed door, pressing himself against me in every way he possibly could.

The kiss was unlike any other we had shared. It was passionate and unhinged, and I worried briefly that someone might try and open the door just to find out what the noise was.

"Maeteo," I breathed when he pulled back from me for air, his forehead resting against mine and his breaths coming in quick pants. "What — what are you — "

"Shh," He screwed up his face, his eyebrows furrowing against my forehead, "Please, just let me…"

He did not finish his sentence, but instead began to pepper short, chaste kisses across my cheeks and nose, and I let my hands move from the muscles in his arms to the warmth of his chest. His heart was hammering under my palm, and I attempted to rub small circles over it with my fingers, trying to calm him in any way possible.

Silence passed between us as he kissed every possible bit of my skin he could reach, my fingers continuing their path of circles over his shirt.

"Promise me," Maeteo's voice was gruff when he finally spoke, "Promise you won't leave the back lines. I need you to stay where I know you're safe."

"You know I can't do that," I smiled softly, reaching up to cup his cheek, his stubble scratching at the palm of my hand, "You know as well as I do, they need to see me out there or all of this was for nothing."

Maeteo let out a sigh. His fingers knotting around the hair at the base of my skull and squeezing tightly. I would have winced at the sharp pain, but I focused on the slope of his nose, and the downward curve of his still slightly kiss-swollen lips.

We stood for a minute like that, just holding each other before Maeteo finally let me go. His hand slipping out of my hair and falling to his side as he opened his eyes and looked down at me. I smiled at him lightly, trying to ease the look of fear on his face.

"Kira, if something happens to you while we are out there…I won't be able to stop fighting to come and help you."

"Then something happens." I said softly, shrugging, "You've trained me, Maeteo, I know how to fight. I'm not the best at it, sure, but I know more than enough to get me through."

I hoped my smile was somewhat comforting to him, but his eyes searched my face and for a moment I worried that he might be able to see the guilt I had felt settle into my stomach. He would be fighting for me. As would Hollis, and Tarian, and every other friend I had made within the castle walls these last weeks. They would be fighting while I had a plan of my own.

My heart stumbled in my chest, and I tried to steady my breathing. Maeteo must have mistaken it for anxiety, as he wrapped his arms around me and held me to his chest, his hands stroking through my hair gently.

I wondered as we stood there, Maeteo's hands repeating slow, comforting strokes down my hair, if I was a bad person. The letter from my father had told me to do whatever I had to do to take the Fire Kingdom down from the inside. Tarian's father had repeated the sentiment this afternoon — and whilst I knew this was what I had to do; I could not help but feel the stab of guilt.

I knotted my fingers around the fabric at the back of Maeteo's shirt, breathing in the smell of him one more time before I let him go, placing my hands on his chest and pushing him back lightly. He smiled down at me, but it did not reach his eyes.

28

The war carriages left the castle gates as soon as the sun had started to peek over the horizon.

Emily had clung to me from the second she had arrived in my quarters this morning. Her eyes were rimmed red and her cheeks pink. She had wrapped her arms around me so tightly that I had had to pry her off, laughing lightly.

Now, as I was climbing onto the back of Freya, my armour and weapons packed into the back of a wagon, Emily stood by the stable doors, sniffling lightly and wiping her hands under her eyes. Dread settled into my stomach as I looked at her, and I wished for a second that I could tell her what I was really doing. After all, Cyrus was her half-brother.

I swallowed my discomfort and squeezed the reins in my hand, nudging Freya forward slightly. Emily stepped back just enough to let us through the door before I stopped us again, smiling down at her in, what I hoped, was a comforting way.

"You promise me you'll be safe?" Emily sniffled, placing her hand on my knee. I fought the urge to raise my eyebrows at her.

"As safe as I can be." I smiled, placing my hand on top of hers and squeezing, "I'll be back before you even have the chance to miss me."

Emily smiled sadly, her eyes filling with tears again as she stepped back, crossing her arms over her chest.

I let out a breath, pushing Freya forward through the stable yard and around the side of the castle until we reached the front gates. The carriages full of our tents and weapons had already left, but the soldiers remained. Some on foot and some on horseback, they stood in perfect formation up the long entrance road to the castle. Two single carriages remained at the back of the fleet, and Maeteo's explanation of what they were for came back to me.

The lighter one, with red curtains pulled over the windows, was for if we had to travel during the night and I needed to sleep, or if I needed a break from being on horseback. Gracie would be traveling in that one, and I could see her through the window already, nibbling nervously on her bottom lip and her cheeks still stained with tears from saying goodbye to the man she loved.

The other carriage was darker, and larger. Dark, almost black, wood with tinted windows and pulled by black horses, and my heart sank at the sight of it. While now it held a few of our medical supplies, and my armour and sword, after this was all over, it was intended to bring back the bodies of anyone we lost. Brief flashes of Maeteo, and Hollis, and Tarian, being pulled home in the back of that wagon flooded my mind, and I had to stop myself from shrieking aloud.

A murder of crows flew overhead, and I tried to pay no attention to the ominous feeling they gave me.

Maeteo came up beside me on the back of Fenrir, already in full armour apart from his helmet, which was hung on the side of Fenrir's saddle. He bumped his knee against mine, making my drag my eyes away from the sky to look at him. My breath caught in my throat at the sight in front of me. He looked almost identical to the day I met him, with his hair pushed back and clean shaven.

"Are you ready to go?" He asked, his voice gentle and his face soft. I wanted to reach over and kiss him until my lips hurt.

"Yes," I lied, smiling lightly. He stared at me for a second longer before he nodded his head and turned his attention back to the formation in front of us.

Tarian and Hollis had been sent to the mountains to collect Aepein and Gavrun, and despite my protests,

Maeteo had convinced me that I had to stay here. He did not want to leave my side, but he could not leave his army to move forward without him, so here I stayed. Dark clouds had started to gather in the sky, and thunder rumbled in the distance. It felt fitting that the first rain of the summer would come today of all days.

The castle healer, Merethyl, was shouting from the back of her horse about supplies being packed properly, but the coachman in charge of the carriage just shook his head at her, rolling his eyes.

Maeteo called a chain of commands to the front of the formation, and everyone snapped to attention. The crows had stopped their melancholy singing and were watching us from their perches in the trees, and after another call from Maeteo, the soldiers on foot started marching.

Freya jolted forward at the same time Fenrir did, and I sucked in a breath as we passed through the open gates. Most of the castle staff were gathered at the gates, watching and waving to soldiers as they passed, their heads bowing when I passed by. I tried my hardest to look sure in what I was doing, my shoulders squared and my back straight, I kept my face as calm as I could.

The forest was silent except for the sounds of our parade. There were no singing birds, no scurrying rabbits or squirrels, and no sign of any grazing deer. Dane and I used to sit for hours, hidden in the thickest of the forest's growth, just to watch the deer at the streams. My heart ached at the memory.

We moved through the forest for hours, passing through both the villages that held the tree line, and out into the open fields. The heavens had opened above us about an hour into our journey, and my teeth chattered together as the rainwater soaked through my clothes and into my skin. We were not due to stop for a good while yet, and my only dry clothes were in the carriage in front of us.

Maeteo, who had moved in front of me to keep an eye on a few of the younger soldiers, fell back to my side. His hair was soaked to the point it had started to curl and fall over his face, yet he looked nowhere near as miserable as I expected him to. He smiled over at me, his eyes soft.

"How are you feeling?" He asked, having to shout slightly over the sounds of the rain and of the horses' hooves.

"Cold," I laughed, my voice shaking as I shivered in the downpour. Freya huffed as if she was agreeing with me, shaking her soaking wet mane, and splashing even more cold water at me.

"Do you want us to stop?" Maeteo asked, his eyebrows knotting together as he frowned. I had considered asking him to stop already, but I knew it would put us behind schedule. I shook my head, smiling at him as reassuringly as I could.

"No, I'm okay. How long until we set up camp for the evening?"

"At least another four hours, Princess."

I groaned, my head falling back against my shoulders and Maeteo laughed loudly.

A shadow darker than that of the clouds flew overhead at the same time the rain stopped hitting my face. Looking up, I was greeted with the sight of Aepein's belly, with Hollis leaning to the side and grinning down at me. Gavrun was slightly behind her, and I could see Tarian enough to tell he was shaking his head at his sister.

Laughing loudly, I took comfort in the brief reprieve from the rain, and shifted myself in my saddle, settling myself in for another few hours traveling.

29

When we finally stopped to set up camp, my legs felt like they had the bones ripped from them, and my hands had turned to nothing but pins and needles. My skin had turned pink, and then a bloodless white, and ached as I stretched my fingers out in my gloves.

Pulling open the carriage door, I shook myself off slightly before I lifted myself up into the warm space. A groan fell past my lips as I revelled in the dry heat. Gracie had fallen asleep in her seat, her head leaning on a small, plush pillow, and her mouth parted as she breathed deeply. I knew it was hard for her to leave Callum, and her cheeks and nose were still flushed pink from how much she had cried. My heart still hurt from there goodbye, and I had sworn to myself that I would get her back to him, if it was the last thing I did.

Freeing myself from my soaked clothes, I grabbed the soft, fluffy blanket that was spread across the seat opposite Gracie and wrapped myself up as tightly as I could. Exhaustion had started to seep into my bones, and as I flopped down into the cushioned seat, I let my eyes fall closed. The sounds outside of the carriage were muffled, and I let myself drift into my own thoughts as they carried on — people shouting about tents and food, and someone asking what they were supposed to feed the dragons.

I let my brain wander until I started to doze off, my body finally warming under the comfort of the blanket and my head resting back against the cushioned seat.

The carriage door opening suddenly made my jump in my seat, my hand gripping the blanket to my chest as I jumped out of my seat, my head spinning.

Maeteo stood outside the door, his mouth open and his eyes wide as he took in the sight of me in front of him. My heart hammered in my chest, and I scrambled to make sure every inch of me was covered by the blanket, which, thankfully, was big enough to wrap around myself twice. Gracie did not even stir from where she slept on the opposite seat.

I let my eyes close and pulled my lips into a tight line, taking a breath through my nose as I tried to stop the embarrassment from washing over me. Maeteo, however, did not move. His eyes trailed over my shoulders, the only exposed bit of skin, and down the blanket. My heart hammered in my chest at his gaze.

"Can I help you?" I asked finally, breaking the strange silence between us.

His eyes snapped back up to mine, and a deep flush coloured his cheeks. His hair was still sticking to his forehead, and his shirt had soaked right through so I could see the chain necklace he always wore pressed against the skin of his chest.

"I, uh, I brought you some dry clothes," He stumbled over his words as he stepped up into the carriage. His height seemed to swallow up the space, and he had to hunch his shoulders slightly to stand up straight. I looked at the small bundle in his hands, spotting a dry pair of leggings and a thick, warm jumper that I had thrown into my belongings just in case.

"Thank you," I smiled at him, taking the clothes from him. He nodded, and I watched his throat bob as he swallowed, the expression on his face unreadable. "Was there anything else?"

"Hm? Oh, no... no, nothing else." He flushed, his eyes trailing across my chest again, and I tilted my head to the side as I watched him, "Just... making sure you're okay."

"I'm fine," I smiled, placing a hand on his arm and squeezing the muscle there.

We stood in silence for a minute, the only sound being Gracie's deep breathing. I let myself take in every detail of Maeteo's face; the way his eyebrows curved upwards, the sharp angle of his jaw, and the way he was looking at me as if I was some kind of long-lost diamond.

A soft snore from Gracie pulled my eyes away from Maeteo's face for a second, and seemed to break the trance we had been in. Maeteo cleared his throat, stepping back slightly and running a hand along his jaw.

"I'll let you get changed," he said, his voice rough and thick, though he made no move to leave the carriage. I nodded, a smile tugging at the corners of my mouth as I watched him still stand there, his gaze falling to my blanket again.

"*Maeteo*," I laughed, and his eyes snapped back to mine as his cheeks flushed bright red.

"Right! Yes, okay — I'm going!" He stumbled over his words as he turned on his heel quickly, throwing the carriage door open and leaping back out into the rain. Giggles continued to rack through me even after he had closed the door and I watched him sprint away in the direction of his tent.

Once I had dressed in my dry clothes and had managed to re-braid my hair, I waited for the rain to pass.

My mind wandered over the mid-sea, and to the life that awaited me there. I knew, of course, that I could not kill Cyrus as soon as I arrived, which meant I had to set myself a timeline. If I gave myself a year, was that enough time to get a royal wedding planned and out of the way? Would Cyrus be one of those Princes' that wanted to parade us around every village to celebrate our union?

I pulled my lips into a tight line as I pondered that thought. What would the people of Fire think of me? Would they be as pleased as Cyrus's father would have been about the Kingdoms joining, or would they resent me, the Queen who changed their way of living as they knew it?

The sounds of the rain hitting the carriage eased, and I peered around one of the curtains to see that the field we had stopped in was now basked in the evening sunset. I pulled my — now somewhat dry — boots onto my feet and stood from my chair, wincing slightly at the ache in my legs. Maybe I would ask them if I could stay in the carriage for tomorrow's journey.

Stepping out into the muddy grass, I let the door close softly behind me. Tents had been erected across the field, and soldiers moved between them all, carrying weapons and firewood and rolled up maps. It was the most bizarre feeling to be standing amid it all and know it was all for me.

Straining my neck to try and see above some of the crowd, I spotted Hollis and Tarian slightly to the side of the tents, Aepein and Gavrun lying on the grass with their heads rested on their feet. I started off in that direction, not knowing really what to do with myself.

Aepein lifted her head as I approached and blinked slowly at me. I smiled and ran my hand along her snout, scratching the bridge of her nose just as she liked it.

"How are you feeling?" Hollis asked. Her hair was braided down her back like mine and looked darker than black due to how wet it had gotten. Her armour clung to her like it had been moulded to her body perfectly, and her bow was strapped to her back. She had a sword sheathed at her waist like the rest of the soldiers, but it was much smaller in size than a lot of the others I had seen.

"I'm fine." I smiled, repeating the words I had told Maeteo earlier. I wished I could have told them what I was planning and how it was eating me alive inside, but I knew they would go straight to Maeteo, and he would do everything he could to stop me.

"It's been a long day," Tarian spoke from beside Gavrun, his shoulder resting against the great beast's neck. The pair of them had created quite the friendship between them, and every time I looked at them, I felt my chest swell with happiness. They were so similar in so many ways. "Are you going to join us for dinner, or are you going straight to sleep?"

As if in answer to his question, my stomach growled loudly. Tarian raised his eyebrows while

Hollis laughed loudly, linking her arm through my own and dragging me towards the best smelling tent in the field.

The catering tent had been set up the same way the great hall in the castle had been, with long tables filling the main space. The only difference here were the food stands at the far end of the tent. My mouth watered at the smell of cooked meats and vegetables filling the space, and Hollis weaved us through the packed space to grab ourselves plates.

My eyes wandered the room as we sat at one of the long benches. Maeteo was nowhere to be seen, and my stomach lurched at his not being there. I knew he was probably in his own tent, resting after the long day we had, but my heart missed his presence.

Gracie, to my surprise, plopped down onto the bench next to me, her eyes still half closed with sleep and her hair wild. I nudged her with my shoulder and shot her a small smile, which she returned half-heartedly.

As the catering tent filled with even more people, my eyes kept flitting to the entrance, hoping with all my heart that I would see Maeteo.

30
Maeteo

The journey from the castle to Ebonfort took us nearly three full days. After how wet everything had gotten during the first day of travel, we had to stop for longer to dry off, putting us behind by an annoyingly large amount. Then, after the second day of travel was so hot, one of the newer soldiers fainted in the afternoon sun, forcing us to set up a medical tent right there in the path.

If you had asked me, we should have just strapped him to the back of a horse and kept moving, but Merethyl said that was unethical.

Now, as we drew close to the evening of our third day traveling, all of us were growing tired. I had moved with Kira to the front of the parade, leading us to where we would be setting up out base for the foreseeable. Ebonfort stood silent around us as we passed through, the only sounds the marching of feet and the hooves of horses, and the occasional groan from the carriages. All the shutters on the windows were closed, and houses sat

in darkness. There were no children in the street
playing, and even the taverns stood silent.

Kira sat strong atop of Freya, but even she noticed
the strange atmosphere; her bottom lip pulled between
her teeth and her eyes scanning every alleyway. Her
hair had grown knotted and tangled, so she had pulled it
back off her face, and her eyes were heavy with
tiredness, but she sat with her shoulders back,
determined not to show weakness. My heart still beat
wildly at the sight of her.

Tarian and Hollis had stopped about three miles
ago, keeping Aepein and Gavrun as hidden as they
could until they were needed.

I pulled Fenrir to a stop, and the whole parade
stopped behind me. Kira turned to look at me, but I had
already jumped down from the saddle and started
walking. I heard the grumbling of voices behind me,
but I ignored it as I took cautious steps in the quiet
village.

Ebonfort reached its end at the top of a hill, and
from there you could see for miles over empty fields
and abandoned farms — that was where we were
intending to cut off the Fire Kingdom army.

Kira's small body came up beside mine as I walked,
and I looked down at her. Her eyes were focused ahead
of us, and she had her arms wrapped around herself.
The wind was harsher here, with how high up Ebonfort

was, so I shifted to her other side, shielding her from the harsh breeze. She smiled up at me in thanks.

My heart sank into my stomach as we reached the top of the hill and gazed out at the fields.

Several of the fields closest to us stood empty still, however the rest were full of tents. Fire Kingdom flags flew high in the air, and from where we stood, we could see thousands of soldiers moving around, flitting from tent to tent, gathered around bonfires, and playing tunes on instruments even though the music was lost on the wind.

Kira grabbed my arm, her eyes wide and panicked. We had lost a day traveling, and it had cost us the advantage of having a decent base camp. I drew in a breath through my nose, running my tongue over my teeth and pursing my lips as I considered the options.

There was an opening slightly to the east of where we stood now, which would take us to the other side of the small river that ran through the fields in front of us. If we had the advantage of being over water, it might give us back some of our lost time.

"We cross the river." I said to Kira, who simply nodded in response. I turned on my heel, jogging back to where Fenrir was standing waiting for me.

Crossing the river took us another hour into the setting sunset. When we finally started the set-up of our camp in the fields, the sounds and smells of Fire's camp had begun to float over the river, and my stomach growled unhappily with hunger. The catering tent was always the first to be built, and thankfully it was almost finished. I made sure the Fenrir was settled and comfortable in his makeshift stable and made my way across the field.

Kira's tent had been thrown up as quickly as possible, and I could see her shadow inside, back lit by candles and the orange glow of her lanterns. She was letting her hair down, her arms stretched above her head; I tripped over my own feet just watching her.

A hand clapping onto my shoulder drew my eyes away from Kira, and to Tarian's face. His cheeks were flushed red, and his hair was windswept. Hollis was a few steps behind him, her face pale with exhaustion already. I smiled at Tarian lightly and tilted my head in the direction of the catering tent, and he nodded in response, waiting for Hollis to catch up with him before he started walking. The three of us walking together, reminded me of our first war games together. Tarian and I had teamed up as soon as the games begun, and, of course, wherever Tarian went, Hollis followed. They had been my closest, most trusted friends since.

The tent was almost empty when we reached it, and Hollis grabbed us a spot at the table nearest the far wall while Tarian and I filled up three plates with as much food as we could manage to squeeze onto them.

"What's the plan, then?" Hollis asked as we sat down across from her. I slid a plate full of meat and potatoes over the table to her, and she dug in hungrily, barely stopping to take a breath.

"We rest for tonight. Tomorrow…" I bit into a perfectly roasted potato, my eyes rolling back slightly at the mix of crispy skin and fluffy insides, "Tomorrow, we fight."

"Sounds easy enough." Hollis chuckled through a mouthful of food.

The warmth of someone else's body came up beside me on my right, and a plate slid onto the table beside mine. I looked to the side, finding Kira sitting herself down beside me. Her hair had been re-braided, and she had changed out of her riding clothes. The skin on her cheeks was kissed pink from the wind and sun, and I wanted so badly to reach out and run my fingers along the freckles there.

"Your Majesty," I said, my voice coming out thick.

"General," Kira smiled at me, but her eyes flickered to Hollis, who was suddenly much more interested in the plate in front of her.

We fell into a comfortable silence, the four of us eating beside each other quietly as the tent filled with more weary soldiers looking to fill their stomachs with food before our battle.

Anxiety crept down the back of my neck as I thought about what was coming when the sun rose tomorrow morning. I would lose some of the people in this room. People I had trained with, laughed with, and grown with. It was the hard part of being in charge — getting to know people on a personal level and then having to send them to war, as if they meant nothing to me.

Kira's hand on my arm pulled me from my thoughts, and I looked up in time to see her standing from the table, taking her plate to where they were washed, and heading out of the tent. She stopped at the entrance, her eyes locking to mine for a second before she left. I shoved myself away from the table, nearly knocking over a boy named Cian as I did so.

"Try not to be so obvious, Maeteo." Hollis laughed, shaking her head.

"Bite me, Holl." I muttered, taking my plate from the table, and leaving it on top of the small pile waiting to be washed. Hollis was still laughing as I made my way out of the tent, my eyes trained on Kira's retreating figure as she crossed the field towards her tent.

My boots squelched against the grass as I followed her across the field, not letting her out of my sight once. She looked over her shoulder once to make sure I was following her, and her face broke out into a smile when she saw that I was.

Kira's tent was set up immaculately. Her bed had been set in the middle of the space, with plush pillows and thick blankets. There was a small writing desk against the far wall, and the rest of the space was filled with rugs, a vanity, and several trunks. Her armour was stood waiting in the corner, alongside her sword and a bow that I had yet to see.

I stepped through the light fabric of the entrance, taking in the sharp smell of citrus that seemed to follow Kira everywhere. She had already taken off her boots and was sat on the edge of her bed, staring at me with her head tipped to the side. My stomach flipped uncomfortably in my stomach.

"Wipe your feet." Kira smiled, leaning back on her hands.

"Wipe my…" My words cut off as I looked down at the small mat I was standing on. My boots were black with mud, and Kira's had been discarded close by the entrance. "It's a war tent."

"And I must sleep in it. Wipe your feet, please."

I shook my head, laughing as I wiped my boots across the small mat, trying my hardest to get most of the mud off them before I stepped farther into the tent.

Kira held out her hand, and I slipped my fingers through hers and pulled her up to standing.

Her lips were on mine in an instant, and I groaned, letting my free hand wrap around her waist as I placed her other on the back of my neck. Her body was soft against mine, and I relished in the feeling of it pressed against me. Her soft sigh against my mouth made my heart burst into a sprint, and my stomach flipped into a frenzy. I tightened my grip on her t-shirt, my knuckles turning white from the strength I was holding her with.

The sounds of the camp were drowned out by the sounds of our breathing, and for the first time in days I did not think about anything apart from the feel of Kira's lips on mine, how some of her hair had fallen loose from her braid already and feathered around her face, how her fingers felt twisted in the strands of my own hair at the nape of my neck.

I let out a groan as she pulled away from me, her forehead resting against mine as she caught her breath. I had to bend my head down a fair distance to reach her, and that was with her on the very tips of her toes. Kira's fingers stroked through the hair at the back of my head, and I basked in the silence of the tent, knowing that after tonight silence would be something I would find rarely.

"Are you okay?" Kira asked, her voice thick. I let my eyes flutter open, pulling my head back so I could look down at her properly. She stared up at me with big, worried eyes, and my heart ached in my chest.

"I'm fine, Princess." I smiled, lying through my teeth to try and settle her nerves. I had been trained for this since I was a child — she needed to believe I was fine to keep her confidence in me. She needed me to be fine. The whole of our army *needed* me to be fine.

"What will happen tomorrow?" Kira stepped away from me, linking our fingers together and sitting herself down on her bed. I sat next to her, wrapping my arm around her shoulders, and pulling her into my side, my nose instantly burying itself in her hair.

"We're hoping to take them by surprise. We'll make the first move before the sun rises. They won't be expecting it that early."

Kira nodded her head, and the smell of her hair weaved its way into my brain, cementing itself into my memories.

I put my finger under her chin, tilting her head up to look at me, and pressed my lips to hers.

31
Kira

The golden glow of dawn had not yet touched the skyline, and we were stood on the side of the river, watching as the first of our soldiers made their way through the waist deep water.

My eyes nipped uncomfortably as the morning wind whipped past my face. I had not slept last night, once Maeteo had left my tent and left me to my own thoughts — my skin had felt too hot, and my bed had felt far too empty after the time we had spent in it together.

Hollis and Tarian had left to retrieve Aepein and Gavrun an hour ago. Maeteo and I wished them good luck, and I had tried not to tear up at the sight of Maeteo hugging his two closest friends goodbye. I knew that what I was doing was the right thing but watching him say goodbye to the only people in his life who had been there for him — my heart had broken in my chest.

Now, my eyes searched the clouds above our heads, hoping to see the shadows of two great beasts flying above, ready to attack when we needed them to.

We were at the very back of our army. Bands of soldiers both on foot and horseback were stood in formation in front of us, the nerves rolling off every single one of them in the early morning haze.

Maeteo bumped his shoulder against mine, the metal of our armour hitting together noisily and making me look up at him. He had not yet put on his helmet, and his hair was still down around his forehead. His stubble had come back in while we had been traveling, and his eyes were rimmed red from lack of sleep. I reached out a hand and placed it on his cheek. His head tipped into my hand slightly, and he placed the lightest of kisses to the skin of my palm.

I wondered if last night was burned onto the backs of his eyelids like it was mine.

A shout from behind us had Maeteo's head snapping up, his eyes wide suddenly as he searched the camp to see where it had come from.

Fenrir was galloping towards us, his reins dragging on the mud as he ran, and his poor handler tripping over himself trying to catch him. Maeteo frowned, moving directly into the horses' path and catching his reins quickly, managing to pull him to a stop despite the strength of him. Fenrir's head reared up, and he let out a loud whine, bumping his nose against Maeteo's chest.

Maeteo smiled lightly, running his hand up Fenrir's nose to the space between his ears and slipping the reins back over his head.

"He wants to join in." Maeteo laughed, looking at me. I raised an eyebrow, shaking my head in disbelief.

Maeteo turned to the handler, telling him to go and fetch Freya, and jumped up to mount Fenrir. He looked the picture of the perfect General sat on top of his mount, his chin lifted, and his helmet hung on the side of his saddle.

Freya was led to me by the same handler, his cheeks flushed pink and his hands shaking as he handed me her reins. I thanked him and smiled as I took them, settling my foot into the stirrups and hoisting myself up into the saddle.

I looked over to Maeteo when I was settled comfortably, and flushed when I realised, he was already watching me with a small smile on his face.

"Staring is rude, General, you should know better." I teased, trying my hardest to lighten the mood slightly. Maeteo chuckled lightly, his eyes dark despite the laughter.

"Just taking in the sights." He smiled lightly, "I'll see you on the other side, Princess."

As he spoke, the sound of screaming carried over the river to us. Plumes of smoke had started to snake towards the sky, and our second band of soldiers started to move, jumping down into the river and making their way to the opposite bank — over to where they would fight for me.

I swallowed harshly, nodding my head, and with one last look at Maeteo, I urged Freya forward.

Water lapped at my ankles as we crossed the deepest part of the river, my fingers turning white with how tightly I had them wrapped around Freya's reins. The smells of burning had started to travel on the wind as we made our way towards the fields. I could hear the ringing of swords clashing and it made the hair on my arms stand on end.

The armour Tarian had made for me fit like a glove. The stainless steel of the chest piece was covered in smaller, metal leaves, painted green to match the forest trees. Silver vines wound their way across the bodice, and it had taken my breath away when I first laid eyes on it. Gracie had helped me into it before anyone else was awake, and for the first time since I arrived at the castle, I felt every bit the Queen I was.

Now, as I sat atop of Freya and moved into the back lines of battle, I felt like a child who had fallen into the deepest part of a fast-flowing river and could not find their footing.

My breath left me in one sharp burst as we broke through the trees, and I was finally faced with the battle in front of us.

Tents were burning. Men were yelling. Swords were clashing, and arrows flew in every direction. I froze on the back of Freya, my heart stopping in my chest.

"Look at me, Kira." Maeteo yelled, slipping down from Fenrir's back and hurrying over to me, "If this is too much, turn around and go back to your tent. No one would —"

Maeteo was cut off by an arrow flying an inch past his face. He swore loudly, unsheathing his sword and spinning on the spot and swiping upwards blindly. His sword sliced across the front of an oncoming soldier's face, knocking him to the ground in a pool of his own blood.

My eyes went wide as I flinched on Freya's back, moving to Maeteo's side and unsheathing my own sword from where it was on my saddle, my hands shaking as I held it in front of me.

Maeteo stared up at me, a glint in his eyes that I did not recognise as he smiled lightly. His face was splattered with blood already, and his lips were turned upwards into a small smile.

"That's my girl."

I grinned to myself as I steered Freya away from Maeteo, throwing us both headfirst into the fighting with a scream.

32

Sweat dripped down the back of my armour as I stepped back into my tent.

The fighting had lasted all day, through the mid-afternoon heat and the ridiculous rainstorm that had followed. The field along the river was littered with bodies, both soldiers from Earth and from Fire. The river itself had taken on a dark red tint as their blood seeped through the soil.

My limbs felt like jelly from throwing myself around the battlefield. Freya had her legs swiped out from under us as we had moved across to help a fallen soldier, and I had been thrown ten feet away from her. She had managed to get back up but bolted in the opposite direction. Mud coated my legs right up to my knees, and my hair was plastered to my head with a mix of sweat and blood.

I had spotted Maeteo at one point locked in combat with another soldier. His teeth were borne, and his sword locked above his head, but his other hand held a small dagger that had not been spotted, and he ran it upwards into the other soldier's ribs, releasing himself from the dangerous dance he had been trapped in. His eyes locked with mine and he grinned wildly before turning on the spot and disappearing into the thrall. I had not seen him since.

Hollis and Tarian had arrived in a flurry of fire and blood-curdling screams. They tore strips of the field apart from the backs of Aepein and Gavrun, burning hundreds of Fire soldiers where they stood.

Cyrus's second in command had finally called a reprieve once they realised they were losing. They had retreated to their tents, their tails between their legs, and we had made our way back across the river.

My stomach growled loudly as I let my helmet drop to the ground and pulled my feet out of my muddied boots. Food had been the last thing on my mind this morning as we had readied ourselves for battle, and I was starting to feel lightheaded.

Voices from outside of my tent piqued my interest, and as I looked over my shoulder, Gracie pushed her way through the fabric doorway, her hands carrying a tray full of delicious looking roasted potatoes and meat covered in gravy. I groaned out loud, the sight of the food in front of me the best thing I had seen all day.

Gracie laughed lightly, letting the door fall closed behind her and heading across the tent to place the tray on my bed. I followed close behind, my mouth watering at the smell, not even bothering to take off my armour.

"Have you already eaten?" I asked Gracie when I noticed she had only brought one tray. She nodded.

"I ate with Chef," She explained, "I was driving myself crazy stuck in my tent."

I nodded, pulling the tray of food onto my lap as I sat on the edge of the bed and shovelling a fork full of potatoes into my mouth. My eyes rolled closed as the taste of them filled my senses, and my stomach growled in appreciation.

Gracie sat herself on the bed next to me, her eyes on the ground as she scuffed her feet against the tent floor. Her lips were pulled into a tight line, and her fingers worried in the bedsheets. I frowned, furrowing my brows and bumping her with my shoulder, careful not to hit her with my armour too hard. She looked at me with glassy eyes.

"Are you sure you're doing the right thing?" She asked, her voice loud in the quiet tent. I stared at her for a second, her question sinking into my brain before I moved my tray off my lap and pulled her into a tight hug.

"I have no choice, Gracie." I sighed, squeezing her as tightly as I could with my armour still on. She sniffled but nodded against my shoulder.

"I know, I do know that. I'm just —" She shrugged, pulling away from me to wipe under her eyes, "I just don't like it, I guess."

"I don't either." I smiled a little, trying to reassure her. "It's definitely not how I imagined this whole Queen thing going, that's for sure."

Gracie laughed lightly, shaking her head. We fell back into comfortable silence as I finished off the food on my plate, sliding the tray across the floor to beside the door to remind me to take it back to chef when I could.

The evening passed with Gracie and I working in silence. She helped me out of my armour, and we went to work making sure all my things were packed away in a trunk. We knew we would not be able to take them with us, so anything that could not be hidden on our bodies or could fit into the one shared trunk we were taking with us, was packed into the trunk at the end of my bed.

Maeteo popped his head in to say goodnight at one point, and Gracie excused herself to give us a bit of privacy. His eyes had scanned the tent, confusion crossing his features when he saw the trunk open, but he did not say anything about it, instead he simply kissed me goodnight and promised he would see me in the morning. My heart shattered in my chest at his words, but I nodded and smiled at him anyway.

Little did he know that Gracie and I would be making our move as soon as the camp fell into the hands of sleep.

Gracie had gone back to her own tent to get her own belongings sorted, with the reminder to keep it light as we would only be able to take what fit into one case. She had nodded, her eyes still glassy with unshed tears as she ducked out of the doorway, her feet silent in the muddy grass.

I could not leave without saying goodbye, and with a sigh I stood from my bed, turning my attention to the writing desk that had been placed at the back of my tent. I had been confused when I had seen it initially, but now I was glad it was there. Sitting myself down in the wooden chair, I picked up a clean sheet of paper and a feathered pen and started writing.

33

Crossing the silent camp under the light of the moon had my hair standing on end.

Gracie's hand was clutched tightly in mine, and we worked our way silently over the muddy field, the trunk full of our clothes dragging behind us. Horses whinnied from the makeshift stable, and my heart tugged in my chest at the thought of leaving Freya behind. If it would not attract too much attention, I would go and tack her up and take her with us.

I pulled the trunk up to the edge of the river, making sure it was sturdy standing by itself and slid down into the water, shivering at the frigid temperature seeping through my trousers. Gracie slid down next to me, and we held the trunk above our heads as we crossed over, our steps slow and sluggish through the current. I tried to ignore the dark red tint to the water.

Throwing the trunk up onto the edge, Gracie hauled herself up onto the opposite bank first, reaching her hand down to help me and pulling me up alongside her.

The ground here was less grass and more mud; more blood. We stood for a second, shivering, wondering how best to avoid the bodies littered across the battlefield.

Weaving our way in and out of the tree line, we made it around the field without too much hassle. My fingers felt numb against the metal handle of the trunk, and my teeth were chattering together painfully. An owl screeched overhead, making both Gracie and I jump in fright, the trunk slipping out of our hands and into the mud with a wet thud.

The sound of footsteps coming towards us made me stand tall, my shoulders squaring themselves and my face falling into one of perfect indifference.

Two Fire soldiers broke through the trees, their swords drawn, and a flaming torch held above their heads. Gracie's hand grabbed the top of my arm, her fingers squeezing almost uncomfortably. I did not turn to look at her, but I lifted my opposite hand to rest on top of hers, hoping that the soft squeeze I gave her fingers in return was enough to comfort her.

"Where do you think you're going?" One of the soldiers in front of us leered, his voice clipped with an accent. He stood taller than his companion, but they both shared the same greasy hair and unkempt appearance. I swallowed, hoping my voice would not fail me now.

"I am here to see Prince Cyrus." My voice carried with more confidence than I felt, and I heard Gracie take a sharp breath. The guards looked us both up and down, smirks on their faces.

"The Prince does not deal with swamp rats." The smaller of the two guards chuckled, and the corners of my vision turned red. I lifted my chin, my fingers balling into fists.

"I am Queen Kira Dagon of the Earth Kingdom, and I demand to see my betrothed."

The guards stared, their eyes wide and I could see the cogs in their heads turning as they digested the words I'd just spoken. The silence stretched between us for an uncomfortable minute before the two guards leaped into action. Their voices overlapped as they both lunged forward, both reaching to take the trunk from behind Gracie and me.

I slipped my fingers through Gracie's, squeezing them tightly as we followed close behind the two men, who were apologizing so vehemently it was almost funny.

The orange glow of the campfires lit the path in front of us, and I locked my jaw as I took in the camp we had just entered.

The tents were triple the size of ours, and the smells coming from their catering tent smelled like much more than just the meat and potatoes we had. Gracie must have noticed it also, because her eyes were wide as she whipped her head back and forth, taking in the new surroundings.

Soldiers stopped in their tracks at the sight of us crossing through their camp. Some stood up from their seats around the campfires to get a better look, and I felt Gracie squeeze herself closer to me. I kept my chin tipped slightly upwards, making sure none of my nerves showed through.

You are their Queen, Kira, and Queen's do not weep.

Eyvlin's voice filtered through my subconscious as I tried not to let myself slip; my eyes trained on the backs of the two guards in front of us.

When they stopped suddenly, Gracie and I ground to a halt behind them. The tent in front of us was larger than the rest, with a peaked roof and Fire flags waving in the late-night breeze. A soft orange glow came from inside the fabric walls, and a figure was moving around inside, their shadow cast against the cream wall. One of the guards spun on his heel, narrowing his eyes as he stared at us and his friend disappeared inside the tent, letting one side of our trunk fall to the muddy ground.

I frowned at the retreating guard's back, watching as his shadow crossed through the tent and stopped by a table. The other person inside had stopped their pacing, their hands leaning on the table as they leaned forward to listen to him.

A sharp laugh came from inside the tent, and the guard stuck his head out of the door, gesturing with his hand for me to come inside. Gracie moved alongside me but was stopped in her tracks.

"I'll only be a minute." I smiled at her before throwing a glare to the guard still outside. "Fetch her something to keep her warm." He nodded, taking off at speed towards a different row of tents, letting our trunk fall into the dirt fully. Gracie sighed through her nose, but sat atop of the lid, crossing her arms over each other and watching me as I stepped inside.

I let the fabric doors swing closed behind me. The warmth of the tent hit my skin and made me sigh through my nose; I still had not regained feeling in my fingers. I let my eyes wander the interior of the tent quickly, taking in the plush cushions, the rugs, and the neatly made bed in the corner of the room.

A table took up a significant portion of the middle of the room, and leaning on his hands against the wooden top was Cyrus. His hair was loose around his face, and his lips were pressed into a tight line. He had his shirt untucked, and the sleeves rolled up to the elbow, and I noted the black tattoo banded around his forearm. I blinked, pulling my eyes away from his arms to look at his face again. His cheeks were gaunt, and he had bags under his eyes.

"Are you so unsatisfied with the mockery you're making of my men on the battlefield, Sweetheart, that you've come to mock me in person?" He asked, his voice clipped as he looked me up and down, his brows furrowing at the sight of me covered in mud.

I lifted my chin, clasping my hands in front of myself to try and centre myself.

"Actually, Cyrus, I've come to talk about our... betrothal."

One of his eyebrows quirked upwards, and he pushed himself off the table and into a standing position. He stuffed his hands into his pockets as he stared at me across the tent. I felt his gaze on every inch of my skin, but I did not dare break our stare first.

When he finally looked away first, I let out a breath. I could have sworn there was sweat dripping down my back.

Cyrus crossed the tent quickly, towards where he had a small teapot and cups sitting beside a cast iron fire. He looked over his shoulder at me, a small smile on his face.

"Do you take one sugar or two, Sweetheart?"

34
Maeteo

I threw open the curtains to Kira's tent, my chest heaving as I struggled to take breaths in the humid air. My legs burned from running.

I had gone to her tent this morning before the sun had risen, but it had been empty, and I had assumed she would be in the catering tent. Crossing the camp quickly, I chewed on the inside of my cheek, worry overtaking me at her disappearance. She had not been in the catering tent either, but my anxiety did not have the chance to come to a head, because it was at that moment that one of the younger soldiers had come and grabbed my arm and told me one of Cyrus's men was at the entrance to our camp, and he wanted to speak to me.

I had gone to meet with him, Kira momentarily placed in the back of my mind. The man waiting for me had a smirk I wanted to slap off his face. He sat on top of a pure white horse, their feet muddied and splattered with river water.

"Can I help you?" I asked, crossing my arms over my chest and narrowing my eyes. He grinned at me, not answering my question but instead holding out a rolled-up piece of paper. I glanced at it quickly, my brows furrowing as I unrolled it and took in the words in front of me.

Cyrus had called a ceasefire.

We had won.

By the time I lifted my head again, the messenger had already crossed the river again and was galloping across the battlefield. I grinned, twirling the rolled-up letter in my hand as I turned back to the camp to let them all know the good news.

My jolly mood had not lasted long when they informed me that no-one had seen her since the fighting stopped yesterday and she had returned to her tent. Hollis and Tarian had been in the medical tent since Hollis took a fall off Aepein mid battle, and Tarian had been slashed in the face by an arrow that narrowly missed his eye, so I knew neither of them would have seen her either. I felt my heart fall into my stomach and took off at a sprint towards her tent.

Empty. Her tent was empty. I let my helmet drop to the floor, stepping forward onto the fabric of the flooring, catching the toe of my boot on the small rug she had placed inside the opening to catch dirt. It had made me roll my eyes when I had seen it the day before yesterday — she was so, so infuriatingly precious about keeping a war tent clean.

Now the sight of the rug, askew and covered in mud, made my heart twist in my chest.

Her bed was made up as if she hadn't slept in it last night. I moved over to it, passing around the table set up with our maps, and ran my fingers over the soft cotton of the pillowcases. The soft fabric beneath my fingers felt wrong. Turning on the spot, I looked over everything in the space.

Nothing had been knocked over, nothing had been damaged, and nothing seemed out of place — even the small figures on the maps hadn't moved since we were last in here. My heart started to hammer in my chest, fearing the worst had happened.

Her writing desk, that sat against the far back wall of the tent, was the only thing that looked different. A small, thin slip of white paper fluttered in the breeze that came through the open entrance, and I snatched it up, my throat tightening up as I recognized her handwriting scrawled across the paper.

M,

I went with him willingly. Nothing was forced.

I need to marry him — please, please do not follow me.

Yours,

K.

I crumpled the paper in my fist, my breathing coming hard and fast as her words sunk into my brain.

My legs moved on their own accord, and a roar that sounded like an animal ripped from my throat as I kicked over the map table, throwing the crumpled ball of paper on the ground and grinding it under my boot as I stormed out of the tent. The hot air engulfed me as I moved across the grass, blood and mud mixed even this far back.

The medic tent sat to the left of the field, and it was overflowing with people. Bodies lay on cots, holding their wounds, while some people cried beside their fallen brothers.

All this. All of this was for her, and she went with them.

A new rage started to bubble in my stomach as I moved across the tent, towards where I could see Tarian and Hollis sitting together. Hollis's arm was in a cotton sling, and she sat stone faced beside where Tarian was getting prodded by Merethyl, his face scrunched up in pain as she stitched a wound above his eyebrow.

Hollis turned her head towards me, the commotion of my speed through the tent drawing her attention, and her face perked up momentarily until she saw the anger sketched on my features. Her mouth fell open as if all the breath in her body had left her. Tarian opened his eyes as I stopped behind Merethyl, looking up at me and frowning.

"She's not there?" He asked, his voice thick with emotion. Merethyl turned to look at me, and Hollis stood from where she sat, her good arm dangling by her side and her mouth pressed into a tight line. I shook my head.

"No. No she's not there," I started, clearing my throat and pushing my hair back from my face. "She — she went with them."

The words didn't land for a second, and the three of them in front of me frowned, questions written over their faces.

"What do you mean, she went with them?" Merethyl asked, her eyes flitting from me to Hollis and then to Tarian, both of whom were looking at me like I'd murdered her myself.

"I mean," I started, taking a deep breath and trying to keep the rage in my stomach down, "She went with Cyrus. She left a note — she wants to marry him, and she left with him whilst we were being slaughtered."

Hollis was the first to move, her legs giving out from under her as she sat back down on her chair with a heavy thud. Silence filled the tent, and I knew everyone around me had heard my words as angry whispers started to fill the air. I took a breath, closing my eyes for a second before I turned on the spot and met the eyes of every one of my men, where they lay either injured or mourning.

"Her Majesty is with Prince Cyrus." I called, my voice carrying around the silent tent easily. "She went of her own accord."

"So, what now?" A voice called from somewhere to my left, I looked over but couldn't place where the voice came from.

What now?

I mulled the question over in my head for a second before I spoke again, my voice thick with anger as I remembered the words of her letter. *Please, please do not follow me.*

"We go to them." I started, squaring my shoulders. "We go, and we get her back."

"Cyrus won't let us near her, Matty." Hollis's small voice came from behind me, and I looked over my shoulder to meet her blue eyes, the same blue as her brother's, completely void of all their usual spark.

Anger bubbled uncomfortably in my chest at the sight of her looking so broken.

"He won't have a choice." I growled, "I'll kill him before he even knows we're there."

Epilogue
Kira

My hair whipped around my face as I stood on the upper deck of our ship.

The coastline of Earth pulled farther away as the ship sliced through the choppy waves of the mid-sea, and I crossed my arms over my chest, trying to shield myself from the frigid temperature. Autumn had barely kissed the ground on land, but out on the water, the wind was harsh, and the temperature had dropped dramatically.

Gracie had disappeared inside almost as soon as we had boarded, her hands clutching tightly to the fabric of her dress as Cyrus's men lifted our single case of clothes down the stairs into the deck below and to our cabin, her eyebrows knotted together in the middle and her lips pressed into a thin line. I would've laughed at the look on her face if my heart hadn't lodged itself into my throat the second we left the castle grounds two days ago.

Reminding myself that this was all part of my plan was the hardest thing. Maeteo's gaze from last night in my tent still burned on the backs of my eyelids, and I could still feel the scorch of his hands on my waist. I closed my eyes, breathing in the cold air and willing myself not to think of him. Him, or Tarian, or Hollis, or even Fenrir.

A hand touched my upper arm, and I snapped my eyes open. Turning my head, I met Cyrus's eyes. His lips were turned up into a small smile, and a blue scarf was draped around his neck, tucked into his jacket. I schooled my face into a smile.

"Are you alright?" He asked, his hand still on my arm, and I nodded my head quickly.

"Yes! Yes, I'm fine." I smiled, turning my head to look at the coast growing ever smaller. "Just... thinking. How am I to still rule over Earth if I'm not there?"

I had thought this through, of course. Emily would take care of everything immediately, and I would deal with as much as I could from afar.

Emily. My heart tugged at my thoughts of her. The last time I'd seen her was two days ago, before the army moved through the open castle gates; before I'd lied to her about what my plan was. Before I had waved her goodbye from Freya's back as we rode out of the castle gates towards the waiting battlefields.

Cyrus shook his head, his smile growing slightly more as he turned me away from the edge of the ship, his arm wrapping around my shoulders. I tensed; the close contact more than I wanted.

"No need to worry about that right now, Sweetheart." He said softly, "Let's get you into the cabins; you'll catch your death up here."

I nodded my head but glanced back over my shoulder at the still burning fires along the coastline. The sounds and sights of the bodies left dying on the field still plagued the inside of my mind, and I could barely breathe as Cyrus led me down to the lower deck with the cabins.

I had to remind myself, over and over, that this was all part of my plan as the ship moved across the uneasy mid-sea. I was their Queen, and Queen's do not weep.

I would go to Fire.

I would marry Cyrus.

And then?

I would kill him.

To Be Continued

Acknowledgements

When I decided I wanted to be an author, I was ten years old.

I spent a lot of my childhood in difficult situations, and reading was an escape for me (Shout out to The Suitcase Kid by Jacqueline Wilson especially.)

I have written many a thing over the last seventeen years, from my teenage fanfictions to the first idea for this novel, my journey as an author would not have been possible without the love and support of the people I'm about to mention.

To my Beta Readers – Lyndsie, Leah, Alex, Arlene, Sophie, Diane, Beth and Becca. The Whatsapp chat has kept me sane the last few months of writing this novel, and I can't wait to see what you all have to say when it comes to the second novel. Also, I promised there would be no animal deaths, didn't I?

Mum -- look what I did! Thank you for never ever giving up on me, even if you didn't understand everything I was talking about, your support has been never ending.

Danielle, Eve & Kimberley – I have no words for how special you three are to me. Our friendship has grown and blossomed over the last two decades and I hope you always remember how colossal your impact on my life has been.

Papa – I'm sorry you're not here to see this, but I promised you I would do this one day. I miss you and I hope you're proud of me.

Lastly, and most importantly –

To James, William & Caelan – Everything I do in this life, I do for you. The best husband and children a woman could ever ask, your support and understanding whilst I've spent hours at the computer has been absolutely unmatched. I love you with every inch of my soul.

Printed by Amazon Italia Logistica S.r.l.
Torrazza Piemonte (TO), Italy